The Weaver's Heir

Book One: Crafter

TS McCarthy

© TS McCarthy 2023

First printed in Australia by Mountain Way Publishing 2023.

The moral rights of the author have been asserted.

All rights reserved. Except as permitted under the *Australian Copyright Act 1968* (for example, a fair dealing for the purposes of study, research, criticism or review), no part of this book may be reproduced, stored in a retrieval system, communicated or transmitted in any form or by any means without prior written permission.

This is a work of fiction. The story, all names, characters, and incidents portrayed in this production are the product of the author's imagination and are fictitious. No identification with actual persons (living or deceased), places, buildings, and products is intended or should be inferred.

ISBN 978-0-6459819-1-9

Book Cover Design by ebooklaunch.com

Mountain Way Publishing supports environmentally responsible printing practices. The print version of this book is available on demand.

To my mother, Pamela, an incredible human on every level. Your strength, your 'live life to the fullest' approach and your resilience inspire me always. I hope I am half the mother you are. Thank you.

To my Aunt, Christine, who has believed in me every step of the way. I so enjoy our time together, your observations on life, your humour and our constant projects!

To my wonderful friends and test readers who provided encouragement and feedback. I appreciate you so much.

To my children, Ava and Owen. You bring me so much joy. Grow in creativity and wonder. May the magic never disappear.

For Patrick, who journeys beside me.

Contents

1. A very strange day — 1
2. A very strange night — 18
3. Hesta's request — 44
4. Saturday: Gin's Story — 60
5. Crafter unlocked — 76
6. Into the Void — 91
7. Andera — 106
8. Training a Crafter — 129
9. An oath is given — 157
10. The Lost Crafters — 173
11. Beyond the Manor — 193
12. Varossa — 226
13. The Mountain Man of Groush — 247

14.	Asanya	263
15.	The stones of Mat'drin	280
16.	The Queen and the Sorcerer	288
17.	The rescue of Evie	304
18.	The Tangled Threads	315

Chapter One

A very strange day

Asher Blake sat quietly among the noise and energy of the crowded café courtyard, zealously guarding the two empty chairs she was holding for her friends.

She had tried a few times to grab the attention of the dark-haired waitress who was serving the tables either side of her, but as usual it seemed she was practically invisible, and the young woman simply ignored her in favour of louder, more vocal customers. And there were plenty of those. It was gorgeous weather and Ed's was offering a Tuesday meal 'n movie deal for the school holidays. The place was packed, inside and out.

By some miracle Asher had snaffled a prime table in the brick paved courtyard, right under the huge elm tree. A small fountain off to the right burbled merrily, and the wait staff manoeuvred expertly between the crowded round metal tables and chairs. Every basket chair had a cushion nestled in it to soften the impact of the metal, each one a different colour. Warm throw blankets were draped across the backs of the chairs, and tall gas heaters stood at the ready for when the afternoon Autumn air turned chilly.

She had not seen her friends since they had headed to their own homes after leaving school on Friday.

Asher had not really minded. She had been fully focused on the new piece she was composing, which now needed some strings. What had started as a simple piano melody was now becoming an epic event. She had to be careful it did not totally consume her every waking hour, so she had agreed to lunch with her two closest friends.

It had been so quiet at home, and when she emerged from her music the lack of people around the house had been a little unsettling. Dad was away on conference in Singapore and mum was sequestered in her painting studio – a rather strange turn of events, which had added to Asher's sense of unease.

Evie was out most of the time with her friends. Asher wondered if Evie had a boyfriend that she was keeping far from the family and, more importantly, away from the Beast. Asher had not bothered asking. There was no way Evie would share anything with her, especially after their latest fight on Friday. According to their parents, they had once been close, but that was hard to believe these days. Evie at almost twenty thought she was superior to her fifteen year old sister in every way.

And maybe she is thought Asher sadly, remembering the accusing glare in Evie's eyes, and the disdain in her voice during their ugly argument. *Evie isn't responsible for mum's breakdown and continued migraines. That's all me.*

A shiver ran down her spine. The tingly, unsettling sensation that her Nana Blake used to refer to as 'somebody walking over your grave'. It was accompanied by the distinct feeling that she was being watched.

Ash twisted awkwardly as she scanned the courtyard, but nobody was paying her any attention. Still, she felt uneasy. She slumped further into her chair, hoping to make herself even more unremarkable than she already was.

A few long minutes passed, until, with relief, she recognised the tall, olive-skinned boy and the shorter, mousy blonde girl that were standing in the back doorway of the café, scanning the crowd. She shoved the unsettling sensation to the back of her mind.

"Kate! Levi! Over here."

The new arrivals squeezed their way through the crowded tables.

"Whoa! It is busy in here!" exclaimed Levi.

"Really? I hadn't noticed," Kate responded drily, as they joined Asher at the table.

"Everyone making the most of the last great weather before we slide into short, dark days" said Asher happily.

She loved winter. Coats, scarves, gloves... all the layers made it super easy to just blend in unnoticed. Or better still, stay warm at home with little pressure to be out and about at all.

"You guys all sorted for tonight?" she asked her friends.

Kate and Levi nodded. "We've left our packs at the front, they said it was too crowded to bring them back here and they were totally right," answered Levi.

"I'm packed too, my stuff is at home. I was thinking we could head there first to collect it, then go through the back of my place to the woods."

"Sounds like a plan," agreed Levi, "The forecast is fantastic for the next couple of nights. Clear skies too. I've brought my telescope – the small one of course. And snacks, lots of snacks."

The three of them had recently created a school holiday tradition of camping out for three or four nights. The first time had been during the Spring holidays last year, then again in the longer Summer holidays, and now this week. They carried pup tents, sleeping bags and all their food. Levi, who was always hungry, was king of the snacks.

"Speaking of food…" Levi looked around for the rather harassed waitress and smiled winningly at her as he put up his hand politely. Amazingly she came straight over.

As the waitress punched their orders into her tablet a rather forlorn looking woman appeared at the table beside them. Her old grey clothes were well mended, and she was clean, but her eyes were wild with madness. When her restless gaze met Asher's, Asher felt her skin begin to heat and her fingers burn. A confused cacophony of conflicting notes and melodies hammered in her head.

Then the woman looked away and the music eased. The waitress sighed deeply.

"Look, the manager already told you. You can't be in here, bothering the customers. If you'd like a coffee the girls at the front will make you one, on the house. But you can't loiter around out here."

The woman didn't seem to hear her or perhaps she chose to ignore her. Instead she leaned in close to Kate, staring into her blue eyes. Kate pulled back instinctively, surprised but not overly alarmed. The woman then swivelled around to peer intently at Levi. He smiled in a friendly manner.

The waitress huffed. "Okay, I'm going to find Matt." She spun on her heel and strode away.

"The Phoenix and the Sorcerer." The mad woman's voice was raspy and low. Her gaze leapt between them.

"What do you mean?" Levi queried politely.

The woman scowled. She pointed crossly at Kate.

"Phoenix."

Then she poked Levi in the chest.

"Sorcerer."

"What does that mean?" he asked again.

She glared at him and repeated both the words and the action.

Phoenix. Sorcerer. Poke.

Levi threw his hands into the air in mock surrender.

"Okay, okay. What about Ash? Does she get a name?"

The woman turned confused eyes to Asher and frowned. She blinked repeatedly as though clearing her vision.

"Hello Marjorie," said Asher softly, deliberately ignoring the muddled music that had once again burst into life.

The woman leaned close and scowled at Asher. There was no recognition in her eyes.

Levi started in surprise. "You know her?"

"Kind of. Mum always stops and talks with her when we are in town, sometimes helps her back to the boarding house where she stays. The people there know mum quite well, and one of her paintings hangs in the common room. I've wondered before how they know each other, but mum is rather vague about it. Marjorie is always totally disinterested in me, but she really likes Evie. Calls her the Golden Princess. I've never heard her give anyone else a special name."

Nor had she ever experienced the bizarre music or the burning fingers.

She kept her tone light. She didn't want Kate or Levi to think she was upset by, or jealous of, the mad woman's favouritism. She had never been too bothered in the past when Marjorie had been very taken with Evie, patting her skin and stroking her hair. Evie *was* very pretty and charming, and the disparity in their looks and demeanour often drew comparisons, something Asher was well accustomed to.

But to have her friends singled out while she was ignored did sting a little. Quickly she squashed her hurt feelings and told herself firmly that she was being ridiculous. Marjorie's attentions were merely the mutterings of a damaged mind. Besides, Ash preferred being unremarkable. Life was simpler that way, and quieter. Less interruptions and interactions meant more time composing and playing music.

Marjorie soon lost interest in their little group and turned away. In silence they watched her weave through the tables, muttering to herself and sometimes to other customers, before Matt the manager arrived at her side and gently escorted her back inside.

"Well that was odd," Kate broke the silence.

"Indeed," agreed Levi, shaking his head in bewilderment.

A few minutes later and their orders of Classic Ed milkshakes and fries were on the table in front of them. Marjorie was forgotten.

"Yummo," declared Levi, munching happily. Levi could win any eating competition. He held the school fete record for number of hotdogs eaten in sixty seconds, and the town record for donuts. Despite all the eating he did not get any rounder, merely taller. A quirk of nature that Kate openly envied.

Kate's mind had returned to the camping trip.

"I've packed firelighters and matches in case there's not enough kindling to start a fire. We couldn't have one the last couple of times due to fire bans, but tonight should be perfect."

Asher smiled. "Thanks Kate, you are always so organised. I would never have thought of that."

Kate shrugged off the compliment. "I've been camping since I was a kid. My dad was a great teacher." Her voice hitched, but the words were filled with pride.

"Well I've brought cards and a new set of magic tricks," offered Levi, "and fire crackers!"

"Levi, I don't think we're allowed to set off firecrackers at the campsite," warned Kate sternly.

He shrugged, unconcerned. "Well, just in case."

Asher grinned happily as she sipped on her mocha mint milkshake. She was really looking forward to this camping trip. She had been a novice camper for the Spring trip, and she had found more rhythm during the Summer, but Autumn was the time for fires and roasting marshmallows and scarves and ugg boots.

"I've packed my flute, and I have a harmonica in my pocket." She brandished it with a smile.

"Of course you do," agreed her friends in unison, making them all laugh.

Levi slurped greedily on the last dregs of his milkshake.

"Do you think if I ask super nicely they'll give me the recipe for these choc orange milkshakes? They are soooo delicious."

"Absolutely no way," answered Kate confidently, "not even you will charm that recipe out of them. I heard only one person knows all the ingredients and when they are off work nobody can order them."

"I don't want to come on that dark day," declared Levi with a shudder.

The girls laughed.

"We should head off now we're finished so some-body else can have our table," suggested Kate, scanning the busy café.

"So courteous Miss Reynolds," teased Levi, but he stood up and headed out of the courtyard, Kate and Asher close behind.

Inside they bumped into Celia, head of the Year 11 Social Committee. Her lively face brightened even further with a wide smile for Kate and Levi.

"Hi there! Kate, I've been meaning to call you. Are you interested in joining the social committee? Not everyone has great organising abilities and can be trusted to deliver to my high standards, but I think you'd be a great addition to the working group. It's going to be SO MUCH FUN!"

"Sounds like it," smiled Kate, "I'll have a think about it during the holidays and let you know."

"Great!" beamed Celia, bouncing round to greet Levi. Surprise creased her brow when she saw Asher standing there quietly.

"Oh Ash! I didn't realise you were here too!"

Asher shrugged, a half smile teasing at her lips. "Yup, just lingering around."

Celia frowned briefly then smiled apologetically. "Sorry Ash, it's just so crowded in here. Well hi anyway."

"So Kate," Celia said, returning her attention to the task at hand, "give me a call if you want to chat about it. Bye Levi."

Levi rolled his eyes as she strode quickly way, feeling insulted on Asher's behalf.

"Seriously, she doesn't notice anyone but herself."

Asher shrugged. "It's no big deal."

Bill paid and packs retrieved, they headed to the bus stop. They were still fifty metres from the stop when their bus pulled up.

"Should we run?" suggested Ash.

"I don't think I can," said Kate, gesturing at the huge pack on her small back.

"Oh yeah, right."

"Hey look, it's Evie. Evie's getting on the bus. Evie! Evie!" Levi yelled, "hold the bus!"

Evie looked briefly in their direction and then quickly stepped onto the bus, pretending she had not seen them. A few seconds later it pulled away from the curb and trundled passed them.

"Thanks for nothing Evie!" yelled Levi in the direction of the departing bus. "I guess now we wait. At least the bench is empty and we don't have to stand with our packs for twenty minutes," he finished brightly, his natural optimism easily restored.

The time flew by as they laughed and chatted, and before long the next bus pulled up.

"And nowhere near as crowded as the last bus," declared Levi, "we even get seats for our packs. Everything is coming up Levi!"

Ash and Kate burst out laughing at his self-satisfaction.

Happiness seeped throughout Asher's body. After she and Evie had fought on Friday - about mum, her painting, her migraines and Evie's selfishness – Evie had spent as much time out as possible and Ash had retreated to her favourite place, her music room. She hadn't realised how lonely she had been feeling until now. She liked to tell herself that she did not need people, but she really enjoyed being with these specific people.

They settled into their seats on the bus and chattered happily about their camping plans as the bus bounced along.

They were a few stops from home when a buzzing began in her head. It was like the static when a radio station has not tuned in properly. She poked her fingers into her ears and pulled them out in a rush, trying to pop the sound.

It did not work. In fact, the buzzing was getting louder, and now it seemed as though there were words among the buzz. She was sure she heard her name.

Intrigued, Asher focused on the static, trying to clear it. Kate and Levi's chatting faded into the background. It helped to close her eyes. As soon as she blocked out sight the static cleared and she could clearly hear her mother frantically calling for her.

'Asher! Asher! I need you. Where are you?'

Startled Asher opened her eyes and the static resumed. What on earth just happened?

A quick glance around the bus confirmed that no-one was paying any attention to her. Carefully she closed her eyes again.

Jennifer's voice immediately filled her head. *'Asher, Asher, please!'*

'Mum?' she reached out, mentally picturing her mother, *'mum is that you?'*

'Oh Ash,' sobbed her mother in relief, *'thank the stars you can hear me. Come home, come home, I need you now. Asher!'*

'What? Mum what's happening?' Asher yelled back in her mind, panic gripping her.

But the connection was gone. The static cleared and the full sensation of the sounds and sights of the bus rushed back into place. Asher almost toppled off her seat, saved by Kate who grabbed at her just in time. "Are you okay?"

"Yeah fine, thanks," Asher responded automatically, but she didn't feel fine. Did she just have some kind of psychic moment? Or was she going crazy? Worry gurgled in her stomach, mixing uneasily with the fries and shake. Something was wrong at home, very wrong.

"Our stop," announced Levi, standing up and hauling his overstuffed pack onto his back. He glanced at the much smaller Kate who was grimacing at her own pack. "Need some help?"

"Sure."

They were manoeuvring their packs when Asher felt, heard, the static. This time she tuned in faster. *'Mum?'*

'Hurry Ash, hurry,' her voice was weaker.

Seconds later the bus pulled to a stop and Asher leapt off, running almost before her feet had hit the ground.

"Hey Ash!" yelled Levi in surprise, but she did not hear him. She was heading for home as fast as she could, panic and fear fuelling each stride.

Down their street she ran, the normal ten minute meander taking her only a couple of minutes. She burst through their unlocked front door, her body pulsing with dread.

"Mum!" she yelled out loud, "where are you?"

'Lounge room,' was the barely audible response in her mind.

Asher raced there, her heart pounding. Mum lay on the floor, conscious but only just. Asher gathered her up carefully, checking for a wound or blood or damage.

"Mum," she whispered, "what's happened? Where are you hurt? Do you need an ambulance?"

'No ambulance, I need Hesta'.

'What's a hesta?' she asked, but mum did not respond, her eyes flickering shut. Carefully, slowly, Asher pulled her mother upright, but she couldn't hold her steady.

"Whoa!" came a welcome voice at the door, "let me help."

With Levi supporting Jennifer's other side they moved her onto the couch. Kate bustled around in the adjacent kitchen boiling the kettle and grabbing biscuits and orange juice.

"Mum," pleaded Asher, cupping her mother's face with both hands. "What has happened?"

Kate appeared with the juice and a straw.

"Here Jen," she said gently, "drink this. The sugar will help."

Asher moved out of the way, feeling panicked and helpless.

"Is it working?" she fretted.

'Ash,' came her mother's voice in her mind. Asher immediately dropped down next to her and held her hands. Green eyes locked onto her face.

'I am weak. I have over-exerted myself. I was not strong enough to stop the attack. Hesta. I need Hesta.' Tears welled. *'They have taken her'*

'Mum, this isn't making any sense. What attack? And who has been taken?'

Her mother's voice was hoarse and weak.

"Evie, they have taken Evie."

Then Jennifer passed out.

Roaring filled Asher's ears, and then she was no longer in her body, instead she was observing from outside the scene. She felt calm and hyper alert, all the tension and fear she had just been experiencing completely released. She could see mum lying on the lounge, a dark blue woollen blanket draped across her. Levi and Kate standing off to the side, Kate still clutching the glass of orange juice, their dark and light heads close together, whispering anxiously.

She herself, body Asher, was leaning over mum, feeling her head and holding her hand. Spirit Asher could feel the stress radiating from her real self.

'Asher.'

A new voice entered her mind. It was muffled as though far away, but the power was unmistakeable, and in that one word was a command she could not ignore.

'Who are you?' Asher replied.

The woman seemed to tsk in annoyance. *'She's wiped your memory then.'*

Asher frowned. This whole situation was becoming more confusing by the minute. She opened her mouth to ask what was happening.

'I'm Hesta. We have very little time, so don't ask questions. Just listen.'

Asher's mouth snapped shut.

'I'm listening,' she responded to the woman in her head.

'Go find the globe, bring it to her, bring it now.'

The globe? What did that mean? The presence in her head retreated and with a roar she crashed back into her body, her spirit returning with such force she gasped in shock.

"Ash?" called Kate, "Are you okay? Should we call an ambulance for Jennifer?"

'No ambulance,' murmured her mother in her mind. Though her body was not responding, it seemed her mind was still present. Asher felt a surge of relief ease some of the tension.

"No, no..." she stood up, her fingers tingling and her head pounding, "I need to find something, I think it will help her. Mum, mum, please focus. I need to find a globe. Where is it?"

Her mother's eyes fluttered, the effort to talk was clearly huge. "The studio," she whispered.

"Stay with her," Asher directed Levi and Kate, "And don't let anyone in."

Then she raced off, flying through the lounge and bounding up the stairs to the first floor and then to the attic, converted many years ago into a painting studio for mum. Huge skylight windows flooded it with light during the day and offered incredible views of the stars at night.

For most of Ash's childhood the studio was where her mother spent her days and often her nights. The girls had been welcome to come and go, and there were many sleepovers 'camping' on the floor, listening to their mother's fantastical stories about the stars and planets circling the galaxies above them. Asher had loved her mother's descriptions of worlds filled with beings and beasts of all descriptions, some friendly, some fiercesome.

When she was little Asher had totally believed that her mother had visited these places. She had learned over time not to share mum's stories with other children, who had mocked her for being weird. Levi was the only one who had delighted in the stories as much as Asher.

When mum was working on a commission the girls were banned from bothering her, and she would be locked up there for days. She had been highly sought as a portrait painter, renowned for capturing the essence of a person.

Clients often said that having your portrait painted by Jennifer Blake was like a good luck charm. Jennifer chose her commissions with care, and there were some people her mother had firmly refused to paint, regardless of the money on offer.

Once the studio had been a happy place, but now the thought of it filled Asher with dread. It had been three years since her mother had fled the studio in tears and anger, vowing never to paint again. She had refused to talk about it, but the migraines had begun that night and increased in frequency and severity in the months that followed. Her vibrant, clever, carefree mother had been overwhelmed by pain and medication.

For Asher, fear and anxiety had been nagging companions ever since.

None of them had ever returned to the studio, until Friday last week, when Jennifer had started painting again in a frenzy. That is what had prompted the fight between the sisters.

They had said terrible things to each other and had not spoken since.

At the top of the stairs Asher took a few deep stabilising breaths, then she flung open the door to the studio and ran in. Globe, globe... what was she looking for? Quickly she scanned the room, no globe, no picture of a globe, what was it? She paced around, peering under drop sheets and rummaging through collections of paints and brushes.

And then she heard it. A humming, almost a singing.

Mesmerised, Asher moved in the direction of the sound. It was coming from mum's latest painting, a giant canvas balanced on two large easels. The largest work she had ever done. The singing was pulling her towards it.

Her fingers began to tingle.

Filled with apprehension Asher took each step. She knew she should hurry but her steps felt sluggish as though she was wading through mud. Fleetingly she wondered what mum had been painting for the last few days, what had so captured her interest that all else seemed forgotten. Two last steps and she was in front of the painting, but she didn't even glance at it. Her whole attention was captured by the spinning golden globe that hung on a long chain off the edge of the easel.

"Gotcha!" she cried, grabbing the pendant and yanking it off the easel. As she closed her fist around it her head filled with music.

Images burst into life inside her head and Asher staggered backwards as her memory came crashing back.

Chapter Two

A very strange night

Leaving school on Friday afternoon had been a chaotic mass of laughter and talking and yelled farewells.

School was out for the term and the holidays had officially begun. Everyone's mood was high, except for Asher, who had spent the day worrying about her mother. Jennifer had been suffering from one of her energy sapping, vomit-inducing migraines for twenty-four hours. Ash had been anxious to get home and check on her.

Now, finally, the school day was done and she was sitting on the bus heading home, blocking out the chatter of the people around her. Quietly she began to hum, closing her eyes to visualise the music that was tugging at her consciousness, desperate to be shaped. It was a piano piece, and Asher could almost feel her fingers tripping up and down the keys, bringing to life a melody of joy and hope.

As music filled Asher's mind and body, the anxious churning in her stomach eased, and the pressure across her forehead lifted.

She tried to imagine what her mother was doing, imagined her surrounded by Asher's music, her pain wracked mind and body soothed by the soft rise and fall of the notes. Everything was going to be okay. She repeated the phrase over and over in her head, like a mantra. *Everything was going to be okay.*

The music combined with the movement of the bus was actually quite relaxing, until a few moments later when the bus stopped again and the chatter of a group of girls broke into her daydream.

"Hey Ash, almost didn't see you there. Why do you have your eyes closed weirdo?"

The image vanished, the music stopped. Asher sighed deeply, *should have put my earphones in* she thought, and opened her eyes.

"Hi Rebecca."

From behind Rebecca a bright, beautiful blonde with shining blue eyes and small frame pushed forward.

"Don't call her a weirdo Bec," she commanded.

The first girl pouted. "You do it all the time," she complained.

"Yes I do, and that's okay. But nobody else calls my sister a weirdo. Got it?"

Told off by her queen thought Asher. The bright beautiful blonde didn't wait for response, flouncing down to sit next to Asher.

"Hey weirdo," she grinned affectionately.

Asher rolled her eyes at the insulting endearment. "Hey Evie."

The bus ride home took 15 minutes, not long, but it felt like an eon to Asher, trapped in the effervescent gaggle of her sister and her friends. She couldn't even retreat to the solitude of her own mind; the talking and laughing intruded on her thoughts. So instead she popped her earphones in, and amused herself watching the other girls attempt to impress Evie, who was graciously holding court.

When the bus pulled up at the end of their street Asher jumped off with a "thank you" for the driver and a vague wave to the last of Evie's posse. The sisters strode down the street in silence, Evie expertly texting while walking, Ash focused on getting home and checking on her mother.

The house was quiet, but the French doors to the backyard were open to the afternoon breeze. The cool fresh air was a balm after the stress of the day and the noise of the bus. Asher wandered onto the faded wooden deck, breathing in the crisp air, fragrant with the many flowers her mother cared for.

Gardening was one of mum's greatest pleasures. She said it appealed to the artist in her. Creating a garden was similar to creating a painting and gave a person constant purpose and pleasure. As with most things her mother did, it was not an orderly, structured space. Instead, their garden was a treasure trove of colour and plants, pots and old benches, painted tyres and vibrant mosaic encrusted tables.

There were overgrown paths that led to fabulous nooks and crannies, and a pond filled with fish that haphazardly sprouted reeds and grasses.

When Asher was ten, her mother had sculpted a rather lopsided mermaid that perched precariously on the edge of the pond, and named her Mona. Mona's tail was decorated in a mosaic of a thousand tiny, coloured pieces of glass that gleamed and shimmered in the sunlight, and her body was painted a vibrant blue.

"Almost as beautiful as the real thing," mum had declared happily.

Asher thought the garden was a wonderland. Evie thought it was an eyesore and an embarrassment.

Actually Evie thought the whole house was an embarrassment, an opinion she shared freely and frequently.

She did not see the beauty in their scientist father's enthusiastic amateur carpentry projects, or their mother's layers of colours and textures and patterns that imbued every room. She didn't think it charming that the old floorboards creaked and the plumbing groaned. Evie felt they should sell, or worse, knock down 'The Beast' and build something sleek and modern, complete with white kitchen and open plan living.

"You earn more money than half this town, but nobody would ever know it because of The Beast."

And their parents would smile at each other and say "It's not about money Evie, or other people's opinions. It's about love and family and home. You girls were raised in this house, our family was made here. This is home."

Evie would roll her eyes and declare "Well it's embarrassing and you're all bonkers. I can't wait to have my own house. It will be nothing like this old heap."

As for Asher, she held her breath every time Evie pushed to move. She was always slightly concerned that maybe this was the time Evie would convince them to sell, and Asher's heart would be broken. She adored this house and everything in it. Here she could play and write music easily, and even Evie couldn't make her feel weird or out of place. She belonged here, she never wanted to be anywhere else.

"Mum?"

Birdsong greeted her in response. Not outside then.

In the kitchen Evie was making a cup of tea and chatting on her phone to one of her many friends, making plans for dinner and a movie.

Asher wandered through the large, cluttered downstairs rooms. Mum was not in the living room, or dad's study, nor in the book-quake nook – the tiny reading room so named because it was always under threat of being consumed by towering piles of books that seemed to multiply in the night. One misplaced knock and you could trigger a book-quake.

"Mum?"

Upstairs her mother was not in any of the bedrooms, or Asher's favourite space, the music room. A rather grand name for the small space at the end of the hall that was crammed with Asher's assorted instruments. She couldn't resist lingering for a moment there, opening the window and running her fingers along the keys of the old wooden upright piano. The light notes mingled with the quiet breeze. The piano was old and the wood in need of oiling, but it was in tune and the notes were true.

She was bursting to score out the music that had been tickling at her all day, but the nagging anxiety pulsed again and Asher reluctantly pulled her mind back to the here and now. Every room searched. Where on earth could she be? She would not have left the house with the French doors open, and her car was still in the driveway.

There was only one place left to check. The studio. The very thought of it made Asher's heart beat faster. At the top of the stairs the door to the attic studio was open and Asher could hear her mother moving inside.

Uncertainty gripped at Asher, freezing her before she crossed the threshold. She was reluctant to step through, to discover what lay beyond. This room had become such a 'do not discuss' zone that it seemed almost hubris to step inside. Then she heard her mother mutter her name, or what sounded like her name, and she pushed open the door to enter.

Refracted light threw shadows over long discarded paint tubes, glass jars jammed with brushes, easels, canvases of all shapes and sizes, bottles of turps and drop sheets. Dust danced softly in the light, disturbed finally after years of neglect. It felt like the whole room had been holding its breath and was now carefully and quietly exhaling.

It was late in the afternoon, but the huge panes of glass captured as many rays as they could so the artist could work in prime conditions.

In the centre of the space stood her mother, dabbing and swiping paint onto the large canvas held sturdily by two easels pushed together. She was lost in the work, muttering to herself as she painted, selecting colours by touch from the palette in her hand. Asher suddenly felt self-conscious, like she had intruded on some-one lost in prayer. She cleared her throat awkwardly. "Aherm." The painter didn't seem to hear her.

"Mum?"

Her mother leapt around, completely shocked by the unexpected interruption.

"Ash!" she exclaimed, "what are you doing here?"

"Um, I live here..."

"Why aren't you at school?"

Asher raised her eyebrows, "because it's almost 4:30 in the afternoon. Evie's home too, downstairs on her phone."

Her mother's eyes seemed to be focusing, the painting mania easing.

"What about dad?"

Asher frowned, "he's away on conference until next Friday, remember?"

"Oh yes, that's right."

Mother and daughter fell silent, looking nervously at each other.

"How's your head?" blurted Asher, "Has the migraine eased?"

Jennifer rubbed her hand across her forehead, oblivious to the streaks of paint she left behind on pale skin and white hair. She frowned thoughtfully.

"Actually, I haven't thought about it, but it feels much better sweetheart."

Asher felt her body relax, and the tightness in her chest eased. The migraines were often the tipping point for depression, little red pills and days in bed. During those days it was like her bright, brilliant mother was being consumed by shadow.

"What are you working on?" she asked curiously, stepping forward to get a better look at the canvas.

Immediately her mother tensed, her hands quickly reaching out to twist the canvas so Asher couldn't see the images there.

"Don't come any closer! It's none of your business!" growled Jennifer, her voice rough with anger.

Asher froze, eyes wide with shock. Her mother had never spoken to her like that before.

"Mum?"

Her mother blinked rapidly, then sighed deeply. "Sorry darling, I'm tired and quite hungry. It's been so long, I'm not match fit," she finished with a small smile of apology.

Asher glanced around the room. "You always had snacks up here, so you didn't have to interrupt yourself. Did you bring anything up?"

"No, I wasn't really intending to come up here at all. I was on my way to bed after you girls left and some-how I ended up here."

"That was 8am!" exclaimed Asher, "no wonder you're hungry. Do you want to come downstairs?"

Her mother nodded and took a couple of steps towards her, then she stopped, her face contorted almost in pain.

"Actually Asher I think I'd better keep painting. The muse is strong!" she finished lightly, her jolly tone at odds with the grimace on her face.

"Okay, well I'll go grab something and bring it up. Anything in particular?"

But Jennifer was already lost in the canvas and no longer hearing her.

Asher moved slowly down the narrow attic stairs, half listening for any muttering or noises from the studio, but her mother was silent. She felt perplexed and conflicted. It was great to see mum painting again, it felt right, like a missing puzzle piece was found and finally back in place. But the intensity, the anger, was unsettling. It was almost as though her mother was being compelled to paint but was not enjoying it.

Asher understood the compulsion, she always felt that way about music, but she had never not enjoyed it. Music was only ever a happy place, never a hardship or a source of pain. If she was honest, she secretly loved how similar she and mum were, both artists in their own worlds, driven by their creative obsessions. It was something special they shared, that belonged just to them, not dad or Evie.

So when mum had stopped painting, when the dread words 'nervous breakdown' had started to be murmured, Asher had been secretly terrified. Was her mother's art going to destroy her? Would Asher's music one day destroy her too?

As Jennifer had retreated into migraines and nightmares, the unease had grown stronger within Asher. Her focus became being the best she could be, so as not to upset or worry mum. Excellent grades, done. No issues with behaviour at school, of course. No demands or pressures at home, absolutely not. Always a quiet, introspective girl, she became more so – careful not to be too loud or demanding. She kept thinking that if she could just find the way to be exactly right, then mum would be okay.

While Evie's social life expanded Asher felt she needed to stay close to home, especially when dad was away.

To see mum back in the studio was a relief – maybe things were getting better! But it was also unsettling – would today's zealous painting finally push her over the edge into a place that Asher couldn't reach? What had sent her running from the studio three years ago? It was a question Asher had asked many times, but she'd been rebuffed and shooshed by her dad, until she'd learned that it was a topic not to be discussed.

"Be a good girl and let your mother rest. She needs quiet, not all your questions." So Asher had become as quiet as she could.

"Be a good girl and don't be so emotional. Leave your mother alone." So Asher had become as undemanding as she could.

If she ever felt lonely, or scared, or angry, or upset, she pushed the feelings deep inside and focused on playing music that made her feel better, calmer and centred. Evie was the pretty and effervescent daughter. Asher was the quiet and good one.

Only once had she ever pushed against the rules of compliance she had created for herself.

Two years ago, when her mother was resting, Asher had crept up the attic stairs and pushed softly on the door. It hadn't moved. She pushed harder, but still the door did not yield. Confused she had stepped back and then noticed the barrel lock and padlock that had been drilled across the top of the door and frame. The only way in was with a key. Asher had left without answers and not returned, until today.

She made her way down the stairs and along the hallway, faded carpet runners muffling her footsteps, floorboards creaking randomly. It was soothing. The Beast was "full of atmosphere" mum would say, "boring and dull I think you mean" Evie would retort.

Asher usually loved the moody silences, they gave her room to think and create, but today the atmosphere seemed heavy and uncomfortable. Like a breath held too long. She walked into the kitchen, her mind a million miles away.

"Asher!"

Her own breath whooshed out of her as she jumped ten feet into the air.

"Evie! Hells bells, you scared the daylights out of me!"

Evie waved a hand dismissively. "Why are you so jumpy? Actually, I don't want to know. Have you seen mum? I want to tell her I'm heading out for pizza with the crew."

"She's in the studio," replied Asher, saying each word slowly, then repeating them deliberately, "in the studio."

Surprise lit up Evie's face, "wow, wasn't expecting that. Is she okay up there?"

"She seems to be, I guess," answered Asher, reluctant to share her unease with her sister.

Since Evie had become all grown up and superior, they no longer shared their feelings and thoughts with one another.

"Great, well can you let her know I'm out with Josie and Bec and Simon. I'll be home before 10pm and I have my phone. I'm going to get ready then head off."

"Don't you want to go up and see her?"

"Not really." Evie pushed past her, heading for her room.

"Why not?"

"Not interested in the whole crazy painter thing," was the breezy response.

Unexpected anger rose fast and hot within Asher. Her body shook and her face flushed with heat. Asher could not control the words as they burst out of her.

"Oh really? So it's that easy for you is it? Just dismiss mum as crazy and you just live your own stupid, shallow, selfish life with your dimwit friends and not have to worry. Is that it Evie? How nice to be you!" she finished with a shout.

Her heart pounded crazily and she was shocked by the intensity of her reaction. She never let her emotions run out of control. But today she felt... different. Like everything suppressed was bubbling within her.

Evie whipped around, her eyes blazing with surprise at Asher's outburst, and anger of her own.

"That's just what you want to think, isn't it? You are the perfect little mouse, creeping around, making sure mum has a wet compress and a warm tea, while I am the selfish, neglectful, useless daughter who doesn't give a brass penny. Sure. Easy for you to think that, suits you perfectly. I might be selfish, but you are pathetic, a great big suck-up."

"What does that mean?" yelled Asher.

"Nothing weirdo. Nothing." The intensity whooshed out of Evie with a great sigh, but she continued to scowl.

"Look Ash, I don't pretend to understand the whole creative genius thing, but I do know that something happened three years ago that almost drove mum crazy and it happened in that studio. I don't want to go up there, I don't want to be part of it, I don't want to witness it again. It was bad enough that day, I'm not going there again."

Asher watched her sister disappear through the dining room, trying to make sense of what she had said.

"Wait Evie, Evie!"

"What now?"

"What do you mean you don't want to witness it again. Were you there in the studio that day?"

"For crying out loud, you are doing my head in! Seriously? We are still talking about this?" She sighed deeply, clearly annoyed. "Fine. Yes I was there, and so were you. Except you came downstairs for a drink and missed the whole crazy flip out."

Asher felt dizzy; her head was reeling. "So do you remember what happened? What triggered it?"

Evie's bright blue eyes narrowed.

"I find it hard to believe you don't remember. But if you insist that you don't, then let me remind you. She was painting your 13th birthday portrait. You had been up there for a few hours. I went to ask if I could sleep over at Bec's house. Mum was painting and getting agitated. I don't know what you did, but she started yelling at you and you were crying, kept saying you were sorry. She sent you downstairs and then she began yelling at invisible people. I don't think she even knew I was in the room. Then she totally lost her mind and threw paint all over the easel. Next thing she had collapsed on the floor, holding her head and howling in pain."

Asher's chest felt tight and her breath was burning in her throat. "I really don't remember any of this," she whispered, "I didn't know."

Evie shrugged. "Well now you do. Is that all?"

Asher swallowed deeply. "Do you think..." she paused, "do you think it was my fault?"

Evie shrugged again, but she wouldn't look Asher in the eye, sliding her gaze away to stare at her phone.

"I gotta go."

After delivering her bombshell Evie disappeared to her room, then out with her friends. Asher sat for ages in the kitchen, completely forgetting to take food up to the studio. Eventually the cool night air forced her to get up and close the French doors and finally make a cup of tea and toast for mum.

Her mother barely acknowledged Asher when she placed the plate and mug on the table beside her. Asher crept out of the studio without a word.

By 7pm Asher was in her pj's and getting ready for bed. It was ridiculously early, but she felt mentally exhausted. Even her composing was fragmented and difficult.

As she cleaned her teeth and ran a brush through her hair, she went over and over what she knew of that day in the studio. But no matter how hard she wracked her brain, she could not remember any of what Evie had talked about. Why not? How could there be no memory of it when the fall out had such significant impact on the months and years that followed?

Asher had never previously spoken with Evie about the actual Event. Her sister had never offered to discuss it, and

Asher had certainly never imagined they had been part of it. Evie had not opened up to her at all. She had thrown herself into a social life with her friends, spending as little time at home with their floundering mother as possible.

Asher climbed into bed and pulled the soft quilt up under her chin. She felt dazed but her mind would not rest.

If Evie had witnessed it all first-hand, why had she withdrawn from their mother in the weeks that followed? Even now she was rather dismissive of mum's periods of unwellness.

The familiar resentment and frustration at Evie's selfishness and shallowness rose within Ash. This time she did not smother it like she always had before. She had spent years pretending she did not feel abandoned by her sister, pretending everything was fine, that she was fine. Pretending she didn't feel upset that she, the little sister, had been the one who supported dad and made life comfortable for mum. Evie just carried on with her life, largely ignoring Ash... wait, did Evie *blame her? Did mum?*

The ugly thought punched through her hostility to Evie and left Asher with a sick taste in her mouth. Did they all think this was her fault? Had she done something to set this all off?

A text from Kate beeped into her messages around 7:30pm, and Levi tried calling a few minutes later. She ignored the call, sending them both a message saying everything was fine and they would catch up tomorrow.

She stayed curled up in bed. She wasn't hungry; dinner time came and went unnoticed. Instead she lay there, watching the minutes tick by and trying to convince her body to sleep.

Around 9pm her mother came downstairs, pausing outside Asher's room. She tapped lightly on the door before opening it.

"Ash?" queried her mother softly, "you awake?"

Fear and shame and guilt washed through her, *I'm the reason she became so unwell*, and Asher found she couldn't respond. Assuming her silence meant she was asleep, her mother quietly closed the door and headed downstairs, the creaking of the hallway floor registering her departure.

Around 10:30pm Evie arrived home, banging around downstairs for a bit then the bathroom, before heading to her own room across the hall.

At 11:00pm her mother went off to bed and the house and its inhabitants settled into sleep. Everyone except Asher. She was exhausted and cold. Her thin summer quilt was no match for these progressively cooler Autumn evenings.

11:12pm... 11:26pm... looking at the clock just seemed to make her restlessness worse. With a great sigh Asher hauled herself out of bed. Her bladder would not be denied any longer, and she was never going to sleep while she was so cold.

A quick trip to the loo dealt with one issue and a fossick in the linen cupboard in the hall solved the other. On the bottom shelf, beneath the flannel sheets, *note to self,* she thought, *put flannel sheets on bed tomorrow*, was a heavy patchwork comforter, the sort you throw over your existing blankets or quilt. She vaguely remembered it from childhood. It had been her mother's favourite for a long time. The comforter was so big Asher could wrap it completely around herself, almost twice. Snuggly and comforting as the name promised. Just perfect.

Cocooned in the comforter Asher immediately felt better, but a low, persistent grumbling from her neglected tummy raised a third issue which took her downstairs instead of back to bed.

She was munching on vegemite toast and sipping hot tea in the kitchen, enjoying the moonlight streaming through the glass doors, when the first shivers of awareness tickled the back of her neck.

Some-one else was up.

Asher swallowed quickly and sat perfectly still, listening for the footsteps that would identify who was heading her way – mum or Evie. But she heard nothing at all, and the doorway to the kitchen remained empty. Unease gurgled soundlessly in her stomach.

'You're being ridiculous,' she silently scolded herself, but it was half-hearted, and the sense that some-one was in the other room grew stronger.

A quick glance at the clock gave the time as 11:58pm. Almost midnight on a full moon. Asher shivered.

Reason kept insisting that she was imagining things, but intuition told her to sit quietly and listen. Her attentiveness was rewarded a moment later by the creak of floorboards. Aha! Not even the stealthiest of burglars could outmanoeuvre The Beast.

With a surge of adrenaline Asher stood up and tiptoed to the half open kitchen door. If she positioned herself in the right spot she would have a good view into the moonlit living room, while remaining out of sight herself.

Heart pounding, *so loud! Surely the burglar will hear!*, Asher scanned the large room, searching for the intruder. The prickling on the back of her neck was now dancing down her spine, and her hands felt clammy and cold.

Three heartbeats, four, then Asher felt like her heart stopped completely, before resuming again with such ferocity Asher was sure the woman standing in their living room would hear it pounding.

Even though she had suspected some-one was in the house, suspecting and actually seeing the intruder were two completely different things.

She was tall, as tall as Asher, but unlike Asher she didn't seem awkward and too gangly. She seemed the perfect height for herself, and she stood with confidence, exuding strength and grace. A long-sleeved blue dress skimmed over a slim figure and hung in heavy folds around her calves. A narrow gold belt looped around her waist, and multi-coloured leather ankle boots added to the unique elegance that she exuded.

Vaguely Asher was aware that she should have been afraid, but strangely she wasn't. This woman did not seem like any burglar Asher could imagine, and she radiated calm and patience. She seemed to be waiting for something, or some-one. What?

Another breath and Asher had her answer. Light, furtive steps coming down the stairs revealed her own mother, wrapped in her old dressing gown.

If Jennifer was surprised or scared to see a strange woman in her home she certainly did not show it. She crossed the room quickly, her back straight and chin high.

She almost looks defiant, thought Asher curiously.

Eye to eye the two women looked at each other, something silent passing between them. Her mother was the first to speak, her voice low and cool, her tone neutral.

"Hesta. What are you doing here?"

"It's nice to see you too Gin. It's been too long."

Her mother shrugged. "That depends on your point of view."

"That is true for all things," was the response.

"So? What brings you here tonight?"

The older woman laughed warmly, the deep sound filling the room.

"You know perfectly well why I am here Gin. My threads are tangling, there is an energy disruption in the patterns, and all signs lead to you. You are tinkering my dear."

She stared pointedly at the dried paint that was still splayed across her mother's hands. "Did you think I wouldn't know?"

Asher frowned, trying to muddle a meaning from the conversation. None of it made sense to her, but for some reason it seemed to make sense to mum. Jennifer shrugged, seemingly unconcerned, but Asher knew her mother well and could see the tension in her neck and jaw.

"Gin," continued the woman Hesta, and there was no warm laughter now, "what you are doing is foolhardy and dangerous. The threads are tangling, I am fighting to keep them straight. Energy streams are behaving erratically, Crafters are at risk. I need the girl. Destroy the painting."

"No!" the word burst out of her mother. "You have no right to ask that of me. I owe you nothing. You would drag us all into your games and play us as pawns. I will NOT have it, I will NOT. Your grievances and battles are nothing to her, to me."

"These are your people Gin, surely…"

"No Hesta, they are not. These are my people, here in this house, in this town, in this world."

Hesta exhaled impatiently. "What you are trying to do cannot be done. You are not strong enough."

"Watch me," was the grim response.

"Gin! Be reasonable. The price you'll pay is your own sanity, maybe even your life. Surely you know that."

Her mother laughed, a hollow sound lacking all humour.

"Oh I am aware of that. But I believed that once before, and yet, here I am. Still alive, still sane, though in pain much of the time. And that is because I refuse to paint the picture you want me to. How much worse can it be? There might even be relief in painting what I want. The stars know I have felt better today than I have in years."

"Then we are at a stalemate. You paint and I weave, both trying to win. But I am the stronger." Hesta finished, not unkindly, but firmly.

"That may be so, but I have something you never had, something that makes me almost unstoppable," Gin paused, waiting.

Hesta sighed heavily, "Fine, I'll oblige you. What is that?"

"The driving need to protect my child no matter what. The willingness to sacrifice my sanity, my life, to protect her. And that, *mother,* is something you could never understand, and all your weaving cannot change that."

Hesta recoiled back, as though avoiding a blow. For the first time her incredible poise seemed shaken, and her face crumbled.

Asher felt shock hit her hard in the stomach. *Mother?* For some reason she had always thought mum's family were dead. She had never ever mentioned them.

"Gin, I'm begging you please don't do this."

"And why not? So you can fulfil your prophecy and use my child as a soldier in your war?" asked Gin, derision curling around every word.

Hesta shook her head. "No. Because I cannot bear to see you step off into the darkness, to fling your mind, your senses, your very soul into the Void. Because regardless of all that has passed, and all that will come, you are still *my* child."

"I survived it once, decades ago, I will survive it again."

"No, you will not," was the response.

Asher could feel the thundering of her heart in her chest, in her ears, even in her fingers. She wasn't sure she was still breathing. Her mind felt numb and her stomach was tumbling.

"Well then, we're at an impasse. You want her, I don't want you to have her. We'll both do whatever it takes to get what we want. So what now Hesta? Hmmmm? How are the threads woven?"

Asher held her breath. She did not understand any of this, but she knew the next moment was important. Very important. She could feel her mother's tension echoed in her own body.

A movement at the stairs drew all their gazes, as a slight figure wrapped in a blue dressing gown drifted into the room.

"Mum?" asked Evie sleepily, "What's going on?"

Mum's face, already pale in the moonlight, blanched in horror. "Go back upstairs now!" she ordered, fear in her voice.

"But..." protested Evie, confusion jarring her out of sleepiness, "who is she?"

"Go upstairs!"

"Now Gin, stop yelling at the poor girl, you're frightening her. Surely I can speak with my own grand-daughter. Come here child, let me see you more clearly." The words were gently said, but the command was unmistakeable. "My old eyes are not as strong as they once were."

Gin snorted but said nothing. From where Asher was, it looked like mum's eyes were glazed with focus, but she could not work out what she was focusing on. Warily Evie moved closer to Hesta, stopping when the full moon cast her fully into light.

"Interesting," murmured their unwelcome guest, "you are smaller than I imagined, and fairer too. There has not been a blonde Wen in our family for many generations."

Hesta leaned closer, carefully inspecting the young woman before her. Evie threw a questioning look at Gin, who shook her head almost imperceptibly and mouthed 'say nothing'.

"Blonde could be poetry, or perhaps pottery," Hesta muttered to herself, "but is it strong enough?"

She reached out her left hand, palm facing up, fingers extended to Evie. "Blood to blood," she murmured. It seemed to Asher that the tips were crackling, and her own tingled in response.

Evie did not react. Hesta frowned and dropped her hand.

"Gin?" Her daughter's deliberate lack of response drew an impatient 'harrumph' from Hesta.

"Child, what are your talents? Your strengths?"

Evie wrinkled her nose at the strange woman staring intently at her, but true to mum's silent request she said nothing.

Hesta smiled ruefully. "So that's how it's going to be. Well neither of you need to speak to me, now you are here I have plenty to say for myself. And as I am certain those ears are not painted on," she threw an arch look at Gin, clearly delighted with the play on words, "you can hear what I have to say. There are only a few hours until the moon drops and I will be out of time."

Hesta turned to face the window, momentarily distracted by her own thoughts.

Gin caught Evie's eye. "Asher?" she mouthed. "Asleep" was the soundless response. Her mother nodded once, then her face returned to neutral.

"If we have to do this then be brief Hesta. My daughter and I are both exhausted and neither of us are in the mood for an epic story tonight. Let's get this over with."

But Hesta was silent, her clear gaze passing between Gin and Evie. Once more she reached out her hand to Evie and again Asher's fingers tingled and twitched. She rubbed her fingers together to relieve the feeling.

"Something is not right here," murmured Hesta, "there is something you are trying to hide. I can feel your energy Ginarwen, swirling around me. It has been many years and the touch is light, but I would always recognise it. You are attempting a perception alteration on me, and it is working. But why? What you are you hiding?"

Gin shrugged, her face completely impassive. "If you say so."

"And as it is a low energy spend you could keep it up all night until I am out of time. Clever, and frustrating."

Hesta glanced around the room, her eyeline flitting along walls and cabinetry shrouded in shadows.

"There is more than one way to discover what you do not want me to know."

Asher frowned, trying to work out what was going on. This night just got stranger and stranger. She tightened the comforter around her. Hesta began moving, slowly picking up and replacing ornaments and books. Asher's gaze darted back to her mother whose very stillness thrummed with tension. What was mum hiding and how? She had not moved once during this strange, surreal encounter.

Intrigued, Asher watched as Hesta picked up a magazine and peered closely at it, then a pack of playing cards, but for some reason she seemed to ignore the family photos propped everywhere around the room.

Puzzling really. Surely if you were looking for clues about a person you would start with their photos. First rule of social media stalking.

With a flash of insight Ash understood. Mum was shielding the photos! That's what she was hiding! It seemed she did not want Hesta to focus on the photos. With unexpected clarity Asher realised why. Mum did not want Asher to be seen.

She stood as still as she could, not moving, not breathing, as Hesta stepped past the kitchen door and strode back to where Gin and Evie were standing.

Relief flooded through Asher, but then she felt tickling on the tip of her nose. Frantically she rubbed at it, trying to eliminate the urge to sneeze. But it was futile. The sneeze would not be quelled. So she buried her face into the patchwork comforter and turned her body away, hoping to muffle the sound as much as possible.

And when it did happen, it was a tiny, dampened 'hmph' that in any other moment would have been completely undetected. But on this bizarre night, at that exact moment, The Beast and all her occupants fell completely silent and that small, muffled sneeze carried clear across the living room to the three silent women on the other side.

"Ash?" called out Evie, and just like that Gin's concentration was broken and the perception filter shattered. Immediately Hesta's eyes blazed with triumph.

"She's not the one!" she thundered. "She's not..."

"Be quiet Hesta!" stormed mum, fury shaking every word. "Do not say what you're about to say or I will tear apart your threads and throw you into the Void myself!"

Hesta raised her eyebrows, clearly considering the possibility of Gin making good on her threat.

"As you wish. So if she's not-," she paused, "-the one I'm looking for, then who is?"

And Asher knew exactly what she had to do. She had been feeling the energy thrumming in her ears since Hesta had first stretched out her hand to Evie. *Blood to blood...* Even if this night passed without her being discovered Hesta would return again and again. Or mum would do the thing with her painting that was so frightening to both of them. And Asher could not risk mum being hurt again because of her.

She folded the comforter and dropped it over the bench behind her. Then firmly she pushed the door open and strode into the light.

"Me, *grandmother,* you are looking for me."

Chapter Three

Hesta's request

As Asher moved forward everyone started talking at once. Evie pleading for 'somebody to just tell me what the hell is going on', mum yelling at Ash to 'go upstairs and stay there, no matter what', and Hesta crowing that 'destiny cannot be outplayed.'

"QUIET, all of you!" yelled Asher, throwing her hands in the air like a conductor silencing an unruly orchestra.

It felt like energy leapt from her hands, unseen but perhaps felt by the others, for they fell instantly silent.

"Thank you" she mumbled awkwardly, all at once feeling embarrassed and unsure. She had no idea what was happening, or what was going to happen, but every fibre of her being pulsed with the certainty that there was no going back from this moment, and that made her afraid.

"Ahhh," breathed Hesta with satisfaction, "and here she is, at last."

She stepped closer and for the first time Asher got a good look at her face.

"You look so much like mum," she blurted, "except older."

Hesta smiled warmly, "and you look so much like my father did, except younger. And female, of course."

She ran her gaze over the tangled, thick curls cascading over Asher's shoulders.

"And red! That's what I was expecting."

She touched her own auburn hair, still rich with colour despite the silver strands peeking through. Then she pierced Evie with a stern look, as though she was some-how responsible for the mistaken identity.

"So if this is Asher, who are you?" She raised an eyebrow.

"Evelyn," was the proud response, her chin high. Asher felt a surge of admiration. Evie was never cowed by anyone or anything.

"Ash..." mum opened her arms wide and Asher ran into them for a tight hug. She could feel her mother trembling.

"I'm sorry," she whispered, "I know you didn't want me to come out. But how bad can it be? We'll tell her to leave and then we'll go back to normal."

"If only it was that easy," sighed Gin, "nothing is that simple with her."

"What is going on?" interrupted Evie, coming close enough to be pulled into the hug. Mum said nothing for a moment, just kissed them on their foreheads each in turn.

"Hesta is indeed my mother, some-one I haven't seen in many years. I rather hoped I wouldn't be seeing her now either. But here we are. Over the next few days there are identical blue moons in both our galaxies, an astrological anomaly that creates a surge of power. It has allowed Hesta to travel here."

"Where from?" asked Evie, but mum did not answer her question.

"She's come to ask a favour of Asher. A rather large favour actually."

"What sort of favour?" asked Asher.

"Oh you know, the 'will you come with me and save my world from ruin' kind of favour," said Gin light-heartedly, but there was no humour in her tone. "I was really hoping, planning, that this meeting would never come to pass."

Evie shook her head in disbelief. "This is a joke right? A midnight visit from an unknown villainous grandmother-"

"Villainous!" snorted Hesta.

"-veiled threats and outright hostility, suggestions of another world and sinister plots, and somehow Asher is involved."

She did not wait for an answer.

"None of this makes any sense. And Asher is just, well Ash. There's nothing special about her. You don't even know she's there half the time. No offence Ash," she added casually, not even glancing at her sister.

Asher could not even pretend to be offended. It was absolutely true.

Hesta, who had remained mostly silent during their exchange focused her intense gaze on Asher.

"That's an interesting thing to say. Do you feel the energy pulsing from her?"

"Of course", "Nope" replied mum and Evie at the same time.

"Hmmm," mused their grandmother, circling slowly around Asher, *like a lioness trapping her prey*, thought Asher. She pressed closer into mum.

"There is definitely some type of cloaking charm, not too heavy, rather unsophisticated but subtle and hard to detect. Not my handiwork. Yours Gin?"

Mum shook her head and peered at Asher herself.

"I hadn't ever noticed before," she said, wonder in her voice, "How could I miss a cloaking charm on my own daughter?"

"It was not meant for you," dismissed Hesta, "whoever did this has created it over many years, a spiderweb of delicate layers. Very clever indeed. It makes her not invisible, but unremarkable, not worthy of notice, some-one you would struggle to remember or describe. Hiding her in plain sight."

"Well if I had thought to do it I would have made it so heavy and strong she would have been hidden from you until the end of time," retorted Gin tartly.

Hesta ignored her.

Evie stepped out of mum's embrace to look closely at her sister. "I can't see anything different, she just looks like plain old Asher to me."

"Clearly it works on Evelyn," mused Hesta, "so I assume it has a similar effect on other non-Crafters, and maybe even on some of *them*, depending on ability. The question is who laid it and for what purpose."

Asher had no answer to any of this. Fear had evaporated, now it simply felt like some strange dream. Something she was observing without really experiencing, because how could any of this actually be happening?

Deciding it was not real was strangely liberating. Now she could just go with whatever was happening instead of trying to make sense of it.

"Mum, are you guys talking about magic? Are you some kind of witch?"

Evie's voice was small and unsure, not a tone Asher was used to hearing from her bold, super confident sister. Evie had graduated high school with top marks and was studying Law and International Relations at university. She had boldness and confidence by the bucketload.

Gin looked to Hesta, who returned the look with a raised brow. For the first time since this strange encounter began, Asher realised Hesta was deferring to her daughter. She had been so dominating but now she actually seemed to be seeking permission.

Emotions flitted across Gin's face, chasing each other so quickly it was nearly impossible to untangle them. Pain was there. And fear and loss and regret, and something so complex it could not be named.

With a brief nod Gin conceded. Permission granted. Hesta sighed deeply.

"Witch, magic, these are not terms or concepts we use. It's purely energy and levels of ability to manipulate that energy."

"What's the difference between magic and energy?"

"The difference Evelyn is simple in my world and rather over-complicated in yours."

"And that's another thing. What's this talk of worlds? There's one world and we're standing on it."

Evie was getting her courage back. Asher was glad of it, she too wanted to know the answers to these questions and it was always easier when Evie took charge.

"Have you told them nothing?" Hesta asked Gin accusingly. Their mother waggled her brows.

"Well we have a bit of work to do then. Perhaps we should sit down and have a cup of tea."

Ten minutes later and the four of them were seated comfortably in the living room, lamps on, fire lit and steaming mugs of tea in hand.

The scene was so very unmagical, so very familiar and mundane that, with the exception of Hesta, it almost felt like they were going to pull out scrabble and have family game night.

Asher wondered randomly if Hesta and mum had ever done family game nights when Gin was growing up. The thought almost made her giggle. She couldn't imagine her mother as a child playing games with intense Hesta.

"So let's begin," said Hesta, placing her cup carefully on the table beside her.

"Every lifeform is composed of layers of energy. Most humans remain oblivious to this, but some people can see these layers as colours, other people can tap into their own energy and use it, others can tap into the energy of any living being. In my world people manipulate energy through a medium such as sculpture, or in the case of your mother, painting."

Hesta paused while Evie and Asher processed this new information.

"So everyone in your world can do this?" asked Evie.

"No. It is a well-accepted talent but still a rare one. Those people who can do this naturally are called Crafters. We craft energy through a medium. Different mediums have different strengths. Some-one who dyes fabrics is usually not as powerful as some-one who sculpts. Your mother is a painter, a high-level Craft."

"What about you?" asked Asher, curiosity overcoming her shyness.

"I am The Weaver."

The sentence rang with power, and though she spoke softly it echoed around the room, as though she had boomed it through a speaker. It seemed to Asher that the trees outside rustled, and the fire leapt a little higher.

"Hesta," murmured Gin nervously, her gaze darting from the front door to the windows. "Even here..."

"Yes indeed," conceded Hesta, "you are correct. I will be more careful."

"What?" demanded Evie.

"The thing is sweetheart, it is almost impossible for humans to travel between the worlds unless you are an incredibly powerful Crafter..."

"But?" prompted Evie.

"... but it has been done by others and not all of them travel with good intentions. The blue moon power surge makes many things possible. We don't need any *more* un-invited guests."

Hesta pointedly ignored the barb and continued her explanation.

"Crafting is an ancient and noble profession. Crafters co-exist with non-Crafters across my world, each relying on and celebrating the gifts and talents of the other. But the balance is out of whack. Crafters are under attack, disappearing..." she paused, clearing her throat which was suddenly thick with emotion.

"I weave and I weave and there is only one answer in the threads. A war is coming unless the balance is restored. Unless the terrible wrong that is occurring is put right."

"How?" breathed Asher, blood pounding in her ears. It all sounded utterly ridiculous, but somehow she knew the truth of what Hesta was saying, she could feel it pulsing in her whole being. *Blood to blood...*

"I don't know yet," replied Hesta, but there was hesitancy in her voice. She wasn't sharing everything, that much was clear.

Asher cradled her cup of tea between both hands, the warmth seeping into her skin. A solid, familiar feeling in this strange dreamlike encounter. The fire had not yet warmed the room, and shivering a little she thought longingly of the patchwork comforter folded across the bench in the kitchen. She would go and retrieve it in a moment. Hesta was talking again.

"So I have come seeking assistance from the one person I can truly trust, the one Crafter I am sure has not been manipulated or corrupted."

All eyes turned to Gin.

"Mum," breathed Evie.

"So it appears," answered their mother drily, "but what you want from me is not possible."

"Of course it is!" snapped Hesta. "She is a child, you make these decisions, she obeys. That is the way of it."

Gin laughed with true humour.

"Oh mother, you have never understood teenage girls! It's been too long since you were one, and I don't think you even noticed when I was one. On this world, even more than ours, teenagers are hard to compel! And even if I could make her, I wouldn't."

"So this is the part about Ash I gather," Evie cut off their mother's laughter. "The big favour."

Two pairs of green eyes and one set of blue eyes were now firmly on Asher. She tried not to squirm, taking a hurried sip of tea to cover her discomfort. The silence lingered and Asher realised everyone was waiting for her to speak. She swallowed hard.

"So what's the favour then? What do you need from me?"

Hesta smiled, and though it was full of affection and warmth Asher had the distinct sensation she was falling down a hole.

"I am The Weaver," said Hesta, and her voice thrummed inside Asher's body. "I weave the threads of all beings, I tell the stories of a thousand years that have passed and a thousand yet to come. Queens are crowned and kingdoms fall, and still I weave the stories of all time, before and after. I am the history of the five universes and I am their future."

Asher could not look away from Hesta, it was like being mesmerised by the flames of a dancing campfire on a clear, windless night. No other sound intruded on that sacred space, there was only the glow of Hesta and the sound of her voice.

Asher could feel it winding around her body, compelling her to lean closer, to listen harder. Nothing else mattered, only this.

"There has always been a Weaver, maintaining the balance, ensuring the gifts of the Crafters are tied to the fortunes of all. There has always been a Weaver, there must always be a Weaver..." Hesta's voice was hypnotic, Asher could feel it pulling, pulling, "I am the Weaver and you are my Heir."

Blood pounded through Asher's ears, her body felt light, tingly. She was no longer sitting in an armchair in her parents' house. Now she was free of her body, flying through space and time, and though she couldn't see Hesta she could feel her travelling beside her, energy pulsing.

"I am The Weaver," Hesta announced to the planets, and Asher felt their awe and deference.

"I am The Weaver," Hesta thundered to the stars, and Asher felt them tremble with excitement and fear.

"I am The Weaver," Hesta called across the galaxies and all at once Asher felt the presence of countless other energy sources. Moment by moment women started to materialise around her. Some were very young and so beautiful Asher found it hard to look away, some so old and faded they were hard to see clearly.

"I am The Weaver," they responded, a melodious chorus that swelled like a wave through time. And Asher understood. These were her grandmothers, and their grandmothers, and theirs. An unending line of mothers to daughters, generations of Weavers protecting and maintaining the balance of their world, and countless worlds beyond. Shoulder to shoulder they stood, the beginning of the line lost beyond her gaze, the closest to her being Hesta.

Her heart was beating fast, but it was joy not fear that pumped in her veins. The women were smiling at her, holding out their hands, welcoming her.

"We are The Weaver," the many voices sang, melding into only one, "you are The Weaver."

Blood to blood...

Asher felt her tingly, weightless arms reach out in response. *Yes,* she thought, *this is where I belong. Here among the stars.*

Then unexpectedly the images began to shimmer, to fade and disappear. Another voice was breaking into her consciousness, pulling her back to the big, comfy armchair.

"Asher! Asher my sweet girl. Focus on me, follow my voice. Come home now."

Mum.

Sensations and memories rushed through Asher – mum cuddling her when she was little and afraid of the dark, mum changing her pj's when she had vomited in the night, mum laughing with her, and holding her close when she cried. With every beat of her heart she felt mum's love. That's where she belonged, not lost in the stars with memories of long dead ancestors. Mum was real. This was not.

With a rush, like she had dropped from the top of a roller coaster to the very bottom, Asher crashed back into her body. She gasped in shock, taking a few deep breaths to steady herself. Her whole body thrummed with energy.

"What happened?" she gasped, "what was that?"

Desperately she looked to her mother as her vision steadied and her head cleared.

"*That*," replied mum, her voice icy cold with anger and her furious gaze firmly on Hesta, "was a controlling old woman overplaying her hand. A shameful bit of crafting that proves how truly manipulative she has become in her quest for power."

Colour flooded Hesta's cheeks. Asher had the distinct feeling she was not used to being told off.

"Not manipulative Gin, just desperate," she answered, her voice small but defiant. "I'm not doing this for power, I only know that the threads weave always this – Asherwen. She is the answer. Without her all is lost."

"So dramatic," retorted Gin, anger still hot in her words.

"Why me?" asked Asher, "why not Evie or mum? The line of Weavers was clear – mother to daughter. I saw them all but not mum or Evie. Why skip to me?"

"That is a very good question Asher," answered Hesta, but as she said nothing further it was really no answer at all.

Asher turned to her mother who shrugged apologetically but did not say anything either.

Asher was starting to get frustrated. This bizarre, dreamlike encounter was becoming more and more infuriating. So many half-truths and secrets, so many startling revelations and confusions. A magical grandmother seeking her aid, a magical mother trying to thwart her. Asher's whole world was suddenly upside down and inside out. She did not know what to think, what to believe.

It was 2am and she was exhausted and overwhelmed.

Abruptly she stood up. "I've had enough."

Everyone looked at her but nobody said a word. "I'm going to bed now," she announced and headed for the stairs.

"Asherwen," commanded Hesta.

That name again! What does it mean? thought Ash. Reluctantly she stopped walking but did not turn around.

"I know this has all been a shock to you, something I blame your mother for, as she should have been preparing you. But here we are. I cannot command you to return with me, nor can I simply take you. Before your 16th birthday you need to be in Andera. You need to come willingly and of your own free will. I understand what I am asking of you and if I had any other choice, any other option, I never would have come."

Asher could feel the truth in her words but still she did not turn around. She was close to tears of exhaustion and confusion and she did not want anyone to see.

"I am aware I am asking a great deal of you with very little information, but time is of the essence. Even now there are changes in the energy fields of planets far beyond here. We must act with haste. We need to leave tonight. You need training, to prepare for what is coming."

Asher felt as though she had been hit in the stomach, knocking the wind out of her. *Tonight! She had to decide now?*

Her mother's sharp intake of breath drew Asher back around to face them all. Mum looked sick, her skin a yellowy greenish colour. Clearly she was just as distressed as Asher. Evie was silent, as she had been for a long time now, her face totally impassive. Asher had no idea what she was thinking or feeling.

"Mum," her voice cracked.

Gin reached over and enveloped her in a warm, reassuring hug.

"What do I do?" whispered Asher.

Mum shook her head. "I have spent fifteen years trying to change this moment and I have failed. Some Threads are not ours to weave. I am so sorry Asher. I cannot protect you from this choice any longer."

Asher took a great shuddering breath. She felt more than a little overwhelmed. So much about this night was ridiculous and surreal. She wanted to go to bed, not travel across space with a secretive, untrustworthy stranger who wanted to rip her away from everything and everyone she had ever known.

Asher wasn't a Weaver, she did not have magic or powers, and she did not want them. If she was brutally honest with herself, this whole experience had frightened her a little. She just wanted to be ordinary and normal, and not cause any more pain for the people she loved.

"No," she mumbled into Gin's hair.

Asher cleared her throat and grabbed hold of her resolve. She stepped out of her mother's hug and straightened her spine.

"I said no," she repeated, loudly and clearly. "I will not go."

Energy crackled across the room and Asher's gaze was drawn back to Hesta whose face was unreadable.

"As you wish," was the sombre response, "I cannot compel you."

The Weaver stood with a fluid, easy motion and walked over to Asher. Once again Ash was startled by how similar Gin and Hesta were in looks. The same face almost exactly. But such different energy! Gin was an absent-minded earthmother in a worn out dressing gown, while Hesta was a Commander-in-Chief, a Queen.

Hesta reached behind her neck and unclasped a long necklace that had been hidden beneath her clothes.

Hanging from the chain was a heavy gold pendant in the shape of a spinning globe, with countless tiny stars etched on it.

"If you change your mind," was all she said.

On reflex Asher held out her hand and Hesta carefully placed the chain and pendant into her palm. The gold was warm in her hand and Asher could feel its energy pulsing.

"It's singing to me!" she exclaimed, eyes wide with wonder. "I can hear it, I can *feel* it!"

Hesta smiled with pleasure. "You are The Weaver's Heir. It knows you."

Asher stared at the globe for a long moment, then pulled her attention away from its song. She held it out to Hesta.

"Goodbye Hesta, I won't be needing this."

But Hesta didn't take the chain.

"Until we meet again Asher," her grandmother said softly.

Grey eyes met green eyes and Asher saw the endless energy of the universe swirling within the Weaver's steady gaze. It was mesmerising and terrifying. With a quick shake of her head, Asher fled up the stairs and to the safety of her room, the globe spinning from the chain in her hand as she ran.

Chapter Four

Saturday: Gin's Story

It was the persistent pinging of rain on the roof that finally pulled Asher from fitful, troubled sleep. She lay still for a few minutes, trying to clear the hazy residue of her nightmares. She felt exhausted and empty. The strange events of the night, of this morning really, swirled around in her head making it throb and pound.

A glance at her phone on the bedside table confirmed the time to be 8:30am. Not too early for a Saturday but considering she had tumbled into bed after 2am she just did not feel rested.

The patchwork comforter she had discarded downstairs lay heavily across her bed. She strained her memory, but she could not remember how it had arrived there. Probably mum checking on her after she had fled.

Longing for more sleep Asher burrowed deeper under the covers, the warmth a welcome contrast to the cold air on her face. She pulled the comforter over her head and closed her eyes, relaxing into the rhythm of the rain splattering above.

She lay like that for a few long minutes, relishing the sensation of being hidden and cocooned. The happenings of the midnight hours were already starting to fade.

Relax, relax she commanded herself. *Go back to sleep. Breathe in 2,3,4... Breathe out 2,3,4...* Nope, this wasn't working. Against her will she was awake and no amount of counting was going to fool her body.

With a sigh Asher threw back the covers and pulled herself out of bed, slipped on her uggs and wrapped her old grey dressing gown over her pj's. Automatically she scooped up her phone and dropped it in her pocket.

The floorboards creaked beneath the worn patterned carpet as she plodded out of her room in search of mum or breakfast, whichever she found first.

Downstairs the house was empty. Apprehension curling in her gut, Asher walked through the living room, but no strange grandmother waited for her there. In fact there was no sign she had ever been there. The wood and ashes lay cold in the fireplace, no teacup marked where she had sat. The room was bright and cheerful, filled with the morning sun and the light patter of the easing rain. Certainly none of the intensity or drama of only a few hours ago lingered. She remembered how her fingertips had tingled when Hesta had stretched out her hand.

Feeling slightly foolish, Asher pointed a finger at a photo on the mantle.

"Move," she commanded. "Abracadabra."

Nothing happened. Her fingers did not tingle and the picture did not move.

Had it all been a dream? she wondered as she headed into the kitchen and filled the kettle. Maybe she had fallen asleep after collecting the comforter from the linen cupboard and dreamed it all. Now, in the clear light of day, it all seemed so impossible. Magical unknown grandmothers from far off worlds did not appear in the middle of the night and demand you travel with them to save their realm. It was more likely that she had created it all in her sleep, triggered by mum painting again.

Cheered immensely by this likely explanation Asher made a cup of tea and pushed open the French doors to sit on the deck. The furniture and woodwork glistened with moisture, so she pulled a heavy-duty cushion from the storage box and plopped in on a chair.

The sky shone with a pale rainbow and the morning sun was warm on her face. The garden buzzed with sounds of birds and insects and the trees rustled lightly in the breeze. All was right in her world, and she closed her eyes to soak it all in.

"Good morning sweetheart!" chirped her mother, causing Ash to jump and almost spill hot tea all over her lap.

"Mum! You scared the daylights out of me!"

"Sorry Ash. You look so peaceful sitting here. How are you feeling today?"

Was that a loaded question? Asher looked closely at her mum, but she seemed to be smiling normally.

"Not too bad, considering the strange visit we had..."

Her mother looked at her in query, her eyebrows raised.

"You know... Hesta..." Asher dangled the word. "At midnight..."

Her mother shrugged. "I have no idea what you are talking about. Sounds like you had some crazy dream. What was it about?"

Asher grimaced self-consciously. "It's so bizarre, it's kind of embarrassing," she hesitated.

"Go on," encouraged mum.

"You were a magical painter called Gin, and you had a magical weaver mother called Hesta, and you were arguing about me going off with her to save her magical world. I was the only one who could help her," she finished sheepishly.

It sounded completely ridiculous when said out loud.

Mum laughed lightly. "Sounds awesome! I hope it's the sort of magic that helps me clean this house!"

Asher laughed too, relief flooding through her. She realised a small part of her had still been worried that it was real.

Mum turned to head back to her studio and her painting.

"Gin!" she mused to herself as she walked off, "much funkier than plain old Jennifer."

Asher sat for a while longer, thinking about the Hesta dream as she sipped at her tea. It had felt so real, and yet, so impossible.

Once the mug was empty she meandered back upstairs for a shower and to change. Evie was still fast asleep; she was known to have epic Saturday sleep-ins, which meant Ash didn't have to fight her for the bathroom.

A few hours spent in the music room at the piano totally restored her mood and sense of normality. Scoring out the music that had been itching at her yesterday was a huge dopamine rush. Some people loved to run, others loved to dance, for Asher it was all about making music. While she wrote and played she imagined mum painting happily in the studio, and dad working hard on his presentation to his colleagues on Monday in Singapore, and Evie laughing with her friends, a glowing, confident queen. She felt grounded and centred.

Time passed without regard, before the stiffness in her lower back reminded her that she had been sitting still for too long. Standing and stretching Asher looked around for her phone, wondering what time it was. Close to lunchtime judging by the grumbling in her tummy. It took a few minutes of fruitless searching in the music room before Ash remembered she had tucked her phone into her dressing gown pocket.

As she wandered into her bedroom she could hear the phone ringing, muffled by the robe.

That will be Levi, she thought, *goodness knows how many times he's called. We're meant to catch up today.*

She raced over to the bed and grabbed at the discarded dressing gown. The phone continued to ring persistently as she pawed through the material searching for the pocket, then it stopped. Missed it.

Urgency eased, Asher's fingers located the phone, but as she pulled it out of the pocket she found her fingers tangling with some-thing else, something both hard and warm. Carefully she pulled it out with her phone, the two items intertwined.

Waves crashed through her ears and the room seemed to spin briefly before she plopped onto the bed in shock. She threw the phone onto the bed without checking it, the missed call instantly forgotten. Her whole body and mind was completely focused on the other object now dangling from her fingers, humming happily to her.

A long gold chain and a spinning globe, etched with a thousand tiny stars.

"I knew it," she whispered, "that was no dream. But now I want some answers."

Asher leapt to her feet and headed for the attic.

"MUM!" she yelled, racing up the stairs to the studio, "MUM!"

She was breathless, her heart was pounding, her head was pounding, but it wasn't the headlong flight up to the top of the house that made her feel that way, it was anger, pure anger.

Asher burst into the studio, the door slamming against the wall.

Mum jumped around in shock, paint flying from her brush onto the floor.

"What's happened?"

Asher screeched to a halt, puffing heavily as she fought to get her breath and temper under control. So many things she wanted to say! In the end she settled for holding out the chain, the pendant spinning in the light.

"This," she said simply.

The colour leeched from Gin's face and she sighed deeply, almost deflating with the breath.

"Damnation. I scoured your room for that last night, but the rotten thing wouldn't be found. With its energy surrounding you I couldn't clear your memory. Evie thankfully will remember nothing."

The pendant hummed and Asher started in surprise. "It's laughing!"

"Yes," replied Gin dryly. "I can hear it." She pondered the pendant for a moment, then held out her hand palm up. "May I?"

Asher shrugged okay and placed the globe carefully onto her mother's palm. Immediately music flooded her ears and chatter, so much chatter! Asher couldn't really work out what she was hearing, but mum seemed completely tuned in. She was smiling at the golden globe, nodding and murmuring 'aha' at random intervals.

"What's happening?" asked Asher.

Gin glanced at her then focused her attention back on the globe.

"Shhhh," she said gently, "I understand." The music and chatter eased. "She's filling me in on the last few years. We used to spend quite a bit of time together." Gin's voice was filled with affection.

Asher wrinkled her nose. "She?"

"Well it seems impolite to call such an impressive energy source 'it', as she just reminded me."

The globe hummed.

"I hadn't really thought to see this again, I gave it up a long time ago."

Briefly Gin tightened her fingers around the pendant, enclosing it almost like a hug, then she whispered "shush now" and dropped the pendant in the pocket of her smock.

"Mum can you please tell me what's really going on. Honestly."

Gin sighed again. "When the painting is done, this will all be over," she pointed to the easel off to her right, its contents still a mystery to Asher.

"All what?!" Asher practically shouted.

She was so fed up with veiled statements that meant nothing and went nowhere. Her body was thrumming with frustration that threatened to boil over. For years she had squelched her emotions and now it seemed she had little control over them.

"Fine." Mum gestured to the big settee that was nestled along the wall. "Take a seat."

Asher plonked down into the deep blue cushions and immediately sneezed as dust flew everywhere.

"Oh, sorry about that. I should fire the housekeeper," mum joked lamely.

Asher gave her a tight smile but said nothing.

"Okay then," mum cleared her throat, "this is going to sound rather crazy."

Asher rolled her eyes. Seriously?

"Well, I guess I'll start with the pendant then. No actually, with the Weaver, that makes more... no, best to start with energy -" Gin was struggling to tell a story she had thought would never be told.

"Mum," said Ash firmly, "can we start with who you actually are."

That simple request seemed to settle Gin's thoughts. She took a deep breath. Then another.

"Alright. My name, the name I was given at birth is Ginar. I altered it to Jennifer when I settled here just over nineteen years ago." She paused, eyes dark with memory. Asher knew mum was no longer seeing her but looking into the past.

"I grew up on Andera, a world beyond this galaxy. I am, was, the only daughter and heir to the Weaver, and this I never questioned. From Mother to Daughter the role of the Weaver has passed since time began."

Asher found she was nodding. This part she knew.

"There are many worlds Ash, across the Universes, and the Weaver maintains the balance between them. She ensures Crafting, or perhaps magic is an easier way to understand it, is kept alive. It is from that source that all creativity, all inspiration, all wonder is woven." She paused briefly.

"The worlds exist separately, their inhabitants usually oblivious to the energy forces that bind them. The threads are delicate but the ripples from Andera can be felt even here on Earth at times. Travel between the worlds is possible but difficult and highly dangerous. The only way across is through the Void," she stopped.

Asher waited, holding her breath.

"If you are a strong enough Crafter you can hold open a portal and move through the Void without injury. If you are not strong enough, or something goes wrong, you can fall into the Void."

"What happens then?"

"Madness, for those who make it to the other side."

"And for those who don't?"

Mum shook her head. "We don't know. Death most likely."

Asher thought about this for a moment, puzzling through what she had heard last night.

"You said to Hesta that you survived the Void once before and you could do it again. Do you mean when you came here from -"

"Andera, yes."

"But why did you risk it? Why leave and come here?"

For a long time Gin did not respond and Asher was thinking of prompting her, when finally she sighed and rubbed her face with both hands. She sank onto a chair opposite Ash.

"The Weaver maintains balance, and Hesta is right when she said there must always be a Weaver. On many, many worlds energy crafters are persecuted or eradicated, out of fear or jealousy or who knows what. The Weaver works always to restore the threads so magic is not lost from the universes. Andera is the heart of that balance. If power is lost there then the ripples would be unimaginable. This requires a certain -" Gin paused, "ruthlessness. To be the Weaver requires a level of resolve and commitment that makes everyone and everything else merely..."

"Pawns in a game," finished Ash, echoing her mother's words from the previous night. Gin nodded, her green eyes dark with sadness.

"So that's what you were?"

"Worse. I, like all Weavers before me, was expected to be the Chess Master." She smiled sadly. "It turned out I wasn't strong enough. I made a mistake, a big one." Another long pause, then Gin shook her head and exhaled heavily.

"Anyway. I was injured, on the verge of death, no option left but to flee. So I fled as far as I could. As far away from Andera and all the tangled threads as I could go. I leapt across the Void."

"And you ended up here."

"Only just. In my panic and pain I had not prepared properly, had not raised the level of protections normally required for safe passage. It probably would have killed anyone else. But I am a Wen, and my basic measures were enough in the end."

"Wen," mused Asher, the word tickling at her memory. "That's what Hesta called you. Ginar*wen*, and me Asher-*wen*. What does that mean?"

Mum shook her head. "Maybe Hesta, damn her, was right. Maybe I should have been teaching you this years ago. But I really, really thought my leaving had altered the threads and none of this would matter."

"So what does it mean?" persisted Asher.

"Wen is a level of crafting skill, and you are not yet a Wen. Hesta was referring to the potential future you. That's the heir she needs."

"But you just said there always had to be a Weaver, so if that's not you and you don't want that to be me, what happens?"

"Hesta will work it out," said Gin.

"How?" said Asher.

But Gin would not answer, simply shaking her head.

Asher sat quietly for a moment, sorting through everything she had heard, both last night and now. Every explanation only raised more questions. She felt numb, as everything she had ever believed about her mother was shaken to the core. There was still so much she did not understand.

"So what is the Void then? A gap?"

"Yes, you could say that - a gap between worlds, devoid of life, of energy. It is almost anti-energy, and when you are in it," she shuddered, "it is as if all your own energy, your very life force, is being pulled from inside you. As I said, few attempt to cross, fewer make it."

"But Hesta did last night, and she seemed fine."

"She is strong," was the simple response.

"How did she know where you are? And why didn't she come earlier to take you back?"

Mum smiled without humour. "Oh she came once before, many years ago, she wanted to meet her heir. She's had to wait all these years until you were old enough. It's not me she wants. My last trip, well it had a lasting effect," she touched her white hair but offered no further explanation.

"As for knowing where I am, she and I are blood bonded Wens, she can always feel me in the threads, and I her. She knew where I had landed, but hopefully nobody else does."

But as Gin said the words a shadow darkened her face, some-thing clearly bothering her.

Asher did not know what to think anymore. In the space of twenty-four hours her whole world and her place within it had been completely upended. She could not really comprehend that her mother had come from another world, leaving her whole life behind.

"Did you ever regret leaving?" she asked, "did you miss your home and family?"

Mum opened her mouth to reply, but Asher cut her off, another thought jumping into her mind.

"Does dad know?!"

Gin laughed. "Yes actually he does. There have been many," she wrinkled her nose, searching for the word, "*happenings* that required explanation."

She genuinely seemed amused by the memories, but not inclined to share them.

Asher felt like she was watching a movie she had once known well, but now all the actors were muddling up their lines and the characters were changing. Unscripted plot twists were taking regular viewers by surprise. It was incredibly unsettling.

A new thought sprung into her mind.

"The old crazy woman in town, Marjorie – is she...?"

"A lost Crafter, her mind destroyed by crossing the Void?" Gin finished for her. "Yes."

There was so much more she wanted to know, but with one sudden movement Gin stood up, smoothing her paint-stained smock with both hands. "Now I paint."

Asher stood up too, ignoring the dust that accompanied her.

"What is so important about this painting? What are you actually doing?"

Gin considered for a moment then she nodded. "Come on then, come see."

Intrigued Asher followed her across the room, itching to finally see what all the fuss was about. But when she did stop at last in front of the canvas the image there punched her hard in the stomach.

Music roared through Asher's mind, dark desperate music filled with danger. The sort of music used in a movie when there is little hope the hero will prevail, but they choose to fight anyway.

"Oh mum," she breathed, both in awe of her mother's talent, and frightened for her in equal measure, "please don't paint this. Hesta's right, this will destroy you."

Gin shook her head. "No it won't," she declared firmly. "I'm painting carefully, layering the energy. A few more days and it will be done. You will be safe, all will be well. I feel strong, I feel wonderful, don't worry about me."

She sounded so sure, so confident, but Asher was not reassured. She could not pull her gaze away from the canvas.

It was a giant, intricate picture of their house. In the painting Asher was wrapped in a cloak that shielded her from view, safe inside the tiny music room, guarded by glowing instruments. Gin had sketched in dad and Evie, ready to be brought to life with paint. Every detail was exquisite. Outside the house the spirit of Gin surrounded the building, protecting it and Ash from harm.

But that was not the part that caused fear and nausea to roll in Asher's belly.

Spirit Gin was not only protecting the house, she had stretched her arms wide into the sky, and she was holding shut all the portals between Andera and Earth. A lone guardian against the all-consuming, destructive anti-energy of the Void, and anyone who dared to cross it.

"Can you really do that?" asked Ash, rivetted to the painting. Even half-finished it was remarkable, exuding energy. Once complete it would be magnificent.

"Yes."

But Asher was scared. Deep within she understood what completing this painting would do to mum. She would pour so much of her life force into it that she would cease to function in the real world. Her body may live, but her spirit would be gone, locked for eternity in this struggle. Just to keep Ash safe.

She couldn't bear it. She took a jagged, hiccuppy breath and realised she was crying.

Mum pulled her into a tight hug and held Asher as she shook, fighting the tears.

"Shhh my lovely girl, it's all okay. For so much of my life I believed I had only one path. Now I am choosing my destiny, that is an extraordinary thing. I do it willingly."

Asher just shook her head.

"And besides," continued mum reassuringly, "maybe one day when you are ready, and on your own terms, you will be Asherwen, and you will set me free."

What did that mean? She was struggling to pull her thoughts together.

"But not today. For now, it's best you do not remember any of this."

Asher tried to pull back, to disentangle herself from her mother's suddenly firm embrace.

"What do you mean?"

"You are very tired my love, you need to rest," mum's voice was soft and lulling, Asher found herself nodding. Yes, rest, that sounded wonderful. It had been an exhausting couple of days.

"Sleep now Asher, and when you wake you won't remember any of this."

What? No! Asher tried to fight against the cloud dulling her mind, but she was no match for Ginarwen. *Sleep, forget, forget...*

And she had slept. For much of Saturday afternoon she had slept, and when she had woken she had no memory of Hesta, Andera, her mother's paintings or her own strange destiny.

Sunday had passed, and Monday, and all had been forgotten.

But now it was Tuesday, and she stood in her mother's studio as Gin lay almost unconscious in the living room below. In her palm she clutched the golden globe and she remembered everything, Hesta, Gin, her journey from Andera. Asher knew what she had to do.

'HESTA,' she screamed from her mind, sending it as far and wide as she could, imagining the word ringing out across the galaxies, *'HESTA, I NEED YOU'.*

Chapter Five

Crafter unlocked

'*Yes Asher, I am here. You have the globe then.*'

The volume was low, as though she was speaking from far away, but her voice was strong and full of certainty, just as it had been downstairs. Asher immediately felt better. Hesta would make it right.

'Yes. Mum is in a bad way, she's almost comatose but I can't find an injury. And something about Evie being taken.'

'*One thing at a time. I need to see what Gin is painting. Look at the canvas, keep holding the globe, let me see through your eyes.*'

Asher/Hesta stared at the painting, taking in the detail, feeling the energy burning inside it. Long moments passed.

'*This is truly an incredible piece of work. What a Weaver she would have made.*' Asher could feel Hesta's sadness and regret. '*And we need to destroy it.*'

'What? Why?'

'*Your mother's energy, her essence, is captured in that painting, we need to release it. If Evie has been taken then they will come for you soon enough and she will be locked forever in a battle against them. What do you choose Asher? Your mother's life? Or your safety hidden behind her lost spirit?'*

Of course there was no choice. The painting had to be destroyed. She stuffed the globe in her jeans pocket, grabbed a painter's knife from the table and lifted it up to slash through the canvas.

'STOP!!'

She stopped, knife in mid-air.

'You cannot simply slice it open, you will release all the layers of energy in one giant fireball that will consume her, and you, and anyone else within five miles. We need to start carefully, release only enough to rejuvenate her. When she is stronger she can do the rest.'

Asher took a deep breath. *'Okay, tell me what to do.'*

Following Hesta's directions, Asher grabbed a cloth and dipped it in one of the many water containers her mother used to clean her brushes. Hesta had suggested she wipe away the freshest paint, effectively reversing the layering her mother had created, and releasing her energy piece by piece. But when Asher placed the wet cloth on the canvas she was thrown across the room by a huge explosion of energy.

"Ouch," she muttered, lying winded on the floor. She was shocked and rather sore on her hip and bottom, but otherwise unharmed. Wincing slightly she stood up.

'It won't let me wipe it.'

'Damnation! Of course her energy is too powerful. You are untrained, a minnow swimming with a shark. I cannot

counteract her energy from here, it is taking all my concentration to keep this communication open and hidden from prying ears. I don't need a floundering human child, I need a Crafter.'

Asher could feel frustration in Hesta's voice, and fear was swirling around her own body. They were running out of time. She needed to restore mum and work out what had happened to Evie.

Think Ash! And then an idea sprang out of nowhere. Pulling the globe from her pocket she slipped the necklace over her head, making sure the globe was under her clothes, nestled against her skin. Immediately she felt its energy course through her body, but it wouldn't be enough. To counteract her mother's painting she needed to channel the energy, create more power. How could she do that? Her mind was racing over everything she had learned and heard.

What are your talents, Hesta had asked Evie on that long ago night – was it only a few days ago? *We craft energy through a medium,* she had explained. *Your mother is a painter. I am a Weaver.* With a click it all fell into place. There was only one thing Asher was good at, one thing that consumed her waking days and her dream filled nights. Music. She pulled her harmonica out of her pocket.

Raising the small instrument to her lips Asher began to play.

At once the globe fired against her skin, responding to the light notes twirling around her and the painting. Asher's fingers tingled slightly as they held the cool metal, and the fear that had been fuelling her actions was replaced by a focused calm.

'Now, this is interesting,' said Hesta, 'Let's see what you can do. Focus on a small part of the painting, imagine that layer of paint evaporating away.'

Asher stopped blowing into the harmonica and did as Hesta had asked, focusing on the painted image of her mother holding closed the portals. She tried to picture the paint disappearing. Nothing happened. She squinted her eyes, which only made the pounding of her head feel worse.

'For goodness sake child! Keep playing while you do this,' snapped Hesta in exasperation.

Feeling stupid, Asher began playing again, while trying to evaporate the paint. She found it was incredibly difficult to focus on both the tune she was playing and mentally wiping away the paint at the same time. A tiny bead of paint melted down the canvas.

'This is not working,' huffed Hesta 'you are not strong enough, not trained, not focused enough. I have no idea why I am bothering with you. Gin's life-force is fading away while you tinker with your little tune.'

Anger swelled within Asher, rising in a great tide and washing away her fear and fatigue. How dare Hesta insinuate that she was not trying hard enough to save her mother! How dare this stranger from across the universe come into their lives and cause such havoc. Her sister was taken and her mother at the edge of death because of Hesta's machinations.

Asher's chest pounded with fury and the notes blew a ferocious beat. On the canvas the top layer of paint on the image of the house melted away.

'Would you look at that!' Hesta sounded almost sarcastic. *'Perhaps our little mouse can actually Craft. But how well?'*

Mutinous thoughts fuelled Asher's anger and her music, sending loud, discordant notes across the small distance and into the canvas. Another swathe of paint melted away.

'Better. Can you continue? Or do you need a little rest?'

Asher was feeling exhausted, but that mocking tone just spurred her on. Gritting her teeth she channelled all of the emotion of the last few days into the tiny harmonica. Her fury over Hesta and her unreasonable requests, her fear for her mother, not just today, but for the last three years, her frustration and annoyance with her sister, and even with her father. Her constant worry that she was not good enough, not quiet enough, not helpful enough...

Asher played as the paint melted millimetre by millimetre and the great swirl of emotion leeched out of her. She played until she thought she would collapse. She played until Hesta's now calm voice filled her head again.

'Enough now Asher. I believe you have done as much as you can.'

Asher's arms dropped to her side, the harmonica almost falling from her tingling fingers. The painting seemed barely touched to her. Minute sections were melted away, but still so much remained. She hoped with all her heart that she had done enough.

Hesta removed her presence from Asher's mind, leaving Ash to wearily stumble her way back down to the lounge room, slightly lightheaded and a little dizzy.

The last twenty minutes had been excruciating, and she had the distinct impression Hesta the Weaver was less than impressed with her new heir. Still, that was not something she was too concerned about. Her only focus now was her mother and her stolen sister.

In the lounge room Jennifer, *Gin*, was sitting up on the couch sipping at a steaming cup of tea, nibbling on fruit cake that Kate had found in the cupboard. Her skin had returned to a healthy shade of cream and pink, and her eyes were bright and clear.

"Mum," Asher breathed, almost sobbing in relief.

Her mum put down the cake and teacup and opened her arms wide. "Well done Asher. That took incredible courage and strength."

"I barely made a dent. I don't think I'm any good at this."

"Whatever you did, it was enough," assured her mother. "Thank you."

Asher sat wrapped in Gin's embrace for a long minute, savouring the strength of her mother's hug. Then she pulled back, settling into the other end of the lounge. Kate silently handed her a cup of tea.

"So what now? What has happened to Evie?"

Mum took a deep breath. "They came for the Weaver's Heir. Mother to Daughter, everyone knows this. I was in the studio when she opened the door. I could feel the energy charge, could feel the attack against my defences, so

I immediately engaged. I tried to get downstairs as quickly as I could, but my mind was still in the painting and my body was weak."

Her voice caught on unshed tears.

"Mother to Daughter," she repeated. "When Hesta blood-bonded you at birth she tied you into her threads. But for all these years you have been wrapped in a cloak, existing in the threads but unseen by prying eyes. The charm we didn't understand."

Asher screwed up her nose as she recalled the conversation with Hesta on the night she had appeared.

"*You* are the creator Ash. You wove the cloaking charm, layered it tiny piece by tiny piece over many, many years. When you took the globe in your hand the other night you lit up in the Threads, the Heir had been found. But you continued to cloak yourself, remaining invisible."

Asher shook her head in puzzlement. "No I didn't, I have no idea what you mean."

Gin smiled with affection. "Every time you picked up an instrument, every time you played, every time you went to that special place in your head where you create and compose, you layered the charm. You were trying to hide inside your music, to not be noticed, to be hidden in plain sight. You are a Crafter Ash, music is your medium."

Asher nodded as she absorbed the truth in Gin's words. She had felt it as she had battled upstairs. She had felt the energy rise in her and through her as she had created each note.

"Maybe they've been searching for me, or maybe they followed Hesta's trail. However it was done they tracked us down. There is only one daughter blood-bonded into the threads. So when Evie answered the door, when they asked her if she was the daughter of Jennifer Blake, she answered yes, and she was lost."

Fat blobs ran unchecked down Gin's face, the tears she had been swallowing no longer able to be held back.

"And I couldn't save her. I was too weakened by the painting, I couldn't beat them all. They knew I would fight, and they were probably expecting the Heir to be trained. They sent a large squadron. Ash, we need to find her, we need to bring her home."

"We will mum, we will. I swear it." Asher felt the power in her words as she wove that promise into the threads. "Whatever it takes, I will bring her home."

"Aherm," Levi cleared his throat, "sorry to interrupt, but can some-one please explain what is actually going on?"

"Well this is awkward," said Gin.

She gazed at Levi and Kate thoughtfully as though comprehending the reality of their presence for the first time. To be fair, she had been barely conscious when they arrived.

"When I called for Ash I wasn't expecting backup."

Asher said nothing, her face flushed pink with embarrassment. What could she say? There was no simple explanation for what was going on. She could practically hear the gears of Levi's mind turning.

"Sooooo," he said pensively, "just seeing if I've got this straight. Some-one kidnapped Evie and knocked you out, but you somehow contacted Ash before you passed out, and she raced here to save you. Then she went upstairs to get a globe on a necklace, and you came to."

Mum smiled with relief. "That's pretty much it."

"Except nobody has called the police or an ambulance, Ash looks exhausted and is smeared in paint like she was beaten up by a canvas, and it does sound a lot like you are talking about charms and magic."

Silence.

Asher knew from years of witnessing, (and sometimes being the subject of), Levi's bloodhound detecting, that he would wait for as long as it took to get the answer. She kept her gaze firmly on the ground, knowing she would cave if he pinned her with his unrelenting stare.

Mum was not so concerned.

"Levi," she said, and her voice was warm and reassuring, "there is no magic. That's a very strange idea. Everything is fine now, Asher and I can sort the rest out. Thanks for all your help, but it's time for you and Kate to go home now and not worry anymore about this."

He looked unconvinced.

"Be sensible Levi. You've known us pretty much all your life. Do you see anything magical? Have we done anything magical? We don't need the police or an ambulance. This is a family matter and we can sort it out ourselves. A rather intense family feud with Evie caught in the middle, that's all."

Kate was nodding, relief clear on her face, but Levi still seemed hesitant.

"I mean really," Gin was laying it on thick now, "magic? Please."

He considered for a moment, clearly wanting to argue his point, but with each passing minute the strangeness of the last hour was fading. He was beginning to doubt what he thought he had seen and heard. Asher knew that feeling well.

"Yeah, it does sound a bit ridiculous," he conceded.

"How about you two head home and Ash and I will sort out our muddle with Evie."

"What about our camping trip?"

Bother! In all the drama that had completely slipped Asher's mind.

"Another time," mum was saying, "I'm sorry to disappoint you but we really need to go get Evie."

Kate and Levi nodded reluctantly.

"Alright, we'll just grab our packs."

Asher exhaled in relief. Crisis averted. Now they just needed to restore mum's energy levels, find their mysterious magical enemies, cross the Void and bring Evie home unharmed. Piece of cake.

Something sparking in the fireplace caught the corner of her eye. As she turned to look at it more closely the logs burst into flame. Everyone immediately focused their attention there.

"What the?!" exclaimed Levi.

"Oh for goodness sake!" huffed Gin, "could she have any worse timing?"

Asher did not have to wait long for mum's meaning to become clear. Hesta appeared in the flames, a glowing apparition that was both terrifying and awe-inspiring.

"Midnight," she boomed, and her voice vibrated within each of them, "be ready Ginar and Asher. I will hold the portal open. We only have one chance, there is too much unbalance in the threads. Be ready." Then she was gone.

"So much drama," muttered mum shaking her head.

Levi cleared his throat, pointedly.

"Well," began Gin, then stopped, clearly at a loss for words.

Levi raised an eyebrow. "Jennifer, who was the scary woman in the flames? And what's the midnight portal business?"

"Hmmm, about that..." Gin was floundering.

"Levi just drop it," said Kate, uncomfortable with Jennifer's discomfort. "I don't think this is any of our business."

Levi shrugged. He had practically grown up in this house.

"I've never been very good at minding my own business."

Awkward silence filled the room.

"Okay!" burst Ash, unable to bear it, "you want to know? The woman in the flames is my grandmother, and she's like a magical god who controls the world –"

"god is quite an overstatement," murmured Gin.

"- and she wants to train me as her replacement, which is a super dangerous role. Meanwhile some-one has mistaken

Evie for me and kidnapped her. Mum and I need to cross a portal at midnight into another world to save her."

Finally shocked into silence Levi just stared at her, the same confusion and uncertainty in his eyes mirrored in Kate's.

"Yep," said Asher wearily, rubbing her eyes and forehead with both hands, "welcome to my crazy."

***

"So what's the plan?" asked Levi between bites of pepperoni pizza, "it's almost 5pm now. What prep do we need to do?"

Gin exhaled heavily. "Levi, I've already told you a number of times, you cannot travel with us. It is far too dangerous. It is difficult enough for a high-level Crafter, let alone an untrained novice, an injured Wen and two Earth mortals. I couldn't protect you."

The previous hour had passed with Gin and Ash filling in Levi and Kate on Andera and the last few days. There had been plenty of disbelief and questioning, but the vision of flaming Hesta had gone a long way to substantiating their claims.

Once he accepted their situation Levi was enthusiastically all in. Kate was less sure about their involvement, agreeing with Gin that they would just be in the way.

The fire that Hesta had started still crackled in the hearth. Outside the sun was beginning its slow descent sending blushing strands of pink across the sky.

A perfect night for camping, thought Asher regretfully. How quickly and irrevocably her life had changed. And then there was Evie. Every time she thought of her, guilt washed through Asher.

They were looking for me, she kept tormenting herself, replaying the afternoon again and again in her mind. *If only Evie had missed that first bus... if only I had left Ed's two minutes earlier and made it onto the same bus... if only I'd not gone for lunch and been home...* but such thoughts were useless. Evie was gone and they had to focus on bringing her back.

"What Ash and I need to do is rest," Gin was saying. "Every minute I'm feeling better, but a good sleep is required to help restore me. I highly suggest Ash that you try and sleep for a while. Put your phone on the charger and set your alarm for 11:00pm, then 11:15pm, then 11:30pm. I'll do the same. We cannot oversleep. Levi and Kate – go home," she finished firmly.

She walked over to where they sat on the sofa and lay a hand on each of their heads.

"You cannot remember any of this. When you leave this house the details of the afternoon will start to blur and fade. Tomorrow when you wake in your own beds this will all be forgotten."

The teenagers closed their eyes, unable to resist. After a few seconds Ginarwen released them.

"No fair!" complained Levi.

"Go home."

Gin disappeared up the stairs, three sets of eyes watching her departure. The moment she was out of sight Levi turned to the other two, practically wriggling with excitement.

"So, here's the plan," he began eagerly.

"No Levi," Ash cut him off firmly. "You heard mum. We can't protect you. Enough people have been hurt because of this, because of *me*. Please go home. I'm going to follow mum's advice and get some sleep. I have a feeling I am going to need it. Please lock the door before you pull it closed behind you."

Asher made her way up the stairs, half listening to the rustle of Levi and Kate collecting their things. Then she heard the front door click shut.

At last, she thought with relief, *I need to lie down*. After her battle with the painting she also needed her energy restored.

Collapsing fully clothed onto her bed Ash set the alarms then flicked to the sound recordings on her phone and pressed play on the most recent version of her composition. The mellow sound of her piano filled the room, soothing and energising Asher in equal measure.

She thought of Evie as she snuggled under the comforter and sent a silent plea to the universe to keep her safe. Music swelling around her, it was only a matter of minutes before she was fast asleep.

Downstairs Levi and Kate sat soundlessly, not moving, barely daring to breathe. Long minutes passed before Levi whispered, "I think they are both asleep."

Kate nodded, then frowned. "Do you really think this is a good idea? They were both pretty adamant we should leave."

"Kate, you know Ash. She retreats rather than handle any confrontation. She lives in her head making music. Do you really think she's going to be able to fight the baddies and rescue Evie without us?"

Kate raised her brows as she considered this. "True," she conceded, nodding slowly, "she's not particularly practical or overly forceful."

"Exactly," said Levi smugly, "that's what she needs us for. Practical," he pointed at Kate, "forceful," he pointed at himself. "Though I prefer 'committed and determined'."

"Then I guess we try and get some sleep."

Quietly they unclipped their sleeping bags from their packs and lay them out by the fire.

"Almost like camping," grinned Levi, as Kate carefully set her alarm, "I'm just not sure I can actually doze off this early."

But within thirty minutes, as the room darkened with the sunset, both of them were fast asleep.

Chapter Six

Into the Void

Asher was dreaming. She was in the doorway of her bedroom, but it was not current day. The walls were painted in the soft pinks and creams of her infant years, and her bed and dresser were missing. Asher tried to move forward into the room but she was held still, merely a spectator for this moment.

The room was dim and quiet, undisturbed except for the shaft of soft afternoon light that illuminated the cradle in the corner. As the moments passed the shaft began to pulsate and thicken, flickering with light and then with sound.

One long heartbeat passed, and another, then a figure began to materialise. A figure Asher recognised from her own midnight meeting only a few nights ago.

Asher opened her mouth to speak, but in this dreamscape, she was unable to move, to call out. The small occupant of the cradle slept peacefully, unaware of her visitors.

The woman who stepped out of the light and into the room was a woman of power. A woman who had crowned kings and queens and defeated sorcerers. A woman who had defied Death and scorned Fate, who had been loved and reviled in equal measure and who had given up what she loved most for people who would never ever know her sacrifice.

Now she was a woman who had torn a hole in the fabric of space to create a bridge of light from her world to this one.

A hole that would ripple endlessly if she did not hurry. She could not risk anyone following her trail and discovering this child, her most precious secret. Quickly she crossed the small distance to the sleeping baby.

Being careful not to wake the child, Hesta lay a shimmering hand on the small cheek. Sorrow swelled briefly. This small being filled with such innocence and peace. What a burden was to be hers. Gently Hesta loosened the swaddling around the baby's legs to reveal her toes.

The baby squirmed softly but did not wake as Hesta sang.

Daughter to daughter, Blood to blood,
On this day I recognise you.
Child of my child, first and last of my heirs,
I gift you with the blood of your ancestors.
Child of the Earth and Child of the Sky,
With the Universe as witness, I name you.

One quick movement and the tiny needle concealed in Hesta's hand pricked both her own thumb and the underside of the girl's big toe. The slight pain caused the baby's eyes to flash open, but she did not cry out. Blood welled at the sites of the tiny wounds.

Wide grey eyes watched calmly as Hesta pressed thumb and toe together. Blood joined. Hesta felt the power of their blood bonding radiate into the Eternal Weave. One second more and it would be complete.

'Who you?'

The sudden voice in her mind almost caused Hesta to pull back from the bonding in shock. The infant's grey eyes were now filled with curiosity.

'Who speaks?' Hesta asked carefully.

The baby grinned, a funny lilting of a little mouth only just learning to move in such a way.

'Me!' She responded with joy. *'What you do?'*

For the first time in many long decades Hesta was truly taken aback. Asher the watcher felt the Weaver's surprise and wariness as though the feelings were her own. Blood bonding was a powerful energy, greatly misunderstood, sometimes feared, never predictable. Mind sharing was not a skill newborns normally possessed, even those born to shape the Threads.

'I am the Weaver,' Hesta responded, filling her mind with all the love within her.

The baby gurgled with pleasure.

'Who me?' she asked

Hesta smiled, *'You are the Weaver.'*

The baby gurgled again. This made perfect sense.

'With the Universe as witness, I name you. You are the Weaver.'

Asher woke with a sudden start, the alarm on her phone pinging loudly. 11pm.

With a sigh she hit the dismiss button and snuggled deeply, just for a few minutes more. The dream circled around in her mind, so vividly realistic in both image and feeling. She had been the observer, and she had been Hesta, but she knew she was also the baby in the cot. For whatever reason she was being shown the night of her blood-bonding with the Weaver.

Unexpectedly Asher was overcome with sadness. What if she never returned from Andera? What if she never saw her dad again? What if they all got trapped across the Void and he never saw any of them again? He would never know what had happened to his family. She googled the time difference. Singapore was 2 hours behind. Only 9pm there, he would still be up, probably at a conference dinner.

She typed a quick text 'Love you dad, hope you're having a great time. Xx'. Then before she could get teary Asher pressed send and hauled herself out of bed.

The air was cold, so very cold. She decided a warm shower would make a huge difference and headed to the bathroom. Outside her parents' room she paused and knocked loudly.

"Mum, are you up?"

"Yes Ash, just getting dressed, see you downstairs in ten minutes."

Standing under the warm water Asher wondered when she would next shower. Did they even have showers on Andera? She realised how little she knew about her mother's home world. She decided to wash her hair, just in case.

A few minutes later she was back in her room, drying her heavy mass of red curls. She pulled on a favourite pair of well-worn, comfortable dark denim jeans, a long sleeve white t-shirt and a deep green knitted jumper. Her runners were downstairs by the lounge, discarded earlier in the evening. Asher had already decided to take her camping pack with her. It had some clothes, snacks, sleeping gear and some additional musical instruments. She had no idea what else she would need.

She checked her phone - 11:25pm. Time to head downstairs. Asher took a final look in the mirror. She wasn't really one for mirrors; she did not wear make-up or generally style her hair other than to run a brush through it. It had been a long time since she had really looked at herself. The young adult looking back at her took her by surprise. She really did look like mum, like Hesta. She was turning sixteen in a few days and her face was changing. She wondered where she would be for her birthday. Hopefully they would all be home together.

"If I wasn't conserving my energy, I would turn you to stone!" mum was saying crossly as Ash hurried down the stairs. *Oh no, what now?*

She was expecting to see Hesta, or an intruder, but instead a rather sheepish looking Kate and a defiant Levi stood with mum in the lounge room, the targets of her anger.

"This is reckless and foolish and incredibly selfish of you both," continued Gin, "and I am rather disappointed."

"I'm sorry Jen," responded Kate in a small voice, "we really thought we could be of help."

They were both fully dressed, shoes and all. Kate's long mousy blonde hair was freshly brushed and tied, the long plait hanging neatly down her back.

Clearly they were planning to come with them. How on earth did they think they would do that?

Whatever they were going to say next was interrupted by the crackle of the fire in the hearth. Hesta was materialising in the flames, quite real and visible but not actually solid. Unlike the first night when she had sat with them in the flesh.

"Why is she not stepping out of the flames?" wondered Asher to Gin.

"She is on the other side of the portal, still in Andera. She is projecting an image of herself and using the energy of the fire to do so. It's very impactful but actually not too difficult for her to do, particularly as we have the golden globe. She can focus her concentration on that, which leaves the bulk of her power available to create the portal."

Kate and Levi were silently staring at Hesta in the flames. The reality of what was happening seemed to finally be hitting home.

"We have just under thirty minutes before the portal opens," announced Hesta, her voice far less dramatic than it had been earlier, "when it does you must step into it at once, no delay. Once through I will close the portal on your side. No matter what you see or hear, no matter what you experience in the Void, there will be no way back. You can only move forward."

"What will it be like?" asked Asher in a subdued voice.

"It is different for everyone, and the experience really depends on how quickly you move across. The faster you move through, the smoother the process. The stronger your ability, the easier the journey. For a well-prepared, high-level crafter it is barely a moment in time," said Hesta.

"How do we prepare?" Asher asked next.

"The Void is anti-energy, you cannot craft while passing through it. Therefore we use an object of power to store energy in. The stronger the object or the greater the power the more you will be shielded during the journey. You have the globe Asher, that will be your object."

Ash pulled the heavy pendant out from under her clothes, immediately missing its warmth against her skin. "Now what?"

"Now you need to layer your own energy, your own crafting, onto the generations of Weavers that have held that globe before you. I'm not sure how strong the energy created by your harmonica will be against the Void." Hesta seemed to frown, "we need to magnify it."

Magnify a harmonica? Ash wrinkled her nose. Why bother when she could simply play a more powerful instrument. A piano would be best, but... scooping up her pack she rummaged through the front pocket until she located her flute.

"What about this?" She raised the mouthpiece to her lips and blew gently.

A warm melody filled the air. As she played Asher imagined the notes as colours streaming from the flute, surrounding her and the globe, encasing them, protecting them. She could feel herself being pulled into the music, getting swept away.

After a few minutes she reluctantly stopped playing, opening her eyes to see mum, Levi and Kate staring at her in wonder.

"That's incredible," breathed Kate, "how did you do that?"

"Do what?"

"That," said Kate, gesturing to Asher's body.

Asher stretched out her arms, the flute securely held in her right hand. Her body was glowing, shimmering; a thousand speckles of rainbow light reflected in the flames of the fire.

"That should do it," said Hesta with satisfaction. "Play a little longer Asher, the more you can layer the better. Go into the kitchen and take the Terrans with you. I must speak with Gin."

Levi raised his brows.

"Terrans?" he murmured to Kate who grinned and shook her head, as they followed Asher into the kitchen. She settled herself on a stool and closed her eyes, pouring energy into the globe and sending it swirling around her friends as she played.

Kate sat at the dining table, closing her own eyes and breathing in the light and strength that she could hear and feel in Asher's playing. Within moments both girls were lost in the music.

Levi crossed quietly back to the door that separated the kitchen and lounge room. Unknowingly he positioned himself in the same spot Asher had occupied last Friday night. A perfect place to hear and observe without being spotted. In the other room an argument was raging between mother and daughter.

"You must stay behind Gin."

"Absolutely not."

"She comes alone." Hesta was firm.

"No way." Jennifer, *Gin*, was just as firm. "I come too, or she doesn't go at all."

"Then Evie will die." Hesta's voice was flat and cold. "You claim her as your child, surely you don't want to be responsible for her death."

Gin sucked in an outraged breath. "How dare you" she began, her voice shaking with anger. "She is –"

Hesta cut her off.

"Your strength has not yet returned, and you carry an injury from the last time you navigated the Void. If you attempt this crossing you will most likely die, leaving Asher to continue alone, while grieving and potentially panicking. Most likely she will not make it. So Asher dies. Without rescue Evie dies. If you choose not to send Asher, then Evie will still die. Your choice Gin. The death of one or both of your daughters, or you let go of your need to control Asher and let her come to me."

"*My* need to control Ash, oh that is just too much Hesta. You've controlled everyone and everything your whole life. The only thing you didn't control was my leaving, and that has burned at you. Now you see your chance to claim my child as your precious heir. You can't wait to have her there, to ensnare her in your plots and plans. I do not trust you."

Hesta shrugged, completely unmoved by Gin's anger. "One or both daughters will die because of you. But at least if you attempt the crossing you will be dead too and will not have to live with what you have wrought."

"Or perhaps, just possibly, I might survive the crossing. Have you considered *that* Weaver?"

"No. You won't."

"Ha! I don't believe you."

"Then don't believe me. That is of no importance to me at all. But Asher needs to cross safely and she needs to cross tonight. Have you not wondered how Darven could send a squad across the Void? The power that takes is incredible. And how was a squad of four able to defeat *you*?"

Gin was taken aback by this sudden change in topic.

"There were six of them," she said slowly, digesting the enormity of this for the first time. "They had some type of dust, it added to my weakened state."

"Six!" Even Hesta was shocked. "By all the stars that is far, far worse than I had feared. There is only one way he could access the energy required to be able to do that. And now he thinks he has the Heir, and all that power to tap into. Imagine what he is doing to Evie right now."

The words were ruthless, her voice devoid of warmth or sympathy.

Levi turned quickly at the sharp intake of breath beside him. He had been so caught up with his eavesdropping that he had not noticed Asher had stopped playing and crept up behind him.

"Your selfishness will condemn her to a torturous death." Hesta continued relentlessly.

"What a despicable thing to say," railed Gin, but the heat was gone from her voice, now there was only fear and sadness and defeat.

In the kitchen, listening to this horrible exchange, Asher was feeling enough anger for both of them. How dare Hesta talk to mum that way! Asher would have pushed past Levi and stormed into the loungeroom, but his steady hand on her arm held her in place.

"Wait," he whispered.

"Then we are agreed. Asher passes through the portal. You stay behind and try and undo the mess you made with your painting. Perhaps you can re-direct all that *maternal love* into a painting that brings them both home."

The derision in Hesta's voice caused Gin to slump as the fight abandoned her. She stumbled to the lounge and sank her head into her hands. Hesta offered no words of ease or comfort.

In the kitchen Asher took a few long steadying breaths. The anger and dislike flooding her body had to be controlled. All this intense emotion was almost overwhelming, she wasn't used to feeling this exposed. Asher spent most of her life in her own head, putting all her emotional highs and lows into music. *Stay quiet, stay calm and everything will be okay. Be invisible.* It was her life's mantra.

She breathed out and settled her thoughts. She needed Hesta. She needed to get to Andera and find Evie, and Hesta could help her. But that was it, she promised silently, she would never trust her or ally with her. She would bring Evie home and then she and mum would find a way to block Hesta and all the portals forever.

Once she had her temper under control, Asher pushed open the door and walked straight over to mum. All her life she had relied on mum's ready embrace to soothe her fears, fix her hurts and fill her up with hope. Now it was her turn to offer comfort. She wrapped her arms around her mother. Holding Gin tight she tried to pour all her love, her gratitude, her pride and amazement at how wonderful her mother was, into that hug.

"I got this mum, I really do. Don't worry, I'll be home with Evie soon."

Mum squeezed her tightly in response.

"You know Ash, it was always going to be this way," she sighed. "No matter what I've done, or not done, you stepping through that portal without me was always inevitable. It's the picture I kept refusing to paint, the reason the migraines would take hold. You standing in Andera with Hesta. My mind and body were at war with the Threads. And yet here we are." She laughed softly, a strange hiccuppy sound. "Some things seem unchangeably woven into the Threads, but there are always many choices, and we can throw one little surprise into this still."

She glanced over at the clock above the mantel. 11:53pm.

"We have seven minutes to manipulate a few things ourselves," Gin whispered.

Then raising her voice Gin said, "everyone to the kitchen. Oh wait. Not joining us Hesta? What a shame. See you in a few minutes then."

Levi, Kate and Ash followed Gin into the kitchen, all of them bursting with curiosity.

"Okay," said Gin, her words low and fast, her body taut with urgency, "here's the plan."

She winked at Levi who grinned back.

"Kate and Levi, you're up. You are going with Ash. She is going to need friends and helpers on this journey and you two are the best companions she can ask for."

"Woohoo!!" yelled Levi, practically leaping into the air before high-fiving a dazed and grinning Asher.

"Hesta won't be expecting this little adjustment to her plans," added Gin, "so that gives us an advantage. When you step through the portal make sure you are holding onto Ash, arms linked all of you. Don't let go, no matter what. No matter what you hear, or think, or feel. Got it?"

The three of them nodded solemnly, the excitement of only a moment ago evaporating as reality set in.

"You can trust Hesta to guide you in saving Evie, she has her own reasons for wanting to track down Darven, but never forget she has her own agenda very much front of mind. Her focus has and always will be the continuance of the Weaver," she added sadly.

"I don't trust that she will send you home Ash. So take this, you can use it to open a portal back. It's what I used to leave Andera."

Pushing back her jacket sleeve, Gin slipped a heavy silver and enamel bangle off her wrist. The bangle was perhaps 3cms wide, with enamel inlayed flowers intricately crafted and vibrantly painted.

"I recommend you keep this a secret Ash. It is incredibly powerful, not many of these still exist and it's probably best this one remains undiscovered. It is a gatekeeper, it opens the portals."

Carefully, reverently, Asher slipped the heavy bracelet onto her wrist, clasping it shut. It snuggled around her wrist as though perfectly made for her. The silver was warm and strangely also cool to touch.

"It's beautiful," she whispered, "where did you get it?"

Gin smiled. "From my grandmother on my 16th birthday. She was a silversmith. Her sister, my great aunt Bonner, did the enamel work. They were both incredibly powerful Crafters. They created some truly magnificent pieces together, but not many still exist. They had a falling out before I was born and most of their work was destroyed..." her voice trailed off. "Anyway. Now it's yours. Happy birthday sweetheart."

She grabbed Ash and gave her a quick hug. "Remember how much I love you."

"I love you too mum. We'll all be home soon."

"Good, because I won't be able to stall Kate and Levi's parents with your camping trip for more than a few days."

They all laughed at her rueful tone.

"Righto, 11:58pm. Are you ready?"

"Absolutely," replied Asher with a confidence she did not possess. She was excited and relieved that her friends were coming with her, but she was also daunted at the prospect of what was ahead and how she was to bring them all home safely, Evie included.

So many people now depending on me, she thought, uncertainty churning in her gut.

"Remember, hold onto each other and Ash just move towards the light of Hesta's doorway. May the journey be quick and without incident."

Nobody asked Gin what an incident in the Void might be. Unbidden, Asher's thoughts filled with Marjorie.

"Mum..." she said uneasily. "What if... what if we end up like Marjorie?"

Gin shook her head firmly.

"That will not happen. You are not Marjorie. You are Asher el Ginarwen, and you are the Weaver's Heir."

Gin's voice was strong and confident. Asher nodded slightly, trying to feel reassured. She swallowed the "but…" that was burning in her throat.

A few breaths later they were standing in front of the fireplace, three silent figures carrying large packs on their backs, their faces quiet and pensive. After one last hug for each of them Gin stepped back to the edge of the room.

Hesta had disappeared, leaving only the warm glow of the flames reflecting on their faces.

Beside the fireplace the air began to shimmer and crackle. Asher blinked a couple of times, trying to clear her vision until she realised this was the portal opening. Energy pulsed through the air as the very fabric of space was forced apart. Ash grabbed at Levi and Kate, snaking her left arm around Kate's back under her pack, and her right around Levi's. They did the same to her.

The portal opened wider and wider, until they were looking at a glowing door-shaped opening. What lay beyond was hidden behind shimmering cloud. Asher took a deep breath, then another. The globe against her skin was humming, the bracelet on her wrist was heavy and warm, the solid weight of her friends' arms was reassuring and gave her strength.

'Now my darling,' came mum's voice in her mind. Those warm words, strengthening her with love, were the last thing she heard before the three of them stepped forward and into the cloud.

Chapter Seven

Andera

Asher was lost in a dark forest, the trees so dense around her that she could barely see above or in front. Something heavy was holding her arms and she was struggling to move, to escape the claustrophobic trees.

Whispers swirled in the darkness, the words indistinct but the tone menacing.

She was trapped, held down by that invisible weight. Nearby there were people who could help, she was sure she could see their silhouettes, but they ignored her. *As everybody always does* mocked the whispers, and now they seemed to be in her own mind.

Pathetic little mouse, creeping, creeping...

Faster and faster beat her heart, her breath catching in shallow hiccups making her feel light-headed. Panic was setting in. Why couldn't she move?

She had to get out of here! She had something important to do, but what was it? In the distance she could hear Evie calling for her. Evie! She had to find Evie who was lost somewhere in this forest. Asher had done something terrible and Evie had fled into the dark. If Asher did not find her then something bad would happen.

*And how do you think **you** can help?* Tormented the whispers. *This is all your fault. All your fault. All your fault. Everything is all your fault.*

Her chest ached and her mind felt so fuzzy. She tried shaking her head to clear it, but that just made her feel dizzy. She was so tired of fighting against the weight pulling at her arms, every step was a gargantuan effort. Maybe she should just sit here in the dark and rest awhile.

Sit quietly little mouse...

She was working out how to sit down when a strange whimpering at her left made her pause. What was that? Something was pulling on her, almost sobbing.

"Daddy, don't die, daddy," sobbed the girl, "please don't leave me."

Asher strained her ears, she felt like she knew that voice.

"Stay with me daddy, keep listening to my voice, help is coming, daddy please!" it pleaded.

By all the stars that was Kate! Then Asher remembered. They had stepped through the glowing cloud of the portal gate and into pitch blackness. At first she had been able to just keep moving, Levi and Kate holding tightly to her, but after a few steps she had become disoriented and forgotten what she was doing and why. Everything had started to feel unimportant, unnecessary. The whispers had curled around her mind, teasing and ridiculing her. In the dark she had forgotten her friends.

Against her chest the globe pressed heavily, the layers of energy imprinted there infusing her body, clearing her mind.

Kate was caught in the nightmare of the car accident that had killed her father but had spared her without injury. What about Levi?

Asher could feel the weight of him on her right arm, but he was silent. She hoped he was okay and wondered if he too was experiencing his worst moment. She wondered what that might be; he always seemed so carefree and optimistic. She sensed that the globe was shielding her from the worst of it, though the soft refrain of *your fault, your fault, your fault* echoed quietly at the back of her mind. She wanted to ignore it, but the grim truth was that if she allowed Kate and Levi to linger too long in this place of misery then they would lose their minds, and that would be her fault.

She had to get out of the Void, she had to take her friends safely to the other side.

With a deep breath Asher stepped forward. One step then two, dragging her companions with her, though she could not see them. *Look for the light of Andera* she kept saying to herself, moving another step and another. *Look for Hesta's doorway.*

But what if there is no doorway? What if she has trapped us here forever, lost in the dark?

Fear rose quickly, her mouth filling with bile. She was so cold, so cold... except for her chest. Her chest was warm. The globe! Asher focused her attention on the globe and moved forward a few more steps. In the Void it wasn't humming, but she could feel its energy coursing through her body, warming her fingers and toes. She took another step, then another.

Beside her Kate whimpered and sobbed but allowed herself to be pulled forward. Asher wanted to speak, to reassure her friends that they would be okay, but she could not form the words. Her throat felt thick and dry. All her focus and energy was on each step.

How long they moved like this she did not know. Perhaps hours, perhaps minutes. But suddenly, just ahead, Asher could see a light, a glowing doorway.

Hope burst inside her, bouncing around in her stomach and chest. Excitement buoyed her body forward, giving momentum to her sluggish legs. Holding tight to Kate and Levi she pushed forward, each step getting easier as they approached the light. The tightness in her throat eased and she found she could speak again.

"It's okay Kate, it's okay, we're almost out of here, soon we will be far away from this nightmare. It's okay, I've got you. Levi, we're almost through, a few more steps that's all. Everything is okay. Focus on me, focus on my voice. Can you feel the energy of the globe? It's surrounding us, protecting us, we're okay, we're okay. None of this is real, but we are, we are real, and we're okay. Focus on me, move with me."

Words babbled out of her, pouring like a balm onto a wound. The more she spoke, the lighter the load on her arms became. Levi and Kate were responding, they were focusing on her voice, she was giving them hope and purpose. They were moving with her, no longer needing to be dragged.

Twenty more steps, ten… and then, with a huge final step Asher stumbled through the glowing cloud of the doorway and collapsed with Levi and Kate onto the warm stone hearth at Hesta's feet.

Gasping for breath, desperate to fill their lungs with the warm air, the three friends coughed and gulped. After a few seconds the urgency eased and one by one they sat up, leaning on their camping packs like chairs.

Kate was the last of the three to settle, her face grey with grief. Asher reached over and grabbed her fingers. Kate squeezed them limply then let go without a word.

"Well done Asher, that was a good transition across the Void. Even with friends."

Asher raised her eyes to scour Hesta's face for any anger or disapproval at her unexpected travelling companions, but there was none there to see. Her voice and face were neutral, giving nothing away.

"It felt like a very long time," Asher responded, her voice husky.

"Time is fluid in the Void. As I said, good preparation is the key to a smooth crossing."

Hesta gazed at the trio thoughtfully. "Looks like we need to prepare two more rooms, and perhaps a pot of tea. But firstly let's get you off the floor and seated more comfortably."

Carefully Asher and Levi pulled themselves up. Levi reached down to gently help Kate stand, the weight of her backpack and her grief making her heavy and unsteady. She gave him a small smile of thanks. She was not ready to speak yet, but the colour was returning to her face and the dark clouds in her eyes were clearing.

Asher abandoned her pack on the floor and stretched her sore arms and back. Curiously she looked around the large room. The portal had deposited them beside a stone fireplace which was roaring with orange and blue flames.

The walls on either side of the fireplace were encased in floor length curtains, made of gorgeous multi-coloured tapestries of finely woven threads. Ash supposed that behind those curtains there were equally large windows. Briefly she wondered what lay beyond in the world outside.

The room was full of furniture, but the effect was cosy and intimate rather than cluttered. There was a huge sofa draped in woollen blankets and piled with cushions that Kate and Levi were sinking into gratefully. Ceiling to floor bookshelves ran the length of the wall opposite her, encasing a closed door that was the only door out of the room. Warm light from large lamps on the desk and coffee tables chased away any shadows and the lingering darkness of the Void.

Asher had never seen this room before, yet it felt comforting and familiar. The layers of textures, of patterns and colours, were reminiscent of her own home, their own living spaces. With surprise Ash realised her mother had decorated her home on Earth in a very similar way to this room. She wondered whether that was intentional.

"You will need some sleep soon enough. The first trip across the Void is always unsettling. Some people need to sleep for a couple of days to restore their equilibrium. Asher I am hoping a few hours will suffice for you, as we have work to do. Time is not a luxury we can afford right now."

Ash nodded automatically, but weariness was overwhelming her body and the thought of sleeping for a couple of days sounded incredibly appealing.

"Let's forgo tea and biscuits," decided Hesta, looking from one exhausted face to another. Kate was almost asleep on the sofa, curled up into the deep patchwork cushions. Beside her Levi was struggling to keep his own eyes open, determined not to miss a thing.

"Marten will organise your bags, you can follow me to your rooms. Asher, your room is on this floor. I will point it out as we pass. Levi and Kate are on the floor below."

Stumbling with exhaustion the three of them followed Hesta out of the room.

The coolness of the wide hallway after the warmth of Hesta's study was like a slap in the face for Asher. Eyes wide she peered into the dim hallway, vaguely making out more doorways and paintings on the walls. But the lighting was poor and she was too tired to focus on anything in particular.

"This is your bathroom here on the right," Hesta pointed at a darkened doorway, "and that is your bedroom straight ahead. You head in there and get some sleep. I will take your friends downstairs."

Her voice was gentle, almost kind, not what Asher had come to expect in her limited dealings with this strange grandmother.

"Thank you Hesta."

The old woman smiled at her with affection, then unexpectedly reached forward and clasped Asher's chin between her fingers. Startled by the gesture, Ash realised this was the first time she had felt Hesta's touch. It made her seem more human, less otherworldly.

"Sleep soundly Asher. You have done well this night." Then Hesta released her.

The bedroom Asher stumbled into was beautifully warmed by a low fire in the corner and lit by a bright lamp on the bedside table. In the firelight the whole room gleamed golden and cream. A large bed nestled against the far wall and a sofa and armchair were positioned to her right, in front of the open fire. Beyond the sitting area a set of double doors closed the bedroom off from whatever room lay beyond.

Asher briefly considered exploring further but she was absolutely shattered. She could investigate her new surroundings in the morning.

The bed beckoned, and she thought wistfully of the abandoned pack with her pyjamas. A far more comfortable option than sleeping in her jeans. But when she moved deeper into the room she found her pack already lying on the navy and gold sofa by the fire. Too tired to question how or when her belongings had made their way to her new room, Asher merely shrugged and changed her clothes. Who was she to try and make sense of anything in her life right now.

The joyful crowing of an overzealous cockerel woke Asher around 6am. The sun was rising slowly over the horizon, streaks of gold reaching across the sky to tease through a gap in the heavy cream drapes.

Asher lay in confusion for a few brief moments, sorting out where she was and how she got there. She glanced around. Her first impression last night had been of space, and this was confirmed in the clarity of the morning. The dappled light of the sunrise fell on a large oak desk by the window and its matching chair. The walls were covered in gorgeous cream and gold wallpaper, that looked incredibly expensive and hand painted. The bed she was lying in was layered in embroidered quilts of the same colour scheme.

This space was nothing like the cluttered cosiness of Hesta's study. This was a room for a princess and Asher felt both awed and out of place. She wondered how long she would be here, in Hesta's house, in Andera. It all still felt surreal.

She lay snuggled for a long while, listening for any sounds of movement in the house and wondering when she should get up. Her grumbling tummy reminded her that she had no idea where the kitchen was.

Glancing over to where her pack lay open on the deep blue sofa, Asher wondered again how it had appeared there. Perhaps wishing for it had made it materialise. Perhaps breakfast would behave in a similar manner.

"Breakfast please," she said aloud, feeling ridiculous as her voice bounced around the beautiful room.

When nothing appeared after a full minute of counting, Asher pulled back the heavy covers and climbed out of bed.

Bathroom... She vaguely recalled Hesta pointing that out to her last night, so she grabbed some clean clothes and her toothbrush and headed in that direction.

The hallway she stepped into was much bigger than she had realised last night. Indeed it was more of an art gallery, the walls filled with pictures and tapestries. Heavy piled rugs covered the dark wooden floor, and tables laden with glass ornaments, pottery, woven baskets and exquisite jewellery, sat beneath large windows whose thick drapes had already been pulled aside allowing the beautiful objects to sparkle and gleam in the early morning sun.

It felt like an incredibly exclusive artisan's gallery, similar to one she had visited as a child to see her mother's paintings displayed. Then, as now, childish wonder and fear of breaking something made her move carefully, her gaze leaping from one incredible item to another.

A hot shower and scrub of her face and teeth went a long way to restoring her sense of self in this rather overwhelming house. Once she was dry and dressed Asher retraced her steps from last night and found the top of a staircase at the end of the art gallery.

The next floor down she passed a few closed doors before finding a large, heavily polished oak staircase that appeared to flow down into the centre of the house. It was much grander than the simple stairs that joined the second floor with the third floor. This was rather imposing and extremely wide, three people could walk abreast quite comfortably.

Apprehensively Asher made her way to the bottom of the second staircase and what appeared to be a grand entrance hall.

Now she was at a loss. With the stairs behind her she was looking at the double front doors. To her left were open French doors that led into a library type room. To her right another set of French doors led into an enormous sitting room, resplendent in olive and white tones.

Asher hesitated, unsure which doors might lead her to the kitchen and food. After a brief deliberation she decided it was more likely that the kitchen would be off a sitting room rather than a library, so she headed in that direction.

The sitting room opened onto an oversized dining room with a table that could easily seat 24 people, and then finally, off to the right was the kitchen.

She chuckled when she walked in.

"I should have known you would find food."

Levi grinned back at her, a fork laden with scrambled egg and sausages halfway to his mouth.

"Good morning! I was just complimenting Cook on her delicious eggs." Gleefully he shoved the fork in his mouth, making 'mmmmhmmmmm' sounds of appreciation as he chewed.

A generously plump older woman with a large coif of grey hair stood by the stove, smiling happily at Levi as she turned more sausages and bacon in a pan. An oversized white apron was tied neatly over a plain blue dress. She was exactly how Asher imagined a Cook in a grand house would look.

"Good morning," Ash ventured shyly, feeling self-conscious in this house and with a stranger. She longed for Levi's easy nature and ability to charm nearly everyone he met.

"Well you must be Asher," replied Cook with a wide smile, "I'd have recognised you anywhere, you being the spitting image of Ginarwen."

"You know my mum?" exclaimed Ash.

Cook laughed warmly, her short round body shaking with mirth.

"O' course I do. She grew up in this house, in the very room you are currently in, and when she wasn't tucked away in that studio of hers she was like as not in this kitchen begging for treats or badgering for cooking lessons. Now you take a seat here and have something to eat. You must be famished what with travelling here last night."

Stunned Asher sat, absorbing this new information. This grand mansion was her mother's childhood home, and that princess bedroom belonged to her! This had been her mother's world, her people. The whole situation was feeling more real by the minute.

"So who else lives here?" Levi was asking. "There's Hesta, you, somebody called Marten..." he trailed off, inviting Cook to fill in the blanks, which she did readily.

"There's Anetta, Marten's wife," she added, plonking a plate laden with steaming eggs, bacon, sausages and toast in front of a grateful Ash, "she's the general housekeeper. Marten is handyman and odd jobs, plus he'll do butler service when there's a need. Not that there is much these days, we don't entertain like we used to. They have the room next to mine, down that hall." She indicated the other entrance to the kitchen with a tilt of her head.

"We bring in day staff as we need them. Then there's Miss Carowen, Hesta's niece. She's on the second floor, opposite your room Levi. We won't be seeing her for a while yet, she's not an early riser," she chuckled. "And that's us. This big house sure feels empty at times, it's wonderful to have young people around again. How long will you be here with us?"

Levi and Asher exchanged a glance. They had no way of knowing what Hesta had told her staff, and indeed they didn't really know the plan themselves. Levi could read the indecision in Ash's eyes.

"Well that all depends whether the other meals are as magnificent as this one," he waggled his dark eyebrows at Cook who laughed merrily. "I'm partial to cake too..."

Hesta entered the kitchen as they were all laughing, her tall figure imposing in a deep green buttoned dress and multi coloured heels, her back straight and poised, her ageless face calm and almost regal. *Like a queen*, thought Asher, remembering her first impression of Hesta. And now she was in the mansion that matched her.

"Good morning children, did you sleep well?"

They both nodded, mouths full.

"Excellent. Well finish up and join me in the library. Mariah, can you please bring in some fresh hot tea? Thank you," she added, striding out of the room without waiting for an answer.

Knowing a summons when they heard one, Asher and Levi gulped down the last of the food in their mouths and with smiles and thanks for Cook they followed Hesta out of the room.

They walked softly through the large dining room, the sound of their footsteps muffled by the thick cream carpet rug. Not a single floorboard squeaked beneath the wool. Above the endless dining table a huge chandelier danced with the daylight. Ash imagined it would sparkle magnificently in the evening firelight. She wondered if Hesta ate her meals here alone with 23 vacant chairs, or in the kitchen with Cook.

"Phew" whistled Levi softly to Asher as they walked through the sumptuous sitting room, "this is some house! It's like a mini palace. The bedroom I'm in is bigger than my parents' bedroom at home. I wonder if all houses here are like this, or if your grandmother is super loaded."

Asher didn't have time to ponder or reply. They crossed the hall into the library where Hesta smiled at them from an overstuffed embroidered orange armchair. She indicated the large blue sofa opposite her.

"Please sit."

They sat, twisting their heads to gape at the huge bookshelves that ran to the roof, proudly displaying hundreds, thousands of books.

"Let's get started," Hesta began.

"Should we wait for Kate?" interrupted Asher.

"She is still deeply asleep, and likely to remain so for a while. I assume the crossing was traumatic for her?"

Asher nodded, unwilling to speak of it without Kate's permission.

Hesta's wide green eyes were filled with knowing. "The more traumatic the crossing the longer the recovery. She may need a couple of days to feel herself again. I am hoping Evelyn is similarly indisposed. The longer it takes Darven to realise his error the better."

Evie. The lump in Ash's throat thickened. She would adore this house. Asher wondered what conditions she was being held in.

"Do you know where she is?"

Hesta nodded slowly, considering. "I believe I do, but I will make inquiries before I blunder in. From what I know of Darven I'm sure he's taken her to Ostrin Castle, where he has been playing king for the last few years." Her voice dripped with scorn.

Cook arrived with a pot of tea and three gorgeous teacups and saucers balanced on a tray, effectively silencing them all.

With a cheery, "there you are my lovelies," and a wink for Asher, Cook bustled back out of the library and across the hall.

"So who is Darven and why does he want Evie, I mean me? Is he a Crafter?"

Hesta poured three cups of steaming tea, leaving each person to add their own milk and sugar as desired.

"To understand Darven we need to speak a little about the fabric of Andera – our society, our Craftlore." She huffed with exasperation. "I really wish your mother had educated you properly, it is tiresome that we have to discuss this when we should be Crafter training."

Asher said nothing, she would not engage in criticism of Gin with Hesta.

"Crafters are always female Asher, but not all females are Crafters. Most families never produce a Crafter, and even in ancient Crafter families like ours some girls do not have the talent."

"Like Evie," offered Ash.

"Yes."

"Do families *want* Crafter daughters?" asked Levi, "or is it considered a curse?"

Hesta turned to look him squarely in the eye, and Asher braced herself for the derisive comment she was sure would follow. To her surprise Hesta nodded calmly.

"Very perceptive Levi. Indeed not all families want their daughters to be so blessed, or cursed. Crafting is a responsibility and a burden that can be too overwhelming for some. And then there are those that seek to exploit unsuspecting Crafter girls, particularly those from poor or non-Crafter families. They have little experience or protection. I mentioned only females are Crafters, but males can wield power too, of a vastly different type. Men who manipulate energy through non-natural means are called Sorcerers."

"Darven," breathed Asher.

"Exactly." Hesta took a sip of tea. "As with all power, sorcery is neither good nor bad, it is the person who chooses how it is used and for what end. The same is true with Crafting. In my rather long life I have observed that most people live to their own truths and the rest of us label that good or bad, depending on how it impacts us. Darven has chosen to use his power to hurt and manipulate people, to wrest a kingdom from its rightful lineage and to cause death and destruction to those who oppose his quest for domination. Personal impact aside I think we can all agree his behaviour is bad," she finished ruefully.

"So why take Evie?" pressed Asher. She was unconcerned with the politics of this strange world and only interested in rescuing her sister.

"In good time," responded Hesta firmly, "I'm getting there. Darven grew up with powerful Crafters, surrounded by but unable to access their substantial power. Whether it was because of that, or in spite of it, he chose to pursue sorcery we cannot know. We do know that around twenty years ago, he travelled into the Mountains and did not return. There he stayed for many years. Knowing what I now know it seems likely he found a teacher, a sorcerer he could apprentice to." She sighed. "Unfortunately I paid him no mind, thinking him unimportant in the myriad of threads I was monitoring. I was wrong, so very wrong."

She took another sip while collecting her thoughts. "Three years ago he appeared at Ostrin Castle. I had been there only a few days prior, visiting Magda, but he must have timed his arrival to avoid me. I only heard about his appearance there some weeks later in a letter from Freya. Though that was interesting, it was still no cause for alarm. However -"

"Wait up," interrupted Levi, "Who are Magda and Freya?"

"Magda is my niece on my husband's side. Freya is her lady-in-waiting."

"Ordinary people don't have ladies-in-waiting," mused Levi, "which makes Magda..." he paused.

"The Queen of course," was Hesta's tart response.

"Your niece is the queen?"

Hesta inclined her head.

"So that means she is a first cousin of Jennifer's, which means Ash is cousins with a queen!"

Asher sat silently digesting everything she had heard so far. They were cousins with the queen of Andera. By all the stars Evie was going to love this.

"I rather think it is more pertinent that the Queen is niece to the Weaver, and cousins with the Heir. That is a truly prestigious connection for her."

"So Weaver trumps Queen?" pressed Levi.

Hesta looked down her nose at him and did not bother to answer.

"I was unaware of Darven's true influence at Court for the first few months, but then Freya's letters became more concerned and filled with details that were alarming. Darven was now sitting on judiciary sessions, he was appointed head of the army, he had unfettered access to the Treasury, he was allowed to meet with Magda alone and unsupervised. People who protested found themselves out of favour with the queen or exiled from Court. Some simply vanished. And most alarming, the Prince Consort was relentlessly and suspiciously unwell, which meant Magda was increasingly relying on Darven."

"What did the queen have to say about your concerns?" asked Levi.

Hesta ignored him.

"He was clearly making a power play for the throne and while that was concerning it was not enough for me to intervene."

"What!" exclaimed Levi, leaning forward on the sofa. "Some interloper is trying to steal your niece's crown and you don't think you should intervene?"

Hesta pierced him with a hard look and Levi immediately retreated.

"Sorry," he mumbled.

"Understand this," she said sternly. "Kingdoms rise and fall, people are born and they die, great evil and incredible goodness co-exist and jostle constantly for position. This is the way of it. Who is to say which action is the correct one, what should be allowed or not? It is not the role of the Weaver to choose sides in every skirmish, to decide on what should be to suit herself."

Her face was grim.

"So what is the role of the Weaver?" asked Asher hesitantly. She was struggling to understand.

"The role of the Weaver is to ensure magic is protected. Not individuals, but the magical Weave as a whole. She must always maintain balance between the magical and non-magical beings of the universes. She cannot be involved in the day to day arguments and disputes, in the life and death decisions of individuals, unless there is great risk to the balance. If the immense power of the Weaver could be manipulated to serve the purpose of a person or a group than neutrality is lost and the Weaver loses her influence."

It was starting to make more sense to Asher. She spoke quietly.

"People would be scared, wondering when the Weaver or other Crafters would start to take over, imposing their own desires or choices by force. Non-Crafters might rise up and rebel. Energy crafters would be hunted down. Balance would be lost," added Ash thoughtfully, understanding for the first time the delicate tightrope her grandmother was walking.

"Exactly," nodded Hesta approvingly. "Restraint and timing are paramount. I cannot leap to action every time I have a concern. However, more recently Freya mentioned fears that Darven was practising sorcery and that changed things considerably. Using sorcery for his own ends is worrisome enough, more so if he succeeds in stealing the throne. The rulers of the three kingdoms have always been non-magical. It is the accepted way of it. It maintains the balance on Andera. A sorcerer king is certainly cause for alarm and warrants my attention and perhaps even intervention. I began to dig deeper and that's when I really became concerned. In the last six months Crafters have started going missing."

The hairs on the back of Asher's neck were standing on end. Goosebumps had risen along her arms. She dreaded asking the next question, certain the answer was tied to Evie's kidnapping.

"Why are they disappearing? Why is he taking them?"

"Sorcery is not an intrinsic energy power. It requires unnatural means that have to be acquired externally. Rituals, chants, voodoo dolls. He, or she if the sorcerer is a woman, use hair or objects belonging to their victim to cast their charms. Most sorcerers never learn to draw real power from their bits and bobs. But there is one dark aspect of sorcery that most practitioners would never dare to embrace. Blood magic."

The room felt colder all of a sudden and Asher shivered. *Evie, Evie, please be safe. I'm coming for you*, she sent out her plea.

"Some sorcerers have used animals over the eons, and some of the dark tomes speak of blood letting – which is when a person willingly provides their own blood for a charm or a spell. Never before has a Sorcerer used Crafter blood. It is unthinkable, but I greatly fear that is what Darven is now doing. Enhancing his spells and charms with blood from captive Crafters. It's the only way he could send people across the Void. The only way they could defeat Gin. Which is the other big question – how he knew Ginarwen was alive and where to find her. Most people believe she perished in the Void."

Neither Asher nor Levi offered an answer. There was none they could give and Hesta did not seem to expect one.

The Weaver continued. "But stealing Evie just does not make sense. Until now the missing Crafters have been quite low level, not powerful enough to prevail against him one to one. He is not to know that an insider has alerted me to his ambition, so he could assume I would not notice a missing minor Crafter here or there. I do not keep tabs on every person in Andera at every moment, I am maintaining the Weave across multiple universes. He could have continued that while building up his power."

She stood up and began to pace around the room, clearly agitated.

"So why take my Heir, or rather who he assumes is my Heir. Why draw such incredible attention to himself? He must know I will come after him, and that is what concerns me most of all. What can he possible hope to gain?"

Back and forth across the carpet she strode, the heavy green material of her dress swirling around her calves, as she puzzled through the muddle that was Darven.

"Is it the throne he wants? Or is it Crafter power? Perhaps both. A sorcerer king imbued with Crafter blood might be near unstoppable. But neither are possible while the Weaver holds the Threads, and he knows this. Even with stolen Crafter blood he cannot hope to prevail against me. The balance ***will*** be maintained at all costs."

Asher cleared her throat. "Um, excuse me Hesta..."

Hesta stopped pacing and pinned her with a questioning look.

"You just said Darven's goal is not possible while the Weaver holds the threads."

"Yes?"

"So what if the Weaver no longer did. Hold the threads that is. What if he could remove the Weaver and her Heirs, using their own blood as a charm. What would happen then?"

Horror seeped across Hesta's face as her tall body collapsed back into her chair.

"That would be catastrophic, for Andera, for Earth, for all the worlds where people of magic, of power, of energy reside. Factions would form, magical against non-magical. Order would be lost. Without the Weaver..." Hesta shuddered and didn't finish her sentence.

"But why would he?" asked Levi, "Would he really destroy his whole world? For what purpose? You already said you would ignore his throne stealing. He could have just laid low with the whole sorcery thing and made himself king. Why go so large and start a war with the Weaver? It's like he wants you to know. It seems rather personal."

Hesta took a deep breath, her face settling into its familiar poise, but now there was a tightness around her eyes.

"Revenge," she said grimly, "after all these years he is taking his revenge, and I have been too obtuse to even consider it a possibility."

"Revenge for what?"

"For the death of his aunt and the madness of his mother, her twin. My stupid, conceited cousins who overstepped their Crafting and paid the ultimate price. After bringing the wrath of the townspeople upon themselves they begged for my assistance and I refused to help them. For better or worse people make their choices. I am beholden only to the continuance of the Weave."

Abruptly Hesta stood up. Without another word or a glance in their direction she left the room, leaving Levi and Ash wordlessly staring at the empty doorway.

"Well in the end Jen was right," mused Levi, breaking the silence.

"What?" asked Ash, trying to keep up with his mercurial thought process.

"Turns out this *is* a rather intense family feud with Evie caught in the middle."

Chapter Eight

Training a Crafter

For a few long minutes after Hesta left the room, Asher and Levi sat in silence unsure what they should do next.

"So now what?" asked Levi eventually.

"I'd love to explore more of my mum's room, there are double doors off to one side that must lead somewhere."

"Sounds good to me," agreed Levi readily. "We can check in on Kate on the way."

They climbed the large main staircase together, but instead of turning right at the top, Levi headed left into a whole other section of the house that Asher had not yet seen.

"This house just never ends," she breathed, her steps slowing as she peered at the incredible artworks lining the walls. Unlike her floor, this was not a gallery, but a long windowless hall with doors on either side, leading into bedrooms and bathrooms according to Levi.

He stopped at the end of the hall and pointed to a closed door on his left.

"That's my room, and that one," he indicated the door next to it, "is Kate's."

Asher stepped forward and knocked lightly. "Kate? Are you awake?"

Silence greeted her.

Carefully Asher pushed the door open and stepped into the dark room, the heavy curtains blocking any daylight. Deep, even breathing from the bed indicated that Kate was still asleep, so Ash tiptoed quietly out without disturbing her.

Levi's dark eyes were full of concern when she looked at him. "Do you think she's going to be okay?"

Asher nodded slowly. "Yes, because Hesta thinks this is normal."

They began the walk back along the hall, Ash burning with curiosity but hesitant to ask Levi directly. As always he seemed to read her mind.

"You're wondering what it was like for me in the Void? Because Kate's experience was so traumatic."

Asher nodded.

"It wasn't difficult, not like Kate. It was more that I felt –..." he paused, searching for the right words, "It's hard to describe. I felt hopeless, empty, unhappy, without purpose..." he trailed off.

Asher waited, saying nothing.

"I've never felt that way before, and it didn't feel good. But I knew you'd pull us through. I just kept thinking of you playing your flute back home, and your skin glowing with glitter. That's magic Ash, real magic."

The admiration in his voice made her face flush with heat. "It's just music Levi, and energy. Nothing special."

They reached the bottom of the second staircase and began the ascent in silence. Asher was starting to feel anxious again. Why did everyone have such faith in her? What did they think she could do against a sorcerer king?

As they walked into the gallery Levi gasped in surprise.

"This place is incredible! I didn't see any of this last night. Look at that vase, it's like the glass is different colours, but it's actually clear. Is the colour caught inside, or refracting from the outside?" Asher opened her mouth to respond but Levi rushed on.

"What about that sculpture of the two children? Phewee," he whistled in admiration, "It looks like it's made of stone but it feels warm to the touch, I can totally imagine the children laughing and playing. It's like they've been transformed."

Suddenly he lurched away from the sculpture as though bitten.

"You don't think they are actual children that have been transformed?" he asked in horror.

Asher stepped away from the painting she had been perusing to peer at the sculpture in question. Then she reached out her hand to touch the warm stone. Energy tingled beneath her fingers, and she closed her eyes to tune in to it.

"No," she answered softly, "definitely not real children. Just the wondrous creation of a mother depicting her children at play." How she knew, she could not say. She just seemed able to feel the essence of the sculpture.

"Phew," said Levi loudly, "what about those little glass beads? They look like water drops. Hey, that one changed shape!"

For the next twenty minutes they moved around the gallery, Levi's enthusiasm and wonder helping Asher to become more and more comfortable with touching and holding various objects. This morning she had thought this was a display zone, a place to view and not touch, but now she realised each of these artworks was meant to be experienced wholly. The energy within each of them was alive. Levi could feel it too, and he took great pleasure in examining the oddest objects he could find.

She stopped for a long moment in front of a painting she was sure had been created by her mother. It was of two young women laughing in the sunshine, one with gleaming red hair, the other with warm chestnut curls. They were a similar age to Asher and Kate. Ash smiled as she wondered what secrets the two girls were sharing. They looked thick as thieves, caught in a moment of mischief, as though the artist had just discovered them unexpectedly.

Cook had mentioned her mother's painting studio. She guessed that was what lay beyond the doors in her mother's bedroom. Leaving Levi inspecting various curiosities Asher headed along the gallery and into her room.

The curtains had been opened and with a pang of guilt she realised some-one had made her bed. She made a silent vow to do that herself tomorrow morning. Her pack had been zipped up and placed beside the armchair. Briefly she wondered if the mysterious organiser had refolded her belongings that she had shoved in there. Then with a jolt of panic she remembered the globe and bracelet she had pushed deep into the front pocket when she had changed into her pj's last night.

Asher rushed over to the pack and unzipped the pocket. Frantically she felt around inside, her hand searching past packets of tissues, her harmonica, sticks of gum and some muesli bars, until at last her fingers closed around the pendant and bracelet. With a deep exhalation of relief Asher pulled them out. The globe hummed at her reproachfully.

"Sorry, sorry," muttered Asher, clasping the bracelet around her wrist and then the pendant around her neck. She was certain her items were safe in Hesta's house, but leaving them unattended was not a good habit to get into.

"Yo!"

Asher jumped in surprise and quickly pulled her sleeve over the bracelet. She had promised her mother she wouldn't tell anyone about it, and that included detective Levi.

"Yo," she responded. "Ready to see what's behind those doors?"

"Indeed Miss Blake, I choose door number one! And two, considering they are a pair." He let out a low whistle as he looked around the gold and cream room. "Whoa, this is one fancy pants room. I thought my room downstairs was nice, but this is something else. Do you think old Queen Madga has a room this fancy?"

Asher laughed. "I know what you mean. My camping pack seems totally out of place. It's hard to imagine my mother growing up in here. It's such an elegant, grown up space. There are no photos, no personal bits and pieces that you would expect in a bedroom. It doesn't look like a child ever lived here."

"She could have updated it as she grew older. Or maybe Hesta redecorated after she left," suggested Levi.

"Hmmmm, maybe."

The thought made Asher feel unsettled. How long had her mother been gone before Hesta had realised she was not coming back? Before she packed up Ginar's belongings and redecorated her room? Would the same thing happen to Asher, trapped on Andera? She ran her fingers over the bracelet and felt reassured. Gin had not abandoned her here. Asher would always find her way home, mum had made sure of that.

Oblivious to her uneasy thoughts, Levi strode over to the closed oak doors and placed an open hand on each of them.

"Ready?" he called dramatically, "Set... Go!" and with a firm push both doors sprung open and they stepped into Gin's world.

Where the rest of the house was immaculately maintained in colours of gold and ivory, olives and blues, this room was an explosion of colour, with paint splattered on the old grey carpet and well-worn furniture layered with frayed, battered cushions.

This was clearly the long-abandoned painting studio, and unlike the bedroom which had been re-ordered at some point after Gin left, this space seemed untouched. It almost felt like Gin had just stepped out of the room and would return any moment to complete the painting that was propped in the easel.

It was large, like the rest of the rooms, with great panes of glass on two of the walls, ready to catch the full extent of the afternoon sun.

Every available wall space was covered in canvases, some as small as a dinner plate, others as large as a big screen TV. Piles of sketches lay on one table. For a room that was clearly unused it was remarkably clean and fresh. Asher thought of how quickly her mother's attic studio at home had been claimed by dust and general mustiness in only a couple of years. This place had been empty for almost twenty years and yet the air was sweet and no dust flew up to meet them as they walked across the floor. Some-one was still tending it with care.

"Woah," said Levi, his voice hushed, "this is the room that time forgot. It doesn't match the rest of the house at all."

No, thought Asher, *it really doesn't.* But it matched her mother and she could imagine teenage Gin spending her hours in here, turning blobs of paint on a palette into incredible works of art.

Tables high enough to stand at were scattered around the room, laden with paint and brushes. Even in this foreign house on this foreign planet, everything about this space was so familiar.

In one corner boxes were piled neatly on top of each other. Curiosity pulled Asher over to them. In any other room in this house she would not have dreamt of rummaging through things, but this room felt so much like her mother that she did not feel any reluctance at all.

"Well now we know what happened to all of mum's stuff," she called out to Levi, drawing him away from an intense staring competition with a goat in a painting.

He stood beside her as she pulled out clothes and shoes, including a long chocolate coloured, woollen coat with fur trim at the collar and wrists. Unable to resist she shrugged it on, unsurprised that it fit her perfectly.

"Suits you," said Levi approvingly, "though I sure hope the fur details are fake."

Asher grimaced. "Yuck, I hope so."

Still wearing the coat Ash continued to explore the boxes with Levi. As well as clothes there were books and letters, photographs and knick-knacks, jewellery and shoes.

"She quite literally fled with nothing but the clothes on her back," murmured Asher. "Why? What happened?"

'Asher.' Hesta's voice filled her mind.

'Yes Hesta?'

'Come to my study on the top floor. It's time to begin your training.'

"Ah Levi, sorry I have to go meet Hesta. She says it's time for training."

Levi straightened up from the box of books he had been digging through.

"What? When did she say that?"

Asher squirmed. Levi was her oldest friend and so much had happened over the last couple of days she worried he must think she was actually the weirdo Evie always called her. And now she was going to sound even odder.

"Um, she just spoke to me. Telepathically."

He nodded slowly, "hmmm, interesting. Well you do what you need to do. It's time for me to check what's on the menu for morning tea."

Asher smiled gratefully and they left the studio together. As they passed through the bedroom Asher shrugged out of the coat and lay it across a chair, then she followed Levi out of the room, quietly closing the door behind them.

Hesta's study was on the other side of the top floor, she remembered from their arrival last night. As she entered the heavily furnished room Asher was struck by how different this room was to the rest of the home. This private space was warm with layers and textures. Though large it had a cosy feel as opposed to the grand, magnificent formality of the ground floor.

If this were her house she would spend all her time in this room, perhaps with a piano and cello.

Hesta sat at the large desk on the other side of the room, her attention fully occupied by the letters she was scouring through. While Asher stood silently and waited to be acknowledged, she took the opportunity to really absorb her surroundings.

The heavy tapestry drapes had been pulled back, revealing the large windows. Bright sunlight filled the room, illuminating the rich colours of the layered rugs beneath her feet. The carpets were well cared for but showing signs of wear. Asher suspected they had been lying in place for innumerable years, a thousand feet having stood where she now did.

Her eyes were drawn to the large bookcases lining the walls housing hundreds of books, companions to the thousands of books that filled the library below. She wondered if anyone had ever read all of them.

She noted with interest that Hesta seemed just as comfortable in these surroundings as she was in the rooms downstairs. Asher supposed that Hesta would feel at ease in any situation.

With a barely audible sigh Hesta placed the papers neatly on her desk.

"Let's begin." She gestured to the sofa. "Take a seat, close your eyes and breathe in and out for a few moments. I want you to really centre yourself, to feel your breath. Your Crafting experience so far has been wrought from a place of intensity, of deep emotion, and that is often when people find their ability. What I want to teach you is how to access your energy when you are calm. To Craft when and how you choose."

Asher sank into the sofa and nestled into the large cushions. She closed her eyes and breathed slowly. Feeling the air gently fill her lungs, then rush out as she exhaled fully.

As she took the next breath and the one after that Asher felt herself start to relax, anxiety and tension leaving her body with each exhale. In this calm state Asher's thoughts turned automatically to her music composition.

The piano piece was already fully formed, a light melody that evoked a warm Spring day. She could picture her mother potting flowers in the garden, murmuring encouragement to each plant as the sun warmed the earth. Asher breathed in and out, adding the violin. The bright, jaunty notes leapt around in the air like bees buzzing and birds warbling. The composition felt zesty and vibrant. The last element that she wanted to add was the flute. She imagined that would be the breeze, dancing through the garden, teasing at the melody.

"Asher."

Asher opened her eyes, startled by the interruption. She had completely forgotten Hesta was there. With difficulty Ash pulled herself back to present, regretfully leaving the garden and its song behind.

Hesta was looking at her thoughtfully. "What instruments do you play Asher?"

"Well anything really."

"Piano?"

"Of course."

"The violin and the flute?'

"Yes and yes."

Hesta's clear gaze was considering. "What else?"

Asher shrugged self-consciously. "The guitar, cello and the ukulele."

"Hmmm. Energy is emanating from you, swirling around you. Yet you have no instrument in your hand. So how are you doing that?" Hesta sounded almost accusing, as though Asher was some-how cheating.

Asher squirmed under Hesta's intense assessment.

"I don't know. I'm just working on a piece in my head, it's almost finished. I just need to score it and play it to feel it come together."

"So you were creating music in your head right now." It was not a question, but Asher nodded anyway.

"Interesting," mused Hesta. Then with one fluid movement she rose from her chair and walked past Asher to the doorway.

"Where are we going?" asked Ash in confusion.

"To the music room. I want to see you play."

Asher's heart leapt. Music Room. Hesta had said the magic words.

The music room was back on the ground floor and through the library. The large white doors that connected the rooms had been closed this morning and Asher had not realised the wonderland that lay beyond.

A black grand piano had pride of place in front of huge windows that overlooked a manicured flat garden that rolled for acres, beyond Asher's eyeline. Not a single bookshelf, picture or ornament graced this room. It was dedicated entirely to music. Stunned, Ash gazed around the room, drinking in the sight of the cello sitting beside the harp, with three ancient wood violins hanging from a rack on the wall.

The opposite corner was for brass instruments, with a wide selection of flutes, piccolos, recorders, saxophones and trumpets.

Asher felt quite overwhelmed, her eyes darting from one glorious instrument to another. These were nothing like the over-used, under-appreciated battered instruments she had access to at school, or even like her upright piano at home. These were the objects of a Concert level musician. In her world the dollar value would be staggering, but for Asher the real value was in the craftsmanship and the sound she knew lay within.

Her fingers itching, she took a few steps towards the piano and stopped, turning back to Hesta.

"May I?" she asked, struggling to maintain her manners.

Hesta inclined her head, the ghost of a smile dancing on her lips.

"Be my guest."

Asher settled herself on the fine tapestry cushion of the piano stool and reverently placed her finger tips on the cool ivory keys. She played a quick scale up and down the keys to feel the weight and to hear the depth of each note.

Then she threw herself into the First Movement of Beethoven's Sonata Opus 53, one of her favourite pieces. The sound from the Grand was truly glorious. She finished the sonata with a flourish, her whole being thrumming with the music.

"That was magnificent Asher, I have never heard the like."

Asher felt her face warm and her neck flush. She never felt self-conscious while she was actually playing, she never felt awkward or unsure of herself, but afterwards she felt all of those things. She would happily slink away without any applause or praise if that were possible.

"Thank you," she said softly, "but I cannot take any credit for Beethoven's genius."

"The genius of Crafting is in the creation Asher, not simply the raw materials. A Crafter takes the clay and brings to life a sculpture, or tubes of coloured paint and creates a picture that evokes emotion. The quality of the clay or the paint enhance the end result, but the mastery is in the realisation."

Asher kept her gaze on the ivory and black keys, softly running the fingertips of her right hand up and down their length without pressing them.

Hesta continued, "Now play the piece again and imagine the notes as energy. Then focus that energy on something you want to make happen, such as closing those doors."

Obediently Asher began the sonata again. As each merry note rang around the room she stared intently at the doors and imagined them slowly closing together. It seemed to her that they shuddered somewhat, and perhaps even moved an inch or so, but nothing more.

The last notes rose and fell in the room, chasing their fellows away through the house, leaving a full, weighted silence.

"Hmmm..." Hesta looked pointedly at the still open doors and raised her brows questioningly.

"It didn't work," said Ash quietly.

"Indeed."

"Ahem Hesta?"

A small wiry woman appeared in the music room, her entire body vibrating as though she was about to run off to attend to something extremely important. Her gleaming black hair was pulled back into a sensible bun and large black rimmed glasses balanced on her nose, giving her dark eyes are rather owlish look. She was dressed entirely in grey, including her soft leather ankle boots. Everything about her was in direct contrast to her employer.

"You said to inform you when our last guest awoke. I encountered her in the upstairs hall and have just taken her to Mariah for a feed. The chatty young man is with her." She spoke quickly and beamed when she mentioned Levi.

"Thank you Anetta. Let me introduce Asher. She and her companions will be with us for a few days. I am assessing her potential for Wen training. Asher, Anetta is my housekeeper."

Asher smiled shyly at the beaming woman. She was still seated at the piano, but she knew if she stood up she would tower over the small framed Anetta and her gleaming black hair. She resisted the urge to run her fingers through her own tangled curls, in a fruitless attempt to make them behave.

"May I ask how my friend was? It was a very tiring trip."

"Well she seemed in good spirits, full of energy and rather hungry. We're so pleased to have you all here. Good luck with your training."

Then she was gone, moving sprightly back through the library and out of sight. Asher strained her ears for her departing footfalls, but she could not detect them. Anetta moved fast and lightly.

Despite her disappointment over the stubborn doors, Asher found she was grinning. It was a relief that Kate was awake and feeling good. She had been thinking about her as she played, hoping that she would wake refreshed.

"I suspect your music is what woke Kate," said Hesta, her face pensive. "As you were playing I could feel your energy wafting through the house in search of her."

"I didn't mean to do that!" exclaimed Ash in surprise. "I really was trying to close the doors."

"Your mind was on the doors, but your energy was focused on Kate. Do you understand the difference?"

Asher shook her head.

"You need to learn to focus your Crafting. And to be careful of focusing on another person's state. It is quite hard or draining to use your own energy to alter some-one else's state of being. Using your own medium, such as music, can enhance your Crafting without it draining you. However most crafts do not lend to this as it can take many days to complete a piece of pottery or woodwork. Which is why Crafters carry pieces of their work with them, as stored energy. Music is rather unique in its immediacy. It is important to practise using your instruments to direct your energy, however I also want you to practise drawing on energy sources outside of yourself or the music in your head. This is far less draining and more sustainable. And above all, you must avoid taking energy from people. Crafters naturally protect themselves against this, and non-crafters would be most upset."

"How do I do that? Use energy from other sources?"

"We will practise that next, as soon as you have learned to focus your Crafting and your own energy. At the moment it is still raw and rather haphazard."

Asher dropped her gaze back to the keys. She had no real desire to be a Crafter, even less desire to be Hesta's Heir, but she still felt the sting of disappointment that some-how she was not fulfilling her potential. Being an A student was something she took pride in.

"As your Crafting becomes more focused," continued Hesta, "you will learn to tune into the energy of the natural living world, and also into the energy stored in the objects they become. Stored energy is infinite and cannot be depleted, just like a musical composition or a painting. You will always be able to tap into it. That is what makes Crafting so powerful and dangerous. A Crafter can create an object of power, pour their energy into it and then use if forever. Some rare objects can be layered with many different Crafter's energy."

Asher thought about this for a long moment, conscious of the warm globe resting against her chest.

"Can Crafters use each other's works? Could I use the energy my mum paints into her pictures?"

"In theory yes, but it takes years, decades, of training to learn to wield it safely. Crafters often make objects of power for others, or objects that are designed to capture energy for use, but usually their works are accessible only to them. There is only one who can truly access the energy of all Craft." She said it with pride, but without arrogance.

Asher pursed her lips thoughtfully. "So do you become the Weaver because you can access all Craft? Or do you have the ability because you are the Weaver?"

"Very good question," Hesta smiled approvingly. "The role of the Weaver is an inherited one, so I was trained from a young age to not only use my own innate crafting, but to weave the Threads. It is within the Threads that all energy, all magic if you will, is held and woven into the lives of the inhabitants across the universes. Where magic is under attack or at risk of disappearing altogether the Weaver must ensure it is saved. Altering the Weave of the universes is a risky decision, with impacts that are impossible to foresee. It is not something that is done lightly, and it is incredibly difficult. You are quite literally altering the course of millions of life-forms, of the future itself. It is important that the Crafter who becomes the Weaver must be able to manage the strain. Only a handful of times in our long history has the immediate heir proven herself unable or incapable."

"What happens then?"

"The next daughter is appointed. There has never been a break in the line of the Weavers. There cannot be."

"There never will be," a warm voice said reassuringly from the doorway.

Asher nearly jumped out of her skin. This house! With its well maintained floorboards and thick lush carpets a person could sneak right up on you. She thought affectionately of the Beast who would never allow such a thing to happen.

"Caro," Hesta greeted the newcomer warmly, seemingly not surprised by her appearance, "come and meet my new Potential. She will be with us for a few days as she undergoes Wen training. Asher this is my niece Carowen. She lives here at E-Langren."

"Well if that glorious music is any indication of her talent then I am certain we will be celebrating a new Wen very, very soon."

The most beautiful woman Asher had ever seen stepped forward into the room.

Thick chestnut curls gleaming with burnished gold were artfully piled high on her head, framing a round face of flawless ivory skin. Large, rich brown eyes sparkled with warmth and friendship as she approached Asher. Her age was hard to determine. She radiated youthfulness while exuding the mature confidence of a woman who knew exactly who she was and where she belonged in the world.

Asher's gaze flitted between Carowen and Hesta. Though they were different in looks both women radiated poise, elegance and self-assurance.

A wide welcoming smile lit up Caro's face. Asher liked her immediately.

"It is very exciting to meet you Asher. We haven't had a Wen Potential training here for some years. I assume those two young people in the kitchen belong with you."

Asher nodded, feeling a little awed in Carowen's presence.

"Well it is lovely to have such vibrancy filling our rather staid halls."

"Caro is a glass blower," explained Hesta, "she has a workshop in the outbuildings."

"You must come and see it while are you are here," invited Caro, "but do not feel obliged to stay for long. I can be quite obsessive about my glass. Just sneak out when you are ready to leave. I won't be offended, in fact I probably won't even notice." She grinned.

Asher returned her grin, understanding completely. Her mother, Carowen, herself – all driven by their artistic obsessions.

"Speaking of which, I am going to take my lunch down to the workshop. I'll see you at dinner Asher. If I remember..." she winked at Ash, recognising a fellow obsessive.

With a smile for her aunt, Carowen strode confidently out of the room.

Once she was out of earshot Hesta returned to the task at hand.

"Alright, where were we? Ah yes, sourcing energy from outside yourself. This is extremely important."

"Hesta, may we take a break for a little while? I'd like to see Kate."

The Weaver hesitated for a brief moment, then she nodded.

"Alright, but only a short break. We have so much to cover, so much training to do. Return here in half an hour."

Asher smiled her thanks, turning towards the double doors that led back to the library and across the entrance hall.

"Asher," Hesta's voice halted her departure, "try that door, it is a faster route to the kitchen."

The Weaver indicated a dark wooden door that was at the back of the music room. Curiously Asher pushed it open and found herself in a wide hallway. This was much plainer than the hallway on the floor above. It was painted a light cream, with no other artwork or ornamentation. It was a part of the house fancy guests would never see. To the left she could hear her friends talking and laughing so she headed in that direction. She passed a couple of doors on either side and then she was entering the kitchen through the entrance Cook had indicated earlier this morning.

Kate was sitting at the kitchen table with Levi and Cook, sipping hot chocolate and chatting comfortably.

"Ash!" she exclaimed, jumping up to hug her friend. The two girls grinned as they held each other tightly.

"How are you feeling?"

"I'm okay." Kate said softly. "Though I did have the strangest dreams." She wrinkled her nose.

"Like what?" asked Asher.

Kate was silent for a moment, considering how to explain what she had experienced in her long sleep. It seemed to Asher that her friend's deep blue eyes were changing colour. As though the blue was painted over a black base, and the darker colour was seeping through. As Kate hesitated, remembering her Void dreams, her eyes became darker and darker.

Asher frowned uneasily.

"Kate are you sure you are okay?"

Kate laughed and in an instant her eyes were their familiar shade of ocean blue.

"Yes of course. Pretty great actually. Levi's been catching me up – Darven, the Gallery upstairs, your mum's painting studio –"

"Ah Kate," interrupted Asher in a low voice, "Turns out it isn't common knowledge me being Gin's daughter. Hesta's been introducing me as a trainee who she is mentoring."

"Quite right my love," added Cook, "There's dirty deeds afoot in Andera, and it's best you lay low while Hesta works it out. No-one in the house knows who you really are or why you are here. Hesta tried the same nonsense on me, but I wasn't having a moment of it. As if I wouldn't recognise the child of my sweet Ginar. I practically raised that girl. Marten and Anetta didn't live here back then, but Caro grew up with Gin. I think you'll be hard pressed to fool her for long."

"Speaking of Caro, how is she Hesta's niece? And how close a cousin is Darven?"

"Carowen's the child of Hesta's brother actually, long dead now. Oh it's a rambling, but rather sparse old tree that Hesta heads up. Here love, I'll draw it for you."

Cook pulled herself up from the table, the chair scraping on the stone floor as it was pushed backwards. She winced sharply as her back stretched back into shape.

"Beastly old bones" she muttered as she limped to the drawers.

A few minutes of rummaging around produced a thick black texta and some blank paper.

"Righto my love. Let's start with Lyrawen, Hesta's grandmother. No point in going back any further than that."

Cook muttered explanations as she drew, and before long Asher and her friends were pouring over the branches of Ash's newly discovered family tree.

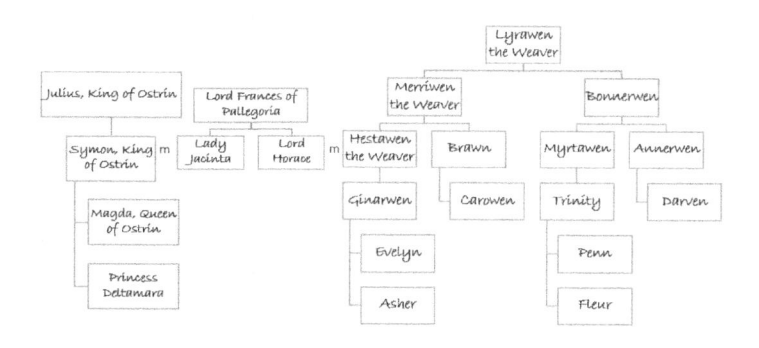

```
                                    Lyrawen
                                    the Weaver
                                        |
                    ┌───────────────────┼───────────────────┐
                    |                                       |
              Merriwen                                  Bonnewen
              the Weaver                                    |
                  |                              ┌──────────┴──────────┐
         ┌────────┼────────┐                     |                     |
         |                 |                  Myrtawen              Annerwen
   Hestawen             Brawn                    |                     |
   the Weaver             |                   Trinity               Darven
         |             Carowen                   |
      Ginarwen                                 Penn
         |                                       |
      Evelyn                                   Fleur
         |
       Asher
```

(Additional family lines shown at left:)
Julius, King of Ostrin — Symon, King of Ostrin m Lady Jacinta — Magda, Queen of Ostrin — Princess Deltamara
Lord Frances of Pallegoria — Lord Horace

"Now out with you all. Go into the sun and fresh air. Enjoy some quiet time before Hesta summons you again."

***

"For goodness sake Levi, not a stone!" Asher fought the urge to duck as he brandished it maniacally.

"The thing is Ash, in a real fight scenario it won't be tissues or socks you'll have to deal with," he raised his brows, "hmmm??"

Asher rolled her eyes. Hesta had allowed her thirty minutes to meet with her friends, but somehow the time had run on, and the Weaver had not summoned her. Asher supposed she was busy with something more important. In truth she did not mind a bit.

They were standing on the flat green lawn behind the house, warmed by the afternoon sun. Large oak trees stood a few metres away, their leaves rustling merrily in the light breeze. In the distance sunlight gleamed off a lake that was big enough for boating or swimming. Various outbuildings were scattered around the property, including

Carowen's workshop. Ash was oblivious to all of this, focused as she was on playing the harmonica to channel her Crafting, as Kate and Levi rather enthusiastically threw things at her.

The pair of socks she had deflected easily enough, though the tissue box had taken a couple of attempts. The piece of cake that Kate had threatened her with from the luscious lunch tray Cook provided might have been messy, but her throw had been halted by Levi moaning about the waste.

Now he stood weighing a stone in each hand, considering whether he should actually launch one at her.

"The more I think about it, the more it makes sense," he continued, and then pelted a stone at her legs as hard as he could.

Kate screamed, but Asher barely heard her. Time slowed down, sounds dimmed, except for the loud, crazy beating of her heart. Asher gazed intently as the stone whirred softly through the air, inching towards her. Calmness descended. Her arms moved in slow motion, raising the harmonica to her lips. The stone inched closer as the first notes rang out.

She considered something Hesta said earlier, about crafting using the energy of the world around her, rather than always drawing on her own internal reserves. Curiously Asher reached out for the energy created by the stone's momentum, directing her music towards it. There it was, a heaviness in the air around the stone, a ripple in space. She tried to focus on that space and spin the stone, hoping to swat it straight back at an unsuspecting Levi. All without moving a muscle.

The air rippled, the harmonica played, and the stone stayed on its collision course to her shin. She yelped in pain as it impacted.

"What were you doing?" exclaimed Levi. "You were supposed to deflect the stone, not let it hit you."

"Oh, was that what I was supposed to do? Thanks for clarifying," answered Asher through gritted teeth. She was doubled over, clutching at her throbbing leg.

"So what happened?" asked Levi.

"Clearly it didn't work," was her brusque response.

"Why not?" he persisted.

Asher glared at him. "If I knew that, then I wouldn't be currently enjoying the sensation of my body bruising."

Levi wrinkled his nose. "More practise," he said with authority, "that's what is required here. Practise makes the witch."

Ash lifted her nose and peered down its length at him. "I believe the word you are looking for is Crafter," she replied haughtily.

"Indeed," agreed Hesta, stepping out of the French doors from the dining room. "Quite right Asher".

Her face aflame Ash threw a reproachful look at Levi, cross that she had been caught by Hesta pretending to be Hesta, and certain that some-how it was his fault.

His own face was the picture of innocence.

"Come now Asher, let us continue with your instruction. Clearly we have much work to do." The Weaver raised a silvery brow at the bruise already darkening on Asher's leg.

Embarrassment bubbled in Asher's stomach and she pulled herself upright, ready to return to the music room.

"Hesta!"

Anetta hurried from the house, her smooth hair completely undisturbed by her quick movements.

"What is wrong?"

"Trinity and the children are here. She's in quite a state, says she must speak with you at once. I didn't mention your guests," she nodded at the three of them.

Trinity... Ash pictured the family tree Cook had drawn for her. Trinity was the daughter of Myrta, Hesta's cousin. Myrta was the Crafter who had died in the Void, sending her twin mad, Darven's mother. That made Trinity Darven's first cousin, and Asher's 3rd or 4th, or something like that.

All the excitement of the last few minutes evaporated. The anxiety and dread she felt whenever she thought of Darven holding Evie captive returned with a thud, lodging itself in her belly, and thickening her throat. She tried to swallow past the lump.

"Then I shall see her at once," replied Hesta calmly, heading back into the house with long composed strides, Anetta trotting beside her.

Asher threw a questioning look at Kate and Levi who nodded wordlessly. Without waiting for an invitation the three of them followed Hesta into the sitting room.

The woman who waited there was pacing around the room, opening and clenching her fists as she inhaled and exhaled rapidly, like she had been running. She was oblivious to the gentle pleas of a young girl who was imploring her to calm down.

Beside the unlit fireplace a tall young man stood, his still presence at odds with the agitation of the woman. His mocha skin and dark hair matched that of the woman and girl and suggested close kinship. *Penn*, Ash decided. His unremarkable dark clothing and determined unobtrusive air resonated with Asher immediately. Like her, he preferred to be an observer.

They all turned as one to face Hesta as she swept into the room.

"Hesta!" breathed the woman in obvious relief, "oh Hesta! It's too terrible!"

Tears that had been barely held at bay now started to drip noisily down her face, as her ragged breathing began to catch and hiccup. Hysteria seemed imminent.

Asher looked to her grandmother wondering if she would embrace and comfort her distraught kinswoman.

"Trinity," Hesta greeted her guest solemnly. In that one deep word Asher heard the echo of a thousand voices, felt the immenseness of a timeless wisdom.

Hesta seemed taller, larger. Trinity felt her presence as surely as Ash did. The tears eased, the fist clenching stopped. Calm settled upon her.

"Weaver," she responded, dropping her eyes in deference.

"Weaver," her children repeated, inclining their heads.

Hesta acknowledged them with a smile. "You are well come to E-Langren, you are welcome in the home of The Weaver."

"We bring open hearts and honest intent to the Weaver. May the Threads always weave true."

Asher felt the words run down her spine as the ancient greetings were exchanged.

Then Hesta strode forward and clasped both Trinity's hands in her own. "Come child, sit and tell me what 'terrible thing' has brought you to my door in such a state."

Gratefully Trinity sank onto the sofa, the girl taking a seat beside her, exuding comfort and care for her mother. The boy remained where he was, watching his mother calmly, his back to Asher and her friends who were still in the doorway to the dining room. No-one paid them any attention.

Trinity took a deep breath. "I don't know where to start, so I'll just launch in at the end. Darven came to the village, after all these years! He wants my children Hesta," tears threatened again and she fought to maintain her composure.

"He said," she paused, her voice catching, "He said, this is the end of the Weaver and we can join him willingly or die."

Chapter Nine

An oath is given

Hesta seemed unfazed by this dramatic announcement.

"Start at the beginning Trinity. Explain to me what happened." The Weaver said calmly.

"If there's a plot to destroy the Weaver I reckon she's somehow involved," muttered Levi so quietly both girls had to lean in to hear him. A rather awkward movement considering they still had their eyes trained on the trio across the room.

"Remember it was her mother who died. If Darven wants revenge for his mother's madness surely Trinity wants vengeance for *her* mother. I know I would." He finished darkly.

Kate and Asher both nodded, it made sense. They remained unnoticed as Hesta asked Trinity to go back to the beginning, when had this happened, who else was involved?

Asher was burning to ask about her sister. Did Darven have Evie with him? Was she okay?

Trinity took a deep breath, and the words came tumbling out.

"It was three days ago that he first appeared. He was travelling alone. At first I didn't realise who he was, it has been so many years since I last saw him. Oh he's a handsome man, so golden and beautiful. Just like his father. He rode in late afternoon and asked some village children for directions to my house. It is peculiar don't you think? How does he know which village I live in? I only moved there after Fleur was born, and I have had no contact with him in since Penn was born."

"So she says," muttered Levi.

"Shhhhh," whispered Kate with a frown.

"He was very friendly and solicitous at first, full of reminisces about our childhood. I had forgotten how much fun we had as children together. We laughed a lot remembering the stories. The first night was a great deal of fun."

She paused to blow her nose, a trumpeting sound that made Levi wince.

"That sounded painful," he murmured.

"Shhhhh!!" whispered Kate and Asher simultaneously.

"He asked a lot of questions about Fleur and her crafting ability, which is non-existent really, isn't it darling?" she patted her daughter's leg reassuringly and continued without waiting for an answer.

Clearly aware that no response would be required Fleur didn't even open her mouth, just smiled affectionately at her mother.

Hesta's intense gaze, which had been fully focused on Trinity, turned its attention to Fleur, and Ash wondered what she was seeing and thinking.

The girl squirmed slightly and dropped her gaze to her hands clasped tightly in her lap.

"Anyway." Trinity cleared her throat, a thick phlegmy noise that drew Hesta's attention back to her. "The second night he became quite insistent that we share with him Fleur's crafting ability and when I explained she was a non-crafter like me, he became very agitated, rather unpleasant really." Tears welled again.

"I see," said Hesta, her calm voice a direct contrast to the dramatic story telling unfolding before her.

"He was insistent that he be allowed to test Fleur for Crafting ability, he said he would be able to tell from her blood. Who ever heard of such a thing? He was becoming quite nasty about it. I think he would have done it by force if I kept refusing to allow it, but then he received a message from Ostrin and he had to leave in a hurry."

"What was the message?"

"I do not know, he did not share it with me. But he was so excited! He said a huge change was coming, that this meant the end of the Weaver and he was offering us the chance, *as family*, to join him willingly. He said the next time he returned it would be with an army. We could join him or die."

Her voice trailed off as she finished her story, her small body slumping into the cushions, all the intensity having been spent.

Hesta sat unmoving, unspeaking, sorting through everything she had heard.

"So he received a message yesterday morning, and returned to Ostrin." She eventually said.

"Oh not to Ostrin!" exclaimed Trinity, "He headed into the mountains."

Hesta stared at her with wide, unblinking eyes.

"Sorry," mumbled Trinity, shifting nervously on the sofa, "Is that important?"

Silence crept around the room, filling the spaces between the still occupants. Hesta was no longer looking at either Trinity or Fleur. Instead her gaze was fixed on something outside, beyond the house. Asher suspected she wasn't looking at anything at all, rather she was considering what she had heard. Her own mind was spinning.

Yesterday morning... if he was somewhere to open a portal in the afternoon then the timing coincided with Evie's abduction. Was the message from Ostrin somehow connected?

Trinity opened her mouth as though to say more, but Fleur firmly took her mother's hand and shook her head. The message was clear. Let the Weaver think. Trinity closed her mouth. Even Levi was silent.

Asher felt the skin on her arms prickle and the hairs on the back of her neck rise. Some-one was watching her. She glanced over at Penn who had not spoken nor moved through the re-telling. He was still standing in the same spot, but was now staring at Asher intently, really seeing her as few people ever did. It was unsettling and confusing to be so completely seen after a lifetime of people glancing at her then looking away.

When her grey eyes met Penn's dark eyes something passed between them, something ancient. It nestled deep within Ash's stomach, spreading warmth through her body.

Penn's eyes widened in surprise and Asher knew he had felt it too.

There was no time to wonder what they had experienced, as Hesta stood up and with a few long strides closed the distance between herself and Penn. He pulled his attention away from Asher to focus on the Weaver.

"May I?" she asked, holding out her right hand.

Penn nodded once.

Carefully Hesta lay her palm on the top of Penn's head and they both closed their eyes. Long minutes passed before Hesta's eyes flew open, satisfaction gleaming in them.

"Thank you Penn. Do you know what I am going to ask of you now?"

He inclined his head. "Yes Weaver."

"Penn el Jesper e Trinity, son of the A'pan, will you willingly swear fealty to me, offering your very life to my service?"

Fleetingly his gaze returned to Asher, the incredibly brief glance burning her, before he dropped to one knee and stretched both arms out to Hesta, palms up.

"Willingly I swear fealty to the Weaver and her true and rightful Heirs."

Asher's fingertips tingled and her heart beat faster and faster. He knew, she would stake her life on it. Penn knew who she was, and this vow he was making was for her. His words wove their way around her heart, the deep rumble of his voice vibrating deep in her being. Unexpectedly tears welled and Ash blinked hard to stop them from multiplying.

Behind Hesta, Trinity and Fleur had also risen, their dark eyes shining with pride.

"Anyone else wondering –" began Levi.

"Shut up!" hissed Kate, jabbing him sharply in the ribs with her elbow.

Hesta reached out her hands with a wide smile, her eyes glowing, clasping Penn's hands in hers and pulling him to his feet.

"Thank you," she said, and Asher felt the sincerity and relief in her words. "You have chosen an uncertain and dangerous path I am afraid, but I am grateful for your courage and loyalty."

Then unexpectedly she leaned close and whispered in his ear, her words for him alone. He nodded once, twice, then "always" he responded solemnly.

Hesta smiled again and squeezed his hands before releasing him and turning to address them all.

"In the presence of witnesses, Penn el Jesper, son of Trinity de Bonner and Jesper el Maris has sworn fealty to The Weaver, and her Heirs. I accept his oath."

With one quick movement she pulled a tiny dagger out of her sleeve and pricked Penn's thumb, then her own. Blood roared through Asher's ears and she staggered slightly, as the two droplets of blood blended.

Across the room Trinity was beaming, practically dancing with excitement. Fleur was also smiling, the magnitude of the moment not lost on her as she clasped at her chest. She reached for the comfort of the sofa behind her and quietly sat down.

Asher took a few deep breaths and felt her body steady. The globe was humming and burning against her chest with such intensity Ash was sure it would burn through her clothes. She sent it a stern mental *'hush'* and to her surprise it cooled down, quieting its noisy hum to a happy whirr.

The formalities must have passed because Trinity flew forward, reaching up on tiptoes to embrace her much taller son.

"Oh Penn! Penn! I am so proud of you. Your father would be so proud of you. Sworn to the Weaver, and you only just of age!"

With a smile he hugged her back, silent in the barrage of her enthusiasm, but his face was filled with affection for her.

"Most warriors could not aim so high! Oh wait till I tell that dreadful Lavisa, who thinks her worthless son too good for my Fleur –"

"Mother." Penn's low voice gently interrupted her. "Thank you. I am pleased you are pleased. As for Fleur, she is only just turned thirteen, let us not worry about potential suitors for her just yet. And certainly not the *worthless son* of Lavisa."

He threw a conspiratorial look to his sister who beamed at him.

Brimming with questions Asher looked for Hesta, desperate to discuss Darven and Evie, but the Weaver was no longer in the room.

Anetta suddenly appeared in the doorway, startling Kate and Levi as she bustled past them.

"Alright then, let's get you upstairs for a wash and a rest before dinner. Trinity you will be in the Royal Suite. Miss Fleur and Master Penn," she nodded at him with a proud smile, "you can share the adjoining room. It is plenty big enough for two beds. Marten has already taken your things upstairs. Come then."

"Oh no, no, no, *no, no*" Trinity was protesting as she was bundled out of the room by the sheer energy of Anetta. "Not the *Royal Suite*! I could never *presume*! The children and I will be just fine in one of the old guesthouses, or perhaps the unused staff quarters…" her futile protests faded out of earshot as they left the room.

Asher stood still, staring long after they had disappeared, hoping Penn would look her way once more. But he did not.

"Phew," whooshed Levi as the three of them slowly made their way back to his favourite spot, the kitchen. "Things sure get intense around here fast, Ash is becoming a witch, Hesta's on the hunt for a murderous, kidnapping cousin, and now we have blood oaths in the mix… and it's only day 1! Best camping trip ever."

He plonked down at the table which was laden with plates of scones generously covered with lashings of jam and cream.

"Is it that time already?" he asked with glee, reaching out a greedy hand. "Don't mind if I do."

"Luckily Marten already whisked a plate upstairs for our new arrivals!" exclaimed Cook. "Help yourself children, but don't spoil your appetite. Dinner is in ninety minutes."

"Not a chance," declared Levi, loading a second scone onto his plate.

Kate hesitated then chose only one.

"Are we creating too much work Cook?" asked Kate suddenly, "can we help you?"

"Oh bless your heart! Not at all. Back in the day we would have week-long gatherings of twenty people or more. A few extra mouths is not a problem for Cook." She smiled happily.

"We'll eat at the big table tonight!" she declared, turning back to the mountains of vegetables on her chopping boards.

Kate and Levi tucked into the still warm scones, marvelling at the freshness of the strawberry jam. Asher found she had no appetite to join them. She felt restless and unsettled, as the energy she had absorbed from the Oath bonding bounced around inside her body.

She stood up abruptly, her chair clattering loudly as it fell backwards on the stone floor.

"Sorry," she mumbled, "I might head out for a walk. I'll be back soon."

Kate and Levi nodded, their mouths occupied with munching.

"Head to the right of the lake my love, you'll find Carowen's workshop there. Seems to me you might want some-one to talk to."

The walk to the lake was idyllic. The flat manicured lawns around the house were intersected by long gravel walkways that headed off in various directions and to various out-buildings. Asher took the one that led to the lake, its waters gleaming in the afternoon setting sun.

On the right side of the lake a large collection of brick buildings were clustered together, smoke rising from the wide chimney of the central structure. Asher pushed open the huge, heavy door and stepped into a warm foyer, sparsely furnished with two unmatched chairs. Three doors greeted her, one on each side and one directly ahead. That one was closed.

Out of tune singing drew her to the small room off to her right. The door was ajar and Ash knocked loudly, clearing her throat deliberately. She did not want to surprise and potentially embarrass the dreadful singer.

"Come in!" sang Carowen merrily.

The room was small compared to the spacious dimensions of the main house, but it was plenty big enough for a large table and three cabinets which displayed various glass ornaments and items. Two overstuffed armchairs upholstered in an eye-catching vivid peacock brocade were placed companionably under a large window overlooking the lake.

The stone floor was heavily covered in layers of thick rugs, which absorbed her footsteps as she walked across the room.

Carowen was standing at the table, a tiny glass butterfly balanced carefully between her fingers. A pair of jeweller's glasses were perched on her nose, the intense magnification allowing her to peer into the tiny object and detect any imperfections.

She smiled with pleasure when she saw Asher.

"Well hello Asher! Welcome to my glasshouse. Others grow plants in theirs, I grow works of glass."

She waved her arms expansively around her head. The tiny butterfly flew out of her hand and landed with a muffled 'plump' on the soft floor by Asher's feet. Asher bent down to scoop it up, worried it was chipped or broken, but the glass creature remained intact.

"That actually happens far more frequently than you would think. For a glass Crafter I am incredibly clumsy. Hence the carpets," Carowen explained, her voice full of amusement.

"It's truly beautiful," breathed Ash, twisting the little creature to and fro, marvelling at the colours that leapt and danced within.

"Thank you. It is part of a set I am creating for Bronwen. A friend of mine," she clarified. "It is a wedding gift for her to give to her sister. The idea is that six, or maybe eight of them will flit around her head as she arrives to meet her mate. Then they will settle into her hair for the promise making, returning to their glass form for all eternity. She can then display them in her home, all the marvellous energy of the day captured within. A good luck charm for their lives together."

Carefully Asher handed back the butterfly. "That's fabulous. Do Crafters usually do that?"

Carowen removed the magnifying glasses, curiosity etched on her face. Asher mentally scolded herself, this seemed to be something an Anderan Crafter trainee should already know.

"You didn't grow up around Crafters?" asked Carowen gently.

Asher shook her head. Which was not actually untrue. She had never heard the term until a few days ago.

Carowen didn't question her further, she simply nodded. "Yes it is common, though Crafter items are rather expensive. I am not the only glass Crafter in Andera but I am the best," she stated simply, "and I choose each commission with care. I want my Craft to really mean something."

She turned to the cabinet behind her and placed the butterfly with three similar ones, already nestled on a shelf.

"Now how can I help you? You look like you have something on your mind. Perhaps you would rather talk than tour the smelting room," she offered kindly.

Asher nodded jerkily, swallowing a lump of tears that had suddenly formed in her throat. Carowen was gesturing to the armchairs and Ash had to fight the urge to pour out her whole tangled story.

Instead she sat down slowly, allowing her thoughts to settle. She had so many questions - about the energy that pulsed around her, and how she was supposed to use it, and whether all Crafters had a defined ability, and why Trinity and Fleur weren't Crafters... but what she most wanted to discuss was Penn.

"Why would somebody be sworn to fealty with the Weaver?' she blurted out.

Carowen blinked in surprise. "Well that was unexpected," she laughed warmly, "I thought you were going to ask me about Wen training."

Asher smiled weakly.

"Well, a Protector is an ancient role, rarely invoked. It is a man or woman from the Ap'an clan who swears an Oath of fealty to some-one of power, usually a clan leader or queen. They are born to the role, trained from birth, all from the same tribe of mighty warriors. An Ap'an child trains their whole life in the hope of being chosen, but it is extremely rare these days. It is usually called upon during a time of war or upheaval."

"Is it a prestigious thing?"

"Oh yes! Many are never selected, only those with the truest of hearts and the noblest of spirits are chosen. Once the oath is sealed with blood it is unbreakable, except by Death. Though there are stories that it survives even that..." she paused, "why do you ask?"

Asher was uncertain what to say. She longed to ask Carowen all about Penn, the urge to talk about him was strong, but she did not know how much of anything Hesta wanted known, even to her own niece.

Confiding in others didn't really come naturally to her. For so long she had felt that she must keep her own counsel and remain unnoticed. Avoiding people's attention was a practiced art, but avoiding their scrutiny was incredibly uncomfortable. She was not a good liar. For a moment she agonised over what to say. Carowen waited patiently, her wide brown eyes calm and non-judgemental.

"Earlier, at the house..." Ash began haltingly. The sudden clanging of a loud bell interrupted her and she jumped with surprise.

Carowen laughed at her shock.

"That is the 'Carowen, tools down' bell. Cook is letting me know there is one hour until dinner. Normally dinner is an informal affair and often I eat here in my study, but the bell means we must be dining together tonight." She stood up and smoothed her plain woollen dress.

"We better hurry. I need to wash and change." She eyed Ash's old jeans and comfy sweater, chosen for their warmth and comfort on the abandoned camping trip.

"We both do. Let's go."

They walked back to the house in companionable silence; Asher relieved that Carowen did not push her for any further explanation. In the dining room they parted ways with a friendly farewell. Asher headed to the kitchen expecting to find Kate and Levi, but only Cook remained. She was bustling around merrily.

"They've already gone upstairs my love. And make sure you change into something nice for dinner, we have company! Marten has hung your mother's dresses back in the wardrobe. Where they belong," she finished happily.

Asher made her way back up through the levels of the house, not encountering any of the other inhabitants along the way.

When she opened the giant wardrobe she found a number of dresses hanging neatly, along with the chocolate brown coat she had been wearing earlier. Tentatively Ash pulled out a cream coloured dress and ran her fingers along the soft wool. It was completely plain, with long sleeves and V neckline that would sit just under her collarbone. The length would drop perfectly to her knees. It was both beautiful and simple, appropriate for dinner in this grand house but not likely to draw attention to herself. She wondered what shoes she would wear, as her boots or runners would look ridiculous. The ever efficient Marten had obviously already considered this, as a quick rummage found her mother's shoes lined up neatly at the bottom of the wardrobe. She chose a pair of green kid boots, slipping them on to test the sizing. Unsurprisingly they fit perfectly, just as she knew the dress would.

When she returned from the shower wrapped in the thick dressing gown that had been lying across her bed, her eyes were drawn to a jewellery box that was sitting on the dressing table. Ash was sure it hadn't been there before.

Inside the box were a pair of sapphire earrings, the large teardrop shaped stones hanging from rose gold hooks that looped comfortably through her ears. There was no note, but she was certain they had come from Hesta.

Asher was dressed and yanking at her tangled curls with a brush when Kate and Levi knocked on her door.

She gasped when she saw them. Casual camping clothes had been replaced by a smart dark suit for Levi, matched with a perfectly fitting white shirt, and a gorgeous scoop neck blue dress for Kate that was covered in a motif of tiny strawberries on green vines. Levi seemed a little uncomfortable, plucking at the collar of his shirt, but Kate was glowing.

She pranced into the room in her white kitten heels, the voluminous layers of the dress flouncing around her.

"Look at us Ash!" she exclaimed. "These dresses are straight out of a 1940's movie! I'm totally in love with the costumes we've been given."

Levi was staring at Ash in bewilderment.

"I don't think I've seen you wear a dress since we were seven and Louise Lively spilt red cordial on your favourite pink dress at her birthday party. You cried and cried. I think it was the trauma that forced you into jeans."

Asher grinned and twirled lightly, the cream dress flaring softly.

"I have to admit it's rather gorgeous. I agree with Kate, they are like costumes. Tonight we are going to a film noir dinner party, filled with mysterious characters."

"Well hopefully there won't be an actual murder," offered Levi with a grin, but the joke landed awkwardly and they all fell silent.

"So what's the plan tonight?" asked Levi, desperate to restore the mood.

"Tonight we don't sit together," commanded Asher, the dress making her feel more confident and assertive. "We sit mixed in with the others, ask questions, find out as much as we can about Andera and Darven and the Weaver – all of it – without giving away the fact that we are not from here. Tonight eat well and rest well, because tomorrow, with or without Hesta, we are going into the Mountains to find Evie."

Her friends nodded solemnly. This might feel like they were on a movie set, but unfortunately it was all too real, and many unknowns still lay ahead.

Chapter Ten

The Lost Crafters

Asher and Kate descended the grand staircase with their skirts billowing around them, grinning madly. Levi brought up the rear, trying not to pull at his collar. Kate had chosen to wear her long hair piled high in a soft bun on her head, and somehow she had managed to tame Ash's wild auburn curls into a bouncing cascade that flowed over her shoulders.

"I hope we're not too overdressed," murmured Asher as they walked through the sitting room, "I can't tell you the last time I was dressed this fancy for dinner. For anything really."

They paused at the entrance to the dining room, drinking in the scene before them.

"I'm going to say we're not too overdressed at all," replied Kate drily.

In the corner the fire was burning brightly, spreading warmth around the room. The large chandelier was ablaze and its light danced across the walls and ceilings, twisting and turning with the firelight.

At the end of the table closest to the fire and furthest from the kitchen, nine places had been set for dinner.

There was one at the head of the table and four either side. Gleaming crystal glasses and silverware lay alongside white china plates edged with gold. The heavy cream curtains had been drawn closed, blocking out the dark grounds beyond and adding an element of intimacy to the oversized room.

Trinity and Fleur hovered near the kitchen door to their right. Trinity's face was crumpled with nerves and uncertainty, as she twisted the material of her red evening dress between her restless fingers. Her daughter stood listening and nodding calmly as her mother whispered frantically in her direction.

Fleur was a similar size to Kate, and while she did not have the height nor presence of her brother, she possessed an air of certainty that gave her the gravitas her mother lacked. There was a quiet beauty in her young face, and a strong sense of self. Her dark eyes flashed with compassion and care, and there was not a trace of mockery as she soothed her nervy mother, assuring her that she looked wonderful in the grand setting.

Fleur had chosen to wear a buttery yellow dress with long sleeves and white lace trim around the neckline and wrists which complemented her dusky skin and gleaming dark hair. It was a simple outfit, well-made and of high quality, which Fleur wore with ease. The two women continued to speak softly to each other, not yet noticing the new arrivals. Nonchalantly Ash scanned the rest of the room, but there was no sign of Penn.

Kate moved into the room to admire the flower arrangements that adorned the tables, Levi close behind. The sudden movement caught at Trinity's awareness, and with wide eyes she spun around to face Asher.

"Weaver," she began, then she screwed up her face. "Oh no! You're not the Weaver. I thought you were for a moment. You look like her. No, actually you don't."

Ash saw the familiar glaze in Trinity's eyes, the look that said *'I don't quite see you...you are fading from my mind'*.

"Who are you? Who is she Fleur? I've made an awful mess of that haven't I?" she babbled.

"I'm sure it is quite alright mother," assured Fleur.

The young girl looked at Asher, her brows raised, asking her to reassure Trinity. Fleur's dark eyes were as direct and piercing as her brother's, clearly seeing Asher through the layers of the charm. It was just as disconcerting now with Fleur as it had been earlier with Penn. Asher had never realised how rarely people really noticed her until these two had. It was unsettling to be so exposed. She took a steadying breath and fought the urge to look away.

"Of course it's fine. No offense taken. My name is Asher. I'm a trainee here. These are my friends Kate and Levi."

Fleur smiled warmly, satisfied with Ash's response.

"I'm Fleur, this is my mother Trinity. We are cousins of Hestawen."

"Oh Fleur!" berated Trinity immediately, "Do not claim such a kinship, and certainly not here in the home of the Weaver. We are nobodies, non-Crafters of no importance. Just simple distant relations, that is all."

Asher thought she saw something swirl in Fleur's eyes but it was gone in a heartbeat, her equilibrium unaffected, and Ash decided she had imagined it. But Trinity was becoming more and more agitated, twisting her dress mercilessly, the fabric tormented by her anxiety that Hesta would think she was claiming importance above her rank.

"There's no such thing as a nobody," Levi interjected, "everybody is some-body, and everybody is important. That's what my gran always said, and she was the most amazing, smartest person I've ever known. It seems to me she was right, I haven't met nobody yet. Which begs the question – if you met nobody, how would you know?"

He grinned at Fleur who offered a small, shy smile in return.

Levi took that as approval to continue. "Just walk in like you own the place, and don't explain, that was another piece of her advice."

"Something he's been doing every day of his life," added Kate, stepping forward to introduce herself. "Levi could crash a wedding and end up giving a speech."

Fleur smiled happily but Trinity looked bewildered at the thought of such a thing happening.

"Speaking of weddings," offered Asher, eager to be part of the banter, "I think the last time I was at a dinner this fancy was for my Aunty Rosalie's wedding two years ago. It was super posh, because she married a banker and his family flew in from..." her voice trailed off, the blank look on Trinity and Fleur's faces indicating she was straying into dangerous territory. Levi was slowly shaking his head at her, his eyes gleaming with warning.

"... and anyway," Asher finished lamely, "the fire is fabulous."

"Yes it is," agreed Kate brightly, "just the right amount of flame to heat ratio. You have to balance the amount of logs used early on to create the coals required to heat a room this size without over-warming the occupants. So far the result is perfect."

Strained silence followed this perky announcement as everyone stared deliberately at the fire.

Asher had no idea how long they would have stood there like that if they had not been interrupted by the arrival of Carowen, gliding into the room in a navy evening dress that almost tickled the floor as she moved.

"Aha!" she cried with glee, her beautiful face warm with welcome and pleasure. "The mystery of the formal dinner is revealed! Welcome Trinity, Fleur. What a joy to have you here with us!"

She swept forward with her arms wide.

Asher watched with interest as Carowen embraced each of her cousins in turn, both mother and daughter smiling with happiness as they returned the hug. For the first time since her arrival Trinity seemed calm and at ease. She chatted merrily with the younger woman, telling her about life in their small village, about Fleur's schooling "such a bright girl, but no Crafting ability, which is not a problem is it dear one, not for a clever girl like you", about the rivalries with the other seamstresses and the challenges of keeping her vegetable garden alive.

Carowen listened intently, laughing and asking questions that kept the conversation flowing comfortably. Her affection for her cousin rippled around them, emboldening Trinity with a confidence she had previously lacked. Asher admired Carowen even more for it.

She was not the only one. Fleur's eyes glowed with adoration as she beamed at Carowen.

"Clearly the other seamstresses cannot hold a candle to your talent dear cousin. The dresses you are both wearing are glorious. So finely made. But what of Penn?" Carowen asked as she glanced around the room, "Is he joining us tonight?"

Trinity puffed up, almost growing two inches with pride. "He is with Hestawen," she declared, "he has taken the Oath of Fealty."

Surprise leapt across Carowen's face. "Already? But he is only just eighteen. To whom has he made such a burdensome vow?"

"The Weaver herself!" crowed Trinity.

"Well, I see." Carowen winked at Ash. "That explains that piece of the puzzle. Huge congratulations to him, and to you. You have done a wonderful job raising him Trinity, I know it hasn't been easy since Jesper passed beyond."

Trinity's face crumbled, pleasure immediately consumed by pain, her body deflating as the joy of the last few minutes leeched from her being. Carowen's face blanched with remorse, and she stepped forward instantly to engulf the older woman in a hug.

"Oh Trinity, forgive my reckless tongue, I am so sorry to upset you."

Her face buried into Carowen's shoulder Trinity shook her head.

"I know Caro, I know. It's not your fault. It's been five years. Anyone would think I could hear his name without succumbing beneath this tidal wave of grief."

She shook herself and stepped back, taking a few deep steadying breaths. Fleur immediately slipped her hand into her mother's and squeezed it tightly.

"It was a great love Trin," said Carowen gently. Her cousin nodded wordlessly.

Unnoticed Ash quietly moved away from the intensely private moment, but not before she saw the wistfulness that glimmered in Carowen's eyes. For all her confidence and self-assurance it seemed she longed for a great love of her own.

A few steps away Levi and Kate were chatting with Anetta who had appeared in her customary quick and silent manner.

Her dark hair was still neatly smoothed into a bun, and she was wearing her grey outfit, but some-how she seemed more formal. Asher ran her eyes over the outfit, puzzling through what had changed. The dress was the same colour grey but it was a longer cut, with a wider neck which allowed for a string of fancy pearls to rest on her collarbone. With a few subtle changes she had dressed for dinner.

Trinity, Fleur and Carowen along with Levi, Kate, Anetta and herself made seven. Hesta and Penn would make up the nine. It appeared that the elusive Marten and Cook would not be joining them.

As though thinking about her caused her to materialise, Cook appeared in the door from the kitchen, her round face beaming with pride.

"Well look at this now! Don't you all look like a pretty picture. Time to take your seats everyone." She clucked around the room, herding them to the seated end of the table.

"Isn't Hesta joining us?" Asher asked, stepping out of the tide to talk to Cook.

Cook winked, lowering her voice conspiratorially. "Planning a grand entrance. Best you take your seat and let her have her moment. Though it better not be too long a moment. Hot soup doesn't keep for anyone, Weaver or otherwise."

Ash obediently sat, finding herself nestled between Anetta on her left and Fleur on her right. The empty seat on Anetta's left side was clearly for Penn and Ash firmly squashed the ridiculous pang that she had missed the opportunity to sit next to him. Across the table Carowen was sitting closest to where Hesta would take her seat at the head of the table, with Kate on her left. Trinity sat between Kate and Levi.

Whether by accident or design they had done as she had asked and spread out among the group. She hoped that tonight they could gather some useful information.

"What is your Craft Asher?" came a quiet query from her right. Asher smiled at the girl.

"I'm a musician."

"Which instrument?"

Asher shrugged self-consciously. "Actually, anything really."

"Wow, that is really unusual."

Asher's cheeks burned at the admiration in the younger girl's voice. Desperately she grabbed at something to turn the attention away from herself.

"What about you Fleur? What's your Craft?"

Immediate remorse slapped Asher hard as she watched the same embarrassed blush creep up Fleur's neck and onto her face.

"I'm not a Crafter," was the soft response as Fleur dropped her eyes to the gleaming cutlery on the table before her.

Asher felt terrible. She had completely forgotten that Trinity had made the point more than once. She wasn't sure what to say next. Should she apologise? Or was that implying it was a shame Fleur wasn't a Crafter? Was it a shame?

Asher felt the familiar awkward anxiety nestle into the pit of her stomach and she wished she could quietly slink away. But across the table Levi was nodding carefully as Trinity spoke, and Kate and Carowen were chatting with great gusto. Ash had asked them to learn everything they could about the people and politics of this world and they were keeping up their end of the bargain. Clearly she had to push beyond her anxiety.

Asher counted silently to ten, imagining her fingers climbing up the piano scale. The churning in her stomach eased a little.

"I'm sorry Fleur, I don't really know much about Crafters or Crafting families," she offered, "I'm sorry for my awkward questions. Is it common that Crafting exists in some female relatives and not others?"

Fleur raised her dark eyes to look squarely at Ash.

"It's really fine, you can ask questions. I am not upset, I just feel bad for my mother."

They both glanced briefly at Trinity.

"She's so proud of being part of the Bonner line and so ashamed that neither she nor I have any Crafting ability. We are the last females of the family branch and I think mum feels we've some-how let everyone down."

"Your Uncle Darven sure sounded cross about it," dug Ash.

"He's not my uncle, he is mama's cousin, and yup, he was really annoyed. I don't think he believed us."

"Why does he care so much do you think?"

Fleur shrugged and Asher believed that she really did not know.

"I had never met him before this week. Most Crafters start displaying Crafter traits quite young, around nine or ten. True Crafting ability has developed by the age of twelve. If you are not displaying signs of ability by then…" she shrugged. "It never really bothered me. Crafting has not been a blessing for our branch of the family tree and I'm happy with my simple life."

Her voice caught slightly on the last sentence and Ash looked away tactfully as Fleur took a long sip of water.

"Anyway. Over the years families have tried to hide their daughters' crafting ability or pretend they had ability when they didn't – you know, for better marriages."

She screwed up her face in disgust and Asher was reminded that for all her poise and intelligence Fleur was only thirteen.

"Mum's cousin Darven was obsessed with some old prophecy that foretells the end of the Weaver. He was badgering mum and quoting lines from it. She was rather confused, I'm not sure she knew what he was talking about. There's some reference to the Weaver's Heir and he was adamant that had to be me." Fleur rolled her eyes. "I mean, really. I think he's a bit bonkers but it was really upsetting mum. And besides, there's the heir." She nodded towards Carowen.

"Weaver Hestawen!" boomed Cook from the kitchen door. Asher jumped so suddenly she banged her knee on the table and jerked her neck.

"Ow!" she yelped. Rubbing the burning neck muscle she twisted around to watch Hesta and Penn stride into the room.

All sound ceased, leaving only the crackle and hiss of the warm flames. The dancing firelight seemed to envelope the Weaver as she regally made her way to the head of the table. Dressed head to toe in shimmering gold it was almost like she was part of the fire's dance, the lace detailing of the sleeves and bodice so fine they sparkled like spider's webs covered in gold dust. Asher could feel the power radiating from her. It was mesmerising. With difficulty she dragged her gaze away from her grandmother, seeking Penn.

The young man was dressed all in black, no frills or fancies to enliven his sombre outfit, but to Ash he seemed just as regal and poised as the woman he strode silently behind. He reached his seat, immediately to the right of the Weaver, and silently sat.

Hesta stood for a long moment at the head of the table, her keen gaze touching each of her guests in turn. What she saw in each of them Asher did not know, but she held her breath and sat a little straighter when those bottomless green eyes turned her way. After a few long moments the Weaver smiled.

"Welcome everyone. It is wonderful to have you all here in my -"

"Well at last!" declared Cook as she pushed a trolley table into the room, its wheels squeaking under the weight of the large serving pot.

The ghost of a smile played around Hesta's mouth. "Speeches later it seems." She sat.

Asher found herself grinning at Fleur as Cook huffed her way around the table, muttering about Fancy Entrances and cold soup.

The silence that had filled the room upon Hesta's arrival was now replaced by blowing and slurping and compliments. Ash savoured each mouthful, enjoying the creamy saltiness as it swirled around her mouth. She glanced at her friends, glad they were here with her.

Somehow Levi was continuing to gobble mouthfuls of soup (his second bowl!) while chatting animatedly to Trinity and Carowen. Kate was carefully blowing each spoonful and contentedly enjoying slow mouthfuls of the steaming liquid.

Love and immense thankfulness swelled in Asher. She was so grateful that these steadfast friends had quite literally leapt across an abyss into this adventure with her and were adapting incredibly well. She found herself blinking away sudden tears, and quickly pulled her gaze away, letting it roam aimlessly around the room until the emotion settled.

Her gaze finally settled on Hesta. The Weaver was turned to her right, her head angled as though she was listening carefully, but Penn was not speaking. He was fully occupied with his soup. Then Hesta responded, her words inaudible to Asher, but clearly spoken into the empty space beside her. Intrigued, Asher stared hard at the spot that so captured Hesta's attention. After a few seconds of concentration it seemed she could see the air crackle and split, like a tiny lightning bolt. Startled, Asher blinked and the effect was lost. The air next to Hesta was still once more and the Weaver was now focused on the bowl in front of her.

Around the table bustled Cook, collecting compliments along with the empty bowls and soup spoons. Ash gulped down the last few mouthfuls before her bowl was whisked away.

The chatter around the table resumed, the low hum of conversation and laughter just as warm as the soup had been.

"Asher," came a chirpy voice from her left, "we haven't really had an opportunity to talk with each other. Your music this morning was glorious."

"Thank you" Asher replied to Anetta.

"So where are your people from? Hesta didn't give me much information, just that we were to prepare for a new trainee, and then suddenly you were all here. Not that I'm complaining," Anetta added hastily, "It is wonderful to have young people in the house."

Asher cleared her suddenly thick throat. *What was the town Cook had said she was from? Wallsend? Wallimoo? Something with a 'W' for sure.* Names swirled through her panicking brain. *Wisteria? Wenton?* It felt like Anetta had been peering at her for ages, was it really only a couple of seconds?

Breathe, think, she instructed her frozen mind. Then like the clear note of a final harmony it was there.

"Hallowsend," she blurted finally, her voice husky with the lie.

"Ah yes," Anetta nodded, "Cook's home town."

"She knew my mother when she was a little girl." That much was true.

"And I suppose they kept in touch and your mother told Cook about your Crafting ability. Cook told Hesta and well here you are!"

Asher nodded, happy for Anetta to draw her own conclusions.

"What about you Anetta, how long have you and Marten lived here?"

The small woman screwed up her nose and eyes, her mouth moving soundlessly as she counted back through her memories.

"Goodness! It must be twelve years now! Where did those years go?"

Across the table Carowen laughed loudly at something Levi said. Anetta's gaze moved from Asher to Caro's glowing countenance.

"She's enjoying herself," said Anetta with satisfaction, "it's wonderful to see. She's often alone here, with Hesta away and only three old people rattling around the house."

"When did Carowen move here?" asked Asher, realising that she didn't know anything about her mother's cousin.

"I believe she came here as a child when her Crafting ability became strong. She was raised with Ginarwen, Hesta's daughter."

Asher felt her mother's name jolt through her like an electric shock.

"Ginarwen?" she croaked awkwardly, taking a quick sip of water.

"Hesta's only child. Dead almost twenty years," said Anetta quietly.

Dead. It was confronting to hear it said. "How?"

"It was before my time here, Hesta never speaks of it. The loss of her only daughter, her Heir, must have been very painful."

Her voice, already quiet and low, dropped further.

"Sometimes very late at night I hear Hestawen talking in her study, as though she is talking with her daughter. Arguing with a ghost, or perhaps her memories. It's very sad."

Guiltily she glanced quickly at her employer and then back to Asher.

"To be the Weaver is a lonely and difficult task. There is a lot of pressure on Carowen now."

Asher stared at the beautiful woman opposite her, so serene yet so animated. Caro exuded a confidence that was at odds with Anetta's concern. For the first time Asher wondered how Carowen would feel about Gin's daughter appearing and making a claim to the Weaver.

Would she be relieved? Or angry?

Asher had no desire to claim Carowen's place as Heir. All she wanted was to find her sister and take her home.

The door to the kitchen burst open and Cook thrust the rattling cart back into the dining room. Levi groaned as the intoxicating smell of roasted lamb and vegetables wafted around the room.

Sometime later, after the dinner dishes had been filled, emptied and cleared away, the fire had burned down low and the candles had begun to release fat tears of wax onto their holders, Hesta cleared her throat.

Immediately the other occupants hushed, and eight heads turned her way.

"Welcome everyone to my home. It is wonderful to be surrounded by family and new friends," she nodded in the direction of Levi and Kate who both beamed. "Tonight we celebrate many things – a new Wen Potential, the visit of my cousin and her family, Penn's oath making, and of course food and fellowship."

Everyone smiled happily at each other, their bellies and hearts full of nourishment.

"There is much to celebrate, but there is also a great danger threatening us and we need to be prepared for what is coming."

Asher's stomach clenched, the delicious dinner no longer sitting quite so well. The faces of the others around the table reflected her same uncertainty and anxiety. Even Levi's effervescent face was still and pensive.

"Trinity brought unsettling news indeed, and I have spent the afternoon confirming my concerns."

Hesta's voice was low and even, customarily calm, but fear snaked up Ash's spine sending cold tendrils of dread into her neck, making her shiver.

"I have previously suspected that Crafters are missing, stolen from their homes and families, never seen again. I have heard murmurings, whisperings. My own enquiries over the last few months confirmed that low level Crafters were missing. I drew my own conclusions and decided to monitor the situation. I had no idea the situation had become so horrific or how bloodthirsty Darven has become. Currently it seems there are perhaps fifty missing Crafters of varying ability. Most frightening is that the kidnappings are becoming more frequent, bolder, more violent in their execution. There arc stories in the last few days of Crafters refusing to meet with Darven's men and then the next day they are gone and their families slayed."

A gurgling sound burst out from Kate, her face pale. "Children too?" she blurted.

Hesta inclined her head in a sharp movement, her eyes unreadable.

"Why has no-one sought your help before now?" asked Anetta, her trembling voice full of anger.

For the first time Hesta's composure failed her.

"It appears the squads have been telling people these atrocities are ordered by ME," her voice thundered across the table, bouncing off the walls.

Behind her the fire roared with fury, flames leaping high into the chimney. Outside an enraged wind buffeted against the house, shaking the windows. Shocked and frightened the assembled group said nothing.

"But he made a mistake." Hesta said quietly, reining in her emotions. The wind ceased, the fire dropped, the atmosphere in the room eased. Asher released a tight breath that she had not realised she was holding.

"He revealed himself to Trinity, certain she would want to be part of his destruction. How wrong he was. He completely misunderstood a heart so true."

The Weaver smiled at her cousin. The shy woman turned red and blotchy under such praise and admiration.

Asher caught a glimpse of Fleur's beaming face and impulsively reached out and grasped the girl's hand that was resting on the table. Around her neck the hidden globe burst into flame, searing her chest. Both girls gasped and Fleur ripped away her hand as though burnt.

Asher took a few deep steadying breaths as the pain eased and the globe cooled beneath her clothes. When she opened her eyes Fleur was staring at her, clutching her own chest.

"What did you do?" she whispered. Asher shook her head, unsure what to say.

"Girls?" Hesta's voice was hard.

"Apologies Hesta, sorry, I just um, banged into Fleur."

Deep green eyes stared her down, but for the first time in her life Asher's face did not flush hot and red with the lie, or the discomfort of the scrutiny. Something strange had happened with Fleur and instinctively she knew she should not share that. For a minute she held the Weaver's gaze with confidence until her grandmother nodded once and turned her attention back to the others.

Maybe I'm becoming a better liar as I become a Crafter, Ash thought ruefully, *just like mum and Hesta.*

Hesta looked deeply at her assembled guests. When she spoke again her voice was dark and deep.

"I am certain that Darven is using Crafter blood for sorcery. He is planning to destroy Crafting, the Weaver, the Balance. For what purpose I cannot say. More is at stake than just his quest to destroy me. Worlds beyond ours exist because of the Balance maintained here in Andera. Darven must be stopped."

"He won't give in easily Hesta," said Trinity, "He was practically glowing with power and ambition. It won't be easy to stop him."

"True," agreed Hesta with a small incline of her head, "but stop him I must."

"If what you say is true and he is using Crafter blood, his sorcery will be getting stronger every day. He has his followers, his squads. You cannot defeat him alone. You will need a group of strong Crafters to support you," added Carowen. "An army. For a war."

Silence followed this. Hesta's face was calm and unreadable. Beside her, Penn's face was still, his emotions carefully contained as always.

Asher looked over at Kate and Levi. Their faces reflected her own fear and uncertainty. When they had linked arms and stepped into the Void the three of them had been aware that what lay beyond was unknown and possibly treacherous, but this felt very real, very dangerous. A war between powerful, magical people, on a strange world far from home.

Levi caught her gaze and threw her a crooked smile.

"I guess we're not in Kansas anymore Toto."

Chapter Eleven

Beyond the Manor

The dinner gathering had wrapped up shortly afterwards, everyone having lost their appetites for dessert and small talk, even Levi. Hesta had asked Carowen, Trinity and Penn to remain, the others had been excused.

"Which is a polite way of saying 'get out'," Levi had fumed as the three of them and Fleur made their way upstairs. "As if we can't be part of making war plans. Go to bed *children*."

"Do you want to be?" Fleur had asked.

"What?" Levi had said, confused.

"Part of making war plans."

That had silenced him.

Now alone in her bathroom Asher smiled a little as she cleaned her teeth, the memory of Levi floundering for a witty response momentarily easing the tension that had been coiled in her belly for the last hour. *War.* Hesta had not uttered it, Carowen had said the word. But it was not the first time she had heard it mentioned.

"So you can fulfil your prophecy and use my child as a soldier in your war?"

What had mum meant? Fleur had also mentioned a prophecy, said Darven was obsessed with it. Asher had the distinct sense she was caught in a rip tide and being pulled out to sea. Fighting it would only make her exhausted. If she didn't want to drown she needed to learn to swim with the rip, and fast.

Asher grabbed a soft flannel, saturated it in cold water and scrubbed her face until it tingled. The blood rushing across her skin invigorated her, and energy pulsed up her spine making her stand tall. Let the grown-ups have their war, she had other things to do.

She yanked the fluffy dressing gown from its hook on the bathroom door, tied it snuggly over her pyjamas and headed downstairs to talk with the people she trusted most.

Unsurprisingly Levi was already sitting on the grey and cream sofa in Kate's room, both of them wrapped in dressing gowns as thick and soft as hers, sipping from steaming mugs of cocoa.

"Finally!" exclaimed Levi when Asher knocked briefly and let herself in. "We've been waiting for you. We are dying to talk about everything."

"Important things first – is there a mug for me?"

Kate grinned and handed her a large blue mug.

"There's a plate of oaty biscuits too," she pushed it towards Ash as she sunk into an armchair. "They remind me of Anzac biscuits."

"They are still warm!" Ash munched happily.

"Yes, Cook brought them up a short time ago. Said she thought we might still be up and in need of something sweet and warm."

"The woman is a Saint!" declared Levi.

The warmth of the fire and the company was soothing and for a few long minutes they sat together completely content, munching and slurping. When they had eaten their fill Kate went off to her backpack and fossicked around, emerging with a triumphant 'aha!' and brandishing a zip-lock bag.

She came back to the table and carefully packaged the remaining eight biscuits into a napkin and then into the bag.

"Let's keep these for tomorrow. We can add them to our supplies."

That single sentence brought Ash back to the immediate issues confronting them.

"Yes," she said thoughtfully, "We need to start planning what we are doing tomorrow. First let's talk about tonight. I'll go first."

Quickly she filled them in on her conversation with Fleur, including Darven's obsession with a prophecy and Fleur being the Weaver's Heir. When she came to the part where she had electric shocked Fleur she hesitated, then decided not to tell them. It felt uncomfortable and weird not to share everything, but she just needed more time to process and ponder what that might mean.

"She also mentioned that Carowen is currently Hesta's Heir, and I did think it was odd that Darven wouldn't know that. It's strange that he's badgering Trinity and

Fleur when there's already Carowen and now he has Evie. Why pursue Fleur as the Heir when he already had plans in place to snatch me... Evie?"

Levi shrugged dismissively. "He sounds like a bit of a lunatic, I don't think we can work out what he's thinking and doing. Interesting about the Fleur thing, I asked Trinity outright who would be the next Weaver and she straight away said Carowen. There was no hesitation. Kate did you find out anything from Carowen herself?"

Kate nodded eagerly. "Yes, she is super friendly and so nice! She was really polite, asking loads of questions about me and us, what we like, how long we've been friends, what are my hobbies. We talked about camping and bushcraft, and I was probably too enthusiastic. She was cool about it but I don't think she's the camping type!"

They all chuckled thinking about the elegant Glass Crafter pitching a tent and sleeping rough for nights at a time.

"Anyway, I didn't want to get too caught up talking about me and us because, you know," she waved her hand around, "the whole Terran thing, so I kept asking about her. It was so interesting! She came here at ten to live with Hesta after her father vanished. Vanished! He went on a trip and never returned. Her mother remarried a couple of years later and had a new family. They are all much younger than Carowen and none of them are Crafters. She visits them regularly, but I think this was actually where she felt most at home. She grew up with your mum Ash, and it was so strange to hear all her stories while pretending

I knew nothing about Jennifer, I mean Ginarwen. Your mum was only two years older than her and they were super close, more like sisters than cousins. I think they ran a bit wild at times, I get the impression Hesta wasn't a really hands on parent. It was hard as Ginarwen got older because she was being trained to be the Weaver and she would go off on 'assignments' with Hesta. Carowen said it was almost unbearable when she died."

Kate's voice trailed off and she stared at her fingernails, blinking hard.

Ash and Levi found other things to look at in the room, trying to give Kate the privacy she needed.

"Anyway," Kate cleared the huskiness from her throat, "I asked who is being trained now to be the Weaver, and this was the strange part, she said no-one. That Hesta had committed to a twenty year period of mourning after Ginarwen's death and that no heir would be named until that period had past. Apparently that anniversary is coming up next year. Don't you think that's odd?"

Asher nodded slowly, trying to take it all in. Why would Hesta commit to a mourning period when she knew full well that Gin was alive on Earth? Why would Darven insist one girl was the Heir while kidnapping another? The more they found out the more muddled it became.

Deciding she couldn't focus on the peculiarities Ash brought her focus back to the most pressing task. Finding Evie.

"Did anyone get a chance to ask about the Mountains, or where Darven might be?"

"Actually I had quite a good chat with Trinity about it," replied Levi enthusiastically. "She knew quite a lot about Darven's time in the Mountains when he first went there, including the town he lived in. It makes sense that he was headed back there after he left her village."

"What!?" shouted Kate and Ash in unison.

"How was that not the *first* thing out of your mouth??" demanded Asher.

"Levi Chandra," admonished Kate sternly.

"Okay, sorry, but to be fair Ash did start the conversation saying the most important thing was hot chocolate," he said.

His dark eyes sparkled merrily in his warm olive face, his tone completely unrepentant.

Ash sighed deeply. "Okay Levi, please tell us what you know."

"Trinity said when they were all much younger Darven went into the Mountains and stayed there for years. The first year he sent her letters talking about their mothers, his grief, his anger and his healing in the Mountains. Turns out he found himself a guru of some sort. My word, not Trinity's. And he built himself a home in an elaborate cave system beyond a village. Trinity wasn't that impressed, thought it was a miserable way to live. Anyway, the letters petered off until eventually he stopped contacting her at all. She thought no more about it, she was newly married, then had Penn and Fleur, so she focussed on her life and put him out of her mind. But she remembered the village he mentioned – Groush."

Kate raised her eyebrows. "Groush?" she repeated incredulously. "That's the name?"

Levi said something in return and they both started to laugh, but Asher missed the exchange. She could not concentrate on what they were saying, her ears were roaring as adrenaline pumped through her body. *Groush, Groush, Groush...* the word thundered on repeat.

"Groush," she said slowly, the unfamiliar word sour in her mouth. "So that's where we are going. I wonder how we find the way."

Levi grinned. "Leave that to us, you do your Witchy training tomorrow and we'll scout the library. I'm sure we can find a map or something."

Kate started to nod in agreement but was overcome by a giant yawn that engulfed her entire face.

"Sorry," she muttered sheepishly.

"No, it's fine," said Ash standing up. "It's definitely bedtime. We need as much sleep as we can get. That sounds good Levi, I'll leave the two of you to ferret out the information we need. You can also be on supplies duty. I'm sure you'll gather enough food," she finished drily.

Levi stood and stretched, his long lean frame reaching smoothly one way, then the next.

"Yup, will do. Now I definitely need some sleep. Good night."

"Good night," echoed Asher as she followed him out of the room. She moved quietly through the silent halls and stairway, collapsing into her own bed with a huge sigh of exhaustion. Her head was whirling with everything that had happened since Trinity and Penn and Fleur had arrived, and questions without answers tormented her sleepy mind.

Mum? Are you there? Silence greeted her plea, as it had every other time she'd tried this over the last two days. *MUM!* She yelled with all her mind, her hand tight around the globe, *please, mum...*

The globe heated beneath her touch as though consoling her, but there was no answer from across the Void. Ash lay heavily in the soft bedding, aching loneliness threatening to overwhelm her.

Breathe in, 2,3,4, Breathe out, 2,3,4.

Then unbidden but most welcome, music crept into her restless thoughts, soothing her anxiety and uncertainty in cocoons of melody. For a few long minutes doubt and fear battled against the hypnotic invitation of the music, until finally she slept.

The sun was high in the morning sky by the time Ash woke feeling refreshed and calm. She had slept deeply, dreamlessly, thankfully undisturbed by the worries of the day. Outside the sun was already warming the windows and the heavy curtains that shielded her from its light.

She lay in bed for a moment, stretching out her legs and wriggling her toes, savouring the supreme comfort of the mattress and pillows. This was the last morning she would wake in this bed, in this house. From now on it would be a sleeping bag, the cool air on her face and the hard ground beneath her body.

With a sigh Asher threw off the covers and swung her feet onto the floor. A hot shower was the first order of the day, then one of Cook's delicious breakfasts, then training with Hesta. Somehow they had to then find a way to leave the estate and find transportation to the Mountains, to Groush. Her gut churned at the name. Groush, where Darven most likely went to open his portal. Groush, where Evie was probably being held prisoner in a cave. There was nothing poetic or inspiring about the name, but for Ash it represented hope – both that she would find Evie, and that they would all be home soon.

Washed, dried and feeling invigorated, Asher pulled on her favourite jeans and blue and white jumper, gave her hair a quick run through with her fingers and headed out of the bedroom. She smiled as she strode through the gallery, its objects alive with sunshine and energy.

Ash walked into the kitchen with a distinct sense of deja-vu. Levi grinned at her, his mouth full of pancakes.

"Morning," he mumbled between chewing. The kettle was boiling merrily and Cook brandished a shimmering green mug in her direction.

"Tea and pancakes Asher?"

"Yes please," she said gratefully, sliding onto the chair opposite Levi. Soon enough the steaming mug was in her hand and Asher sipped carefully, knowing from years of experience that greedy gulping would result in a burned throat. Cradling the mug between her hands, relishing its warmth and comfort, Asher realised it was not actually solid green, but instead was covered in thousands of tiny golden flowers on green vines. The intricate detailing was extraordinary.

"All the cups and crockery in this house are just wonderful," she said, peering at the tiny brush strokes.

"Indeed," agreed Cook, "that's what you get from generations of Crafters living in and visiting this house – potters, painters and ceramicists – they leave behind works of art for us to use as ordinary items. Now, do you want strawberries and cream with your pancakes, or lemon and sugar?"

"I highly recommend both," declared Levi, sighing with satisfaction as he pushed his plate away, "just not together at the one time."

"You recommend what?" asked Kate from the doorway.

Her blue eyes were bright and well rested, her long hair neatly braided. The fancy outfit from last night had been replaced with her customary faded blue jeans and well-worn yellow jumper.

"Pancakes!" replied Levi, Asher and Cook in unison, causing them all to laugh.

"Another plate then!" said Cook with gusto, "Let's get you lot fed for your busy day!"

The three of them exchanged guilty glances, what did Cook mean?

"Is anyone else joining us for breakfast?" asked Kate as Cook piled her plate high with fluffy golden pancakes. "We don't want to be total greedy guts."

"Speak for yourself," grumbled Levi.

"You eat and enjoy Kate," smiled Cook, "Carowen won't be up for a while and the others ate a good hour ago. Which reminds me Asher, Hesta asked that you join her in the study once you had eaten."

"Okay, thanks".

"It is possible to actually brush your hair Levi," Kate was admonishing lightly as Ash left the kitchen.

"Why bother when fingers work just as well?" was the last thing she heard clearly before the heavy walls muffled further conversation.

Feeling slightly scolded by association, Asher detoured quickly to her bathroom and gave her own unruly curls a careful brush. The methodical brushing calmed the anxiety that was becoming a constant companion. It was a low buzz sensation of unease, of pent-up energy that needed to be focused and spent. Her fingers itched to play the piano or her violin, to direct all that energy into the music that was her safe place.

When she felt calmer and her red curls had settled into a soft wave, Asher headed across to the study. There was no need to knock as the door was already open.

Hesta was standing at one of the windows, staring sightlessly at the grounds beyond the house. Today she was wearing a deep green dress with multi-coloured patchwork detailing around the sleeves and hemline, and matching patchwork boots.

Asher cleared her throat. "Hesta?"

The Weaver's face was still and serious when she turned around. "Good morning Asher, did you sleep well?"

It was the sort of question that only required a "yes thank you" response.

Maybe it was the tightness around Hesta's eyes, or the unusual pallor to her skin, but unexpectedly Asher found herself asking "And you Hesta? Did you sleep well?"

The Weaver's eyes widened slightly, and her eyebrows raised in surprise. Asher wondered if anyone ever asked how she was, if it was taken for granted that Hestawen was always okay. Hesta hesitated for a moment as she considered how to respond.

"It was a rather busy night for Marten and myself, not much sleep for either of us I'm afraid." She indicated the sofa, "Take a seat Asher."

Hesta chose the large armchair opposite her, piercing her with a fathomless stare.

"The situation is evolving rapidly," she began finally, "and we are running out of time to train you properly. I need to go to Ostrin as soon as I have organised some things here, which means I will leave in the morning. I do not think it wise that you accompany me yet. Hopefully Darven is still unaware of your being here in Andera. Though I suspect by now Evie has revealed your existence, hopefully he still thinks you are on Earth. It will take him some time to gather the power to open another portal."

"But what about saving Evie?" protested Asher, "that was the whole reason I came here. If you think Evie is at Ostrin then I should come with you."

"I cannot allow that," said Hesta firmly. "You are not ready to face Darven. You will stay here and train with Caro. I will send for you both in a few days."

"A few days!" the words burst out of Ash. "Anything might happen to Evie in that time!"

"There is far more at stake here than your sister."

"Maybe for you, but not for me!" Anger swelled with each word. "Mum was right, you care only for your own schemes!"

Hesta's green eyes swirled with something dark and dangerous.

"Nothing will happen to Evie," she said coldly, "I can assure you of that."

"How? How do you know for sure?" demanded Asher.

Hesta stood abruptly, turning once again to look out the window, her back rigid.

"I will return your friends to Earth first thing in the morning. You will train here with Caro. I will send for you in three days."

Her tone brooked no discussion, no further argument. Clearly the conversation was over. She did not bother to turn around.

Asher leapt to her feet, her face burning with anger, her body shaking. She had never felt anything like this before. Her head was whirling with dark clouds of rebellious music, the notes swirling and pounding like a storm. Around the room objects began to leap from the shelves and the desk, the physical manifestation of the gale inside her body.

Bang! Books whacked into walls. Thump! Cushions flew against the window panes. CRACK! A vase smashed against the fireplace.

Frightened, Asher felt the chaos grow stronger and stronger both within her mind and within the room. Her vision was blurred, her heart was beating so fast she felt like it would burst. The music thundered and she felt herself get swept away within it. She could not control it, could not ease it, she was going to pass out with the pressure...

Then the Weaver was there in her mind.

Sending a cool note to cut through the tempest, gathering all the anger, all the pain towards it. Her powerful presence pulling all the darkness into a small ball in her hands. Asher felt her head clear as the music calmed, and she collapsed exhausted onto the lounge. The wild room eased as the music left her mind, the objects dropping to the floor.

Trembling, Ash buried her face in her arms and sobbed quietly.

After a few long minutes she sat up and rubbed her face with her sleeve. "What happened?" she asked, her voice husky and small. She couldn't bring herself to look at Hesta.

Surprisingly the Weaver's voice was kind and filled with compassion.

"The Crafting grows strong within you and explodes with your anger and fear. You need to learn to shape it, to control it, so it does not drive you mad or destroy you."

"Is this what it is like for everyone?" asked Ash quietly, her voice still hoarse.

"No." Hesta covered the small space between them and sat beside her on the sofa. Asher finally found the courage to raise her tear swollen eyes to look directly at Hesta.

Her grandmother's eyes were clear and unreadable. "It is not like this for other Crafters."

She held out her hand to Asher. Nestled on her palm was the black marble of Asher's fury, gleaming in the strong sunlight. Asher recoiled from it.

"Most Crafters need learn only to channel the talent they have. But for you it is different. You were born to weave the Threads. One day the power of the universes will be yours to command - that is a huge energy load for your body and mind." Hesta's voice was grave. "Right now your Crafting is strong, wild, untrained, driven by emotion rather than consciousness. It exploded within you in a moment of fear and pressure. You have spent your life being small, quite literally making yourself invisible. Now you need to learn to lean into your emotions and control them."

"I don't want this, any of this," whispered Asher. "I just want to find my sister and go home. Please."

The Weaver said nothing for a moment, but there seemed to be sympathy in her eyes.

"One hundred million souls."

Asher was confused. "Pardon?"

"One hundred million souls," repeated the Weaver. "That is how many magical beings exist on the planets of the five universes. And we are responsible for each of them. For ensuring they live and die as it is intended, and that they are woven into the lives and experiences of all non-magical beings. That magic is not lost or destroyed or forgotten or forsaken. Billions of souls, both magical and non, who will never know of you, or I, or the Weave or their own Threads. But their existence is reliant on us."

With a slight flick of her wrist Hesta pocketed the marble. Then she reached out and gently touched a cool hand to Asher's flushed face.

"You can do this. You will do this. It is your destiny. But you must be trained." Her hand dropped away and she stood up in a fluid motion, the patchwork skirt dropping heavily around her ankles.

"Hesta?" Asher's voice was small and hesitant. She wanted to ask a question about her mother, but she was not sure how Hesta would respond.

The Weaver raised a brow.

"Yes Asher?"

"My mother -" she stopped and cleared her throat. "Why are you and my mother estranged?"

Hesta was silent for a long moment and Asher wondered if she would refuse to answer. Or tell her that it was too complicated for a child to understand. But finally the Weaver sighed and shook her head in a small, sad movement.

"I am not really sure Asher. It is something I have asked myself many times over these twenty years. How did we fall so far apart?"

"You were very mean to her when we were planning the crossing to Andera. You said terrible things about her being responsible for Evie's torture and death. Maybe that's why she doesn't want anything to do with you." Asher was shocked at her own boldness.

Hesta smiled a little. "Perhaps. But sometimes it is necessary to be 'mean' as you put it."

Asher wrinkled her nose.

"That makes no sense. She doesn't trust you, she doesn't seem to like you, and you think it's a good idea to be mean to her. Why?"

"Because she would have made the crossing and she would have died. Far better that she is angry at me, than she knots her own Threads before their time. Now, go and spend the day with your friends."

The dismissal this time was warmer, but it was a dismissal all the same. Asher had the distinct impression Hesta had shared more than she felt comfortable with and the conversation was closed. She nodded, her throat still raw, her legs weak and trembling as she stood.

Ash made it to the gallery before the exhaustion overtook her completely. She doubted she would make it down the stairs without falling. So instead she fumbled to her room, and collapsed on her bed, crawling under the heavy quilts.

The globe was warm against her skin, comforting and calming her. The fury of her response still frightened her and she wasn't ready to face her friends. She just needed a moment to ease the pounding in her head and close her bleary eyes. Within a few heartbeats she was asleep, and she dreamed.

It was summer judging by the heated sun on her face and the dryness of the air. She was sitting cross-legged on the rough grass, the ground hardened by long summer days without rain. Not far from her two young girls were playing on the edge of the lake, launching little paper boats into the water. They were laughing loudly as their shoes sunk into the muddy edges of the lake. The sun gleamed off their brightly coloured hair, one glossy brunette and one flaming redhead. Ash knew immediately who they were. Mum and Carowen, or just Caro back then. 'Mum!' she cried. The red-headed girl turned and smiled at her, and within a moment had morphed into the white-haired adult mother she knew and loved. She held out her arms. Ash leapt to her feet, eager to feel her embrace. But as she ran towards her Gin shimmered and disappeared, reappearing further around the lake. Again and again this happened until Ash was howling with frustration. Finally she sank onto the ground breathing heavily. A wave of weariness overcame her and her eyes closed involuntarily.

'Asher', her mother's voice was warm and familiar and so very far away. Ash couldn't open her eyes. 'Find the Mountain Man of Groush. There are answers there. You can trust Cook to help you.'

Asher woke with a start, her head clear and calm. To Groush then.

Levi and Kate were no longer in the kitchen when she made her way back downstairs. Cook thought they were in the library so Asher decided she would head along the service hallway to join them, but at the last moment she decided to detour to the garden for some fresh air.

A few minutes later she was walking along a wide paved path that meandered along the left-hand side of the lake. In the distance she could see a figure that looked to be dancing and twisting by the water. Intrigued she walked closer and soon realised that the tall, male figure was holding a shining broadsword and was moving through the motions of swordplay – lunge, twist, cut and pull. Again and again.

Body and sword moving as one in a hypnotic, rhythmic dance.

Her steps slowed until she was standing still, silently observing Penn the warrior at practice. She realised her heart was thumping madly and she felt slightly light-headed, from both nervous excitement and anxiety.

After a few minutes she considered heading back to the house, but before she could slip away Penn turned and caught her eye.

He did not smile, but he inclined his head in acknowledgement of her presence and held her gaze. It was too late to turn around now. He placed the point of the sword into the earth and stood and waited. His face was glistening with small beads of sweat, but he did not seem like he had overly exerted himself. He was not even breathing heavily.

Her head pounding, Asher walked the final few metres to close the gap between them.

"Hello," she said, trying to sound cool and nonchalant, but desperately wondering if she looked and sounded as self-conscious as she felt.

"Hello," he responded quietly in his deep, calm voice.

Asher realised this was the closest she had ever been to Penn; the first time they had actually spoken to each other.

She stood there for a few silent moments wondering what to say, before blurting awkwardly, "that looks like fun!"

By the stars why had she said that?

He wrinkled his nose. "What does? The exercises?"

"Yes. Are they difficult?"

"Not at all," Penn replied. "These are simple warm ups to strengthen the body. There is not much to them. Would you like to try?"

Asher was about to politely decline, when she realised his dark eyes were twinkling, as though he expected her to say no. Immediately she felt her hackles rise.

"Yes please." She stepped forward and held out her hand for the sword.

"Would you like some assistance?" Penn asked gravely.

"No need," said Ash confidently. *How hard can it really be?*

With a completely straight face Penn flipped the blade out of the ground and handed her the sword, hilt first.

With great bravado Asher grabbed the leather wrapped hilt, ready to brandish the sword for her first big swing. But the swing never happened. With a great thud the heavy blade thumped to the ground, pulling her arm and yanking her shoulder.

"Bloody hell!" she swore, dropping the sword and grabbing at her sore right shoulder with her left hand.

Penn's eyes twinkled and his mouth twitched, but he did not laugh. With one fluid movement he bent and collected the sword from the ground, handling it as though it weighed little more than her violin bow.

"Would you like to try again?" he asked, holding out the offending weapon.

Asher glared at him as she rolled her shoulder, but found she could not sustain her anger for more than a heartbeat. The whole situation was rather ridiculous. Her own mouth twitched and she found herself laughing.

"No thank you," she said emphatically, "I am most definitely not a warrior. I think I'll stick to musical instruments if you don't mind."

"As you wish," said Penn, turning away to lean the sword against a tree. It joined a large curved hunting horn and a dagger in a sheath that looked like it strapped to his shin.

Asher walked to the water's edge and carefully selected a smooth flat stone from the ground.

"I'm not much good with a sword it appears, however I am quite good at skimming stones."

Ash considered the water's surface before angling her wrist and skipping the stone across the water. It bounced once, twice, three times before disappearing into the quiet depths.

"I have not seen this before," said Penn, his tone curious.

"Would you like to try?" Ash couldn't keep the challenge out of her voice.

"It seems simple enough," the warrior responded.

Penn joined her at the water and randomly picked up a stone. Ash noted gleefully it was a rather mishappen looking thing, lacking the smoothness required to skip across the surface. Rather unsportingly she chose to say nothing, and squelched the pang of guilt that immediately followed.

With a flick of his wrist Penn sent the stone across the lake, and it sank at the first contact. He frowned in annoyance and scooped another stone into his hand. Again he threw the stone hard across the water, and again it sank without a single skip.

"This doesn't work," he grumbled, "something is wrong with my stones."

Ash grinned behind her hand, and then relented.

"Here, try a smooth stone, they work much better." She chose one from the ground.

Penn took the stone from her hand and thew it with great gusto. As it disappeared beneath the rippled surface, Asher couldn't help it, she laughed.

"I think we can declare that you have the advantage with the sword, and I have the advantage with the skipping stones. And let's be honest, the ability to skip stones is far more useful than waving a piece of iron around."

Penn rolled his eyes, but he did not stop the smile that crept onto his face.

"Agreed," he said.

They smiled companionably at one another, and Asher felt a strange little flutter in her stomach. She coughed awkwardly to cover the confusing sensation and bent down to tighten her already tied shoelace.

When she straightened up Penn was looking at her seriously.

"You have travelled far," he said softly. "A long journey from where you were to where you are now. And ahead lies an even longer journey for where you need to go. The Weaver's Heir."

Asher knew the surprise was plain on her face.

"What do you mean? How do you know that? Did Hesta say something?"

Penn shook his head.

"I suspected, when I first felt your presence. Then when the blood oath was made, much was revealed to me. For a moment I was part of the Great Weave, part of every Thread. I could see the line of the Weaver, stretching far into history, and coming to rest on you."

Asher stared intently into his dark eyes. Warm eyes, intelligent eyes. Old eyes, in the face of a young man.

"Was there only me? Could another be the next Weaver?"

The desperation in her voice was clear, and she wondered if Penn could hear it too.

Penn screwed up his nose. "Why would you ask such a question?" He sounded genuinely confused. "You are the Weaver's Heir. It is foretold. It is woven in the Threads. Do you not feel this to be true?"

"But I am useless!" burst Ash. "I cannot Craft anything when I need to. And when I am trying to Craft, I cannot seem to control it. It's overwhelming and chaotic."

She was perilously close to tears, swallowing her hiccups and all the confusing, swirling emotion.

"Of course it is," said Penn calmly. "That is the way of it."

"Of what?" His unflustered response both shocked and settled her.

"The Crafting you require to be the Weaver cannot be simple and easy and manageable. It must be wild and strong and push you almost to breaking. You must fight it, contain it, and ultimately control it. You must prove yourself worthy. Only then will you be strong enough to hold the Threads. If it was simple, any Crafter could do it."

"But what if I don't *want* to do it."

"Why would you not want to be the Weaver?"

The words blurted out of Asher before she could consider them.

"Because it is too hard! I just want a normal life, like everyone else."

They stared at each other for a moment, Penn's warm brown face thoughtful, Asher's fair skin flushed and blotchy. Now that the words were said she felt foolish, and somewhat childish. She was also a little shocked at how little control she seemed to have over her emotions these days, and how easily she was sharing her inner most thoughts with a stranger.

"What is it that seems so hard?" asked Penn. Asher could not detect any ridicule or judgement in his tone, simply genuine interest.

"The Crafting. The whole Threads thing. I'm not sure I even really understand that. The power struggles. The pressure. Making life and death decisions. Being wise. Having the answers all the time. The aloneness of it all."

Penn nodded. "Yes, I can see that there are many things that could be hard. But that is true of every path in life. Ignoring your responsibilities and walking away from those that need you and rely on you. That is also hard."

Asher thought of her mother, who had walked away from her destiny, and who struggled against it with terrible physical consequences. Did she ever wonder if she had made a mistake? Did she ever feel regret over her choices?

Penn reached over and took both her hands in his. The warmth of his touch seeped deep beneath her skin, and she knew that Penn was not a stranger. He was familiar to her at her soul's deepest level. As though they had known each other for many lifetimes.

"Being wise and having answers all the time – that only comes with time. Nobody expects that of you, and I am certain every Weaver has made mistakes as she learns. For as powerful and as long lived as the Weaver is, she is only human."

He smiled with true affection, and Asher felt her heart flip.

"And as for being alone – you are surrounded by friends Asher el Ginarwen. Keep them close. There is no requirement that you do this alone. Be patient. Stop forcing your Crafting. Let the music guide you."

Then he released her hands and scooped a flat, smooth stone from the ground. Fluidly Penn twisted his body low to the lake and flicked his wrist. The stone skipped once, then twice, then three times... just as it seemed it might even skip a fourth time the surface of the lake suddenly parted and a gleaming, shimmering blue figure broke through the water and leapt into the air, catching the stone.

Penn and Asher watched in awe as the mermaid spun in the air, and dove back into the lake, her tail glowing and sparkling like a thousand small pieces of coloured glass.

"Hmmm," said Penn, staring thoughtfully at the rippling water. Asher waited for some wise comment on the appearance of the mermaid.

"It seems I am quite good at skipping stones after all."

Ash picked up a handful of decaying autumn leaves and threw them at him. He ducked, which was pointless as the leaves rained down on his head and shoulders, and they both laughed.

***

Asher walked back to the house with her head swirling from Penn's words, and her hands tingling from his touch. The appearance of the mermaid, (Mona, she was sure of it), had reminded her of how little she really knew of the magical world and the responsibilities of the Weaver. She needed to settle her mind and centre her core, and there was only one way she knew how to do that. Penn was right. The music would guide her, it always had.

As she neared the doorway to the music room her fingers started to twitch and she could feel anticipation building in her being. It was definitely time to play.

The music room was flooded with light, stray particles of dust dancing in the beams that shone through the windows. Asher's whole body radiated energy as the instruments greeted her, vibrating with pleasure. She opened the piano lid and ran her fingers along the gleaming keys. Music leapt into her mind, a jaunty jig that she had played for a primary school recital years before. Without hesitation Ash launched into the song, the image of her mother and Caro laughing at the lake dancing in her mind. Soon she was aware of Levi and Kate entering the room, and when they started to jig around Ash couldn't help but laugh, her fingers flying over the keys and ending the tune with a flourish.

"Whooopeeeee," yelled Levi as he finished his jig with a leap. "Encore, encore!"

Kate was laughing and hiccupping as she tried to catch her breath.

"That was so much fun Ash. I couldn't *not* dance, it was like I couldn't control my feet. They just had to join in. Your music has always been amazing, but this time I could actually feel it in my body."

Levi nodded in agreement. "Yep, that's what it felt like for me. Invigorating and energising. I felt like it was pumping through my veins."

Ash understood completely. She felt the same. Playing music, *feeling* music, was always so easy. It was trying to Craft with it that seemed so hard. But she believed now she could practise and focus and she could learn. Here in this house with these instruments her music was magnified, powerful. She wondered if it would be like this once she left, and whether she would be able to develop her Crafting without Hesta to guide her. The thought reminded her of their plan to leave the Manor today.

"I guess we should find some sort of map," she murmured as she closed the piano lid, "something to lead us to Groush."

"Actually we were in the library when we heard you playing," said Levi, "there are so many books we weren't really sure what to look for. We must have checked a hundred books already."

"Let's have another look," chirped Kate, "I'm feeling energised after our jig. It can't be that hard to find a book of maps, surely!"

Forty minutes later Kate's high energy had completely evaporated, and she was cursing under her breath as she balanced precariously on a ladder while shoving a ridiculously heavy tome about the lifecycle of frogs back onto a crowded shelf above her head.

Levi and Asher were completely absorbed in a series of manuscripts about star constellations and planet evolution over thousands of years, and were unaware of the furious scowls Kate was sending their way.

"Look at this!" exclaimed Levi, crouched on the floor beside Asher, papers spread everywhere, "who knew there were so many star systems. These stars are all multi-coloured because of their cellular structure. How is that even a thing?!"

"And the planets," mused Asher, reverently running her fingers over the embossed drawings, "there are very specific notes here about the life-forms, the civilisations, the distance from Andera. Oh my goodness, look at this one! The inhabitants are shapeshifters, taking the form of dragons! It's like reading a fairy-tale, it's hard to comprehend that it is a completely different and real universe."

"Universes," corrected Levi, waving his hand at the various maps and books. "Can you believe *any* of this is real? This would blow the minds of our astronomers on Earth."

Realising that her burning stare was having zero impact on her distracted friends, Kate noisily cleared her throat, "aherrrm."

"Bless you," offered Levi absently, not even looking up.

"Seriously?" Rolling her eyes Kate grabbed the next book off the shelf. A quick flick through the pages revealed it was dedicated to the seed formation of a particular type of flower. Resisting the temptation to throw it at Levi's bent head, it was safely returned to its spot next to the frogs.

The next book was brimming with wildflower recipes. The book next to that detailed birdcalls. The book next to that was a pictorial of swamplands and their edible grasses.

On the floor Asher and Levi continued to 'aw' and 'ah' over their newly discovered space knowledge, contributing absolutely nothing in the search for a map to Groush.

"Right!" exclaimed Kate, leaping off the ladder and landing nimbly on the thick carpet. "That's it you two. Are you even going to help?"

Two sets of guilty eyes met hers, remorse brimming in both.

"Sorry Kate," they chorused.

"It's just all so interesting," offered Levi feebly. "It's easy to get distracted."

"Well get undistracted and focus on finding a map. It's almost lunchtime and we have no idea how we are leaving here, or where we are going, or how long it will take to get there."

Asher and Levi nodded contritely. Then Levi sighed as he looked at the thousands of books they had yet to check.

"This might take longer than we thought. If only we could ask some-one for help."

Trust Cook. Her mother's words seemed to tickle at her ear.

"We can trust Cook," Asher found herself saying. "She might have some answers for us."

"If you think so," agreed Kate readily, eager for some assistance. "It's worth a shot. It could take us days to work this out for ourselves."

We don't have days, thought Ash grimly, *if we can't leave tonight Hesta will send them home tomorrow and I'll be here alone.*

"Does that mean it's lunchtime?" asked Levi hopefully.

"I guess it does. Lead on sir," gestured Kate, ushering Levi to the door. She and Ash fell into step behind him and within minutes they were back in the kitchen savouring the sight and smell of fresh sandwiches loaded with left-over roast lamb and salad.

"Goodness!" exclaimed Cook. "I could set my clock by you Levi."

He grinned happily. "What can I say, I'm a growing boy."

Cook peered up at him, towering above her. "Is that so? Come on then, take a seat all of you."

Asher sat with the others, desperate to ask for Cook's help but also hesitant to share their plans with anyone. What if Cook went straight to Hesta? She swallowed hard to try and clear the thickness of the unsaid words.

Then with the unexpected violence of a sneeze that cannot be contained, the words blurted out of her in a tumbling rush.

"Cook, we need to get to Groush, we need to find my sister before this war happens, or Darven hurts her, or Hesta..."

"Shhhh, calm child. Take a breath." Cook's interruption was soft and firm. She looked carefully around the room, as though checking the very air for unwelcome listeners, then she quietly closed both doors into the kitchen.

"Now Asher. What's going on? And speak quietly. Not all ears are visible to us."

After a few deep breaths Asher shared everything with Cook, making sure to keep her voice low, including the message from her mother she had dreamed earlier that day.

"So we need to leave tonight, before Hesta sends Levi and Kate home and I am stuck here indefinitely, caught up in Hesta's games. The only thing that matters is to find Evie before something really bad happens to her, or my friends. I need to get everyone home safely. Please, please help us." She finished softly.

Still leaning against the counter clenching a tea-towel between her hands, Cook seemed lost in thought, processing everything she had heard. After a few long minutes she limped carefully to the table to sit beside Asher. Levi and Kate re-shuffled their chairs wordlessly.

"Asher this is no game that Hesta plays." The normally congenial Cook was stern and serious.

"Countless people - civilisations, planets - rely on the constancy of the Weaver maintaining the Threads. Most of them don't even know she exists. Those that do are not always disposed to be her friend. It is a lonely, thankless, difficult role, one she did not choose and one she cannot relinquish until some-one else takes her place. There is always, *always*, far more at stake than she will ever explain, or you would want to know. It is important that you understand that."

Asher nodded mutely, the gentle rebuke resting heavily. Her stomach churned with shame but also fear that this only avenue of help would be denied.

When Cook spoke again the sternness had eased, sadness instead now tinged each word.

"A long time ago another young woman came to me, begged me for my help. She too feared it was a matter of life or death. She too feared she was being played as a pawn."

Is she talking about mum? wondered Asher, not daring to ask.

"The Weaver had given instruction to her, just as she has now to you Asher. And the girl disobeyed, just as you plan to do Asher. Things went terribly wrong and she was desperate. So I helped her. The choice was made and the price was paid. And the consequences still ripple across the Threads, between the Worlds."

Nobody said anything. Asher stared at her clenched fists on the table, her eyes brimming with tears.

Calloused hands, wrinkled and scarred with a lifetime of knives and heat, closed warmly over hers. Ash raised her head to meet Cook's kind eyes as a hot heavy tear rolled down her face.

"Come child. Let's not have tears. I will help you just as I helped your mother. Perhaps if I had not done so she would have died as she feared, perhaps not. It's a thread that was never spun so we will never know. Most importantly she survived and here you are."

"Thank you," whispered Ash huskily, the words so inadequate for what she was being offered. She had never considered what it meant for Cook to be caught up in her schemes and how helping her might impact others.

Levi and Kate, silent witnesses for the entire exchange, grinned madly at each other, relief shining in their eyes. Asher snuffled heavily, trying to clear her tear-thickened throat and snotty nose.

"Well you're a right mess!" exclaimed Cook, pushing away from the table to collect a box of tissues.

Asher took the proffered tissues with thanks and noisily blew her nose. Laughter flooded the room, dissipating the sombre atmosphere once and for all.

"Now that's sorted, can we have lunch?" asked Levi hopefully.

Chapter Twelve

Varossa

Asher's body was aching from the tangled strands of her hair to the slightly numb tips of her toes. Her neck was sore from trying to keep her body upright and her lower back was protesting the hard seat. She was not sure when she had been more physically uncomfortable, if ever.

Levi had finally ceased muttering and grumbling thirty minutes earlier and it seemed Kate was asleep on the floor. Her sandy blonde hair was just visible from the pile of heavy wool blankets she had burrowed under, her head cushioned by the softness of her rolled up sleeping bag. Ash envied her the oblivion of slumber.

She breathed deeply, trying to relax into the rocking rhythm of the cart, *just like being on the bus*, until yet another huge pothole sent the rear wheels flying into the air. Asher and Levi bumped along with the cart, grabbing hold of the high wooden sides to avoid being flung too high into the air.

"For crying out loud!" exclaimed Levi, his despondent silence finally broken. "How much longer will we be on this torture device?"

Still holding on with her left hand, Ash leant forward and reached awkwardly into her pack which was safely stowed under her legs. She rummaged around until her fingers closed around the crinkled edge of the map Cook had given them. Grimacing against the pain of holding all her weight steady she pulled herself upright again.

"Okay," said Ash, as she gingerly let go of the side to allow both hands to flip open the folded paper.

"According to the map we are about a third of the way to Mat'drin, the last town before the Mountain climb begins."

"Only a third!" groaned Levi, "We've been travelling for two hours already. That's another four hours. FOUR HOURS Ash! My bones are literally rattled and I cannot feel my butt. I am not having fun."

"Suck it up princess." Her own discomfort didn't make her the most sympathetic of companions.

"Well that's charming," was the wounded reply, but then mercifully he was silent again, burying himself into his blankets and closing his eyes.

For a millisecond Asher felt bad, but not too bad. She had enough to worry about without Levi's moaning and groaning, not least being the numbness in her own bruised bottom.

The conversation with Cook in the warmth and comfort of Hesta's kitchen seemed a thousand miles away, though it had been only four hours since she had helped them hatch their plan, and only a couple of hours since they had actually left the manor.

"Luckily we had no idea how horrendous this cart trip would be or we might never have left. Levi would probably have opted to return to Earth rather than suffer through this." She mumbled, thinking out loud.

"Are you talking to me?" queried the Levi shaped blankets opposite her.

"No, just muttering to myself."

"Fine then." Even muffled beneath layers of wool he still sounded hurt.

Ash rolled her eyes, then immediately felt guilty. Her friends were putting themselves in danger, in uncomfortable situations, just to support her. A rush of remorse washed through her.

"Sorry for snapping Levi, I'm exhausted and worried and it's making me short-tempered. I'm sorry this trip is so awful. Hopefully if we get some sleep it will pass quickly."

He pulled the blankets down to his chin. "It's okay Ash, I know it's not your fault. Just a bit miserable and feeling sorry for myself."

"Ditto," she replied glumly.

"Maybe it will be better if you play something?" Levi suggested hopefully, "something that will make this a more comfortable experience?"

Asher shook her head. "Nope. Cook was particularly clear about this. No *Crafting*", she whispered the word, though there was no way the old driver at the front could hear anything they were talking about. "Too dangerous with the *Darven situation*," more whispering, "we don't know friend from foe."

"Right now I'm not sure if Cook is friend or foe," muttered her companion darkly, "this whole experience is bloody awful." With a loud harumph Levi yanked the blankets back over his face.

The cart trip had been Cook's idea.

There had been limited options for getting to Groush. Apparently cars and trains and buses were not a thing on Andera. Kate's enthusiasm for horse-riding was cut short by Levi, who had never been on a horse and never planned to be on a horse. Walking would simply take too long.

Hesta's normal mode of transport required pinching a driver, some horses and a carriage from her stables and hoping nobody alerted Hesta. It would also have made them extremely conspicuous as her black and gold carriages were rather unique to the Weaver.

But a cart, well that was a boring, common-place way to move from town to town. And when Joseph had rattled his way into the yard, bottles of wine clinking merrily, it seemed that the Threads were weaving in their favour.

Supplies were thrown together, their packs were surreptitiously moved downstairs to the stables and final, hard hugs were exchanged with Cook. It had passed in a blur, which was a good thing. If there had been too much time or planning Asher was sure she would have chickened out. She had resolutely kept her thoughts away from Hesta and how badly she might react when she discovered they were gone. She fiercely hoped Cook would not be blamed.

But now they were actually on their way, hitching a ride with a wine merchant across Andera to the Mountains and to Evie.

The initial hour had been really exciting. Once outside the large wrought-iron gates, she and Levi and Kate had popped out from under the heavy blankets and peered around curiously. They had not really been aware of the discomfort of the cart, as they were so focused on the novelty of the experience.

The road from E-Langren was a simple country lane, lined with trees that shaded travellers from the sun, and created a fence-line between the road and the fields that lay beyond.

The path was blanketed with faded orange and red and yellow autumnal leaves, many of them crinkled and browning with age. They crunched beneath the heavy wheels of the cart.

"Look over there!" called Levi excitedly, pointing between the trees.

In a bright purple field a large plough was being pulled by two red horses, but the unusual colour of the steeds was not what had captured Levi's attention. It was the way they pranced along the ground before leaping into the air to gallop through the sky, pulling the plough smoothly and briskly along the field, that was so captivating. Every few metres they would return to the earth for another run up.

From behind the plough a young girl sat atop another leaping red horse and laughed as she flung handfuls of glittery seeds into the churned earth. Asher could feel the energy the child was imbuing into the tiny seeds as they fell onto the soil. She wondered what they would grow to become.

Before long they trundled into the small village that lay just beyond E-Langren, and which provided the day-to-day necessities and non-live-in staff to the manor. Kate laughed as she surveyed the colourful shop facades.

"Look, there is quite literally a butcher's, a baker's and a candle stick maker, all in a row!"

Asher peered with interest into the window of the candle maker's shop, enjoying the sight of the many different sizes and colours of the candles. Some were shaped like animals, others like trees or flowers, one was a baby's cradle, yet another was a small round ball. The Candle Crafter stood at the front display with a customer and gently blew across the candles. The wick of a candle shaped like a shoe burst into flame and the customer clapped her hands with joy as the Crafter pulled it out of the display and handed it to her.

Next to the candle maker's shop a florist had lined the pavement with buckets of colourful blooms from which customers could choose their favourites to be Crafted together into a beautiful bunch of good luck and well wishes.

Two children playing with a ball turned and waved at them as they passed by, and the three friends smiled and waved back.

The cart rattled on, soon leaving the small village and its peaceful, joyful, uncomplicated life behind.

Their pleasure and excitement had evaporated soon after as the monotony of the journey, and the uncomfortable confines of the cart, started to take their toll.

Now, only a few hours in, they were cross, sore and snapping at each other, and there was still a long way to go.

Deciding Kate had the right idea, Asher unclipped her sleeping bag from the pack and lay on the hard wooden bench seat, the sleeping bag beneath her head. It was supremely uncomfortable in every way, but strangely hypnotic too. The sun still high in the afternoon sky, the cool air on her skin and her racing mind made it impossible to actually sleep, but it was nice to lie there and watch the countryside bounce by.

The rattle of the bottles and the creaking of the cart created their own raw melody and Asher found herself humming along. The music was jaunty and unpolished and her fingers itched to play along on the harmonica, but Cook's warning to lay low was still fresh and Ash settled for tapping her fingers on her palm.

As she lay there on the unyielding wooden bench, the music bouncing in her mind along with her body, a long-forgotten memory swirled into her mind. She remembered being on a carousel when she was very small, perhaps only five, bouncing up and down on the horse's back. She had been squealing with excitement and waving vigorously at her parents on each rotation, becoming more and more complacent with her hold on the handles sticking out of the horse's head. Her enthusiastic twisting and turning finally unseated her and Ash flew off the plastic horse, landing on the floor of the carousel with a huge cry. Within seconds Evie was there, jumping off her own unicorn to check on her little sister. She had cuddled her close, soothed her hurts, which were more shock than injury, and helped her climb back up.

Asher had been too scared to sit on the horse again, desperately shaking her head and crying that she wanted to get off. Evie had climbed up behind her and held her tight, promising that she would be safe. Steady in her sister's embrace Asher had finished the carousel ride.

"I promise you Evie," she whispered fiercely, *"I will find you and bring you home safely. I promise you."*

The globe burned within her palm, surprising Asher. She had not even realised she was clutching it. Her hand tingled with power, and although the energy seared her skin she could not, would not, let go. Asher felt like she was burning the promise into her very being.

Over time they seemed to adjust to the rocking, bouncing, bumping non-rhythm of the cart and the next hour passed uneventfully. Kate woke up and with a groan and an awkward stretch, took her place next to Ash on the seat. Levi was returning to his normal upbeat state.

"Gosh it's super green out here, look at all those fields. It's really just like being at home which is kinda surprising. I think I expected more..." he waved his hand around vaguely, "you know, magic and mystery after Hesta's place and the village outside the manor. This part of the country is actually quite ordinary, like the magic is missing. Look! There's a town ahead! Civilisation! People! Food!!"

"Well your good nature sure bounced back," muttered Asher, rubbing at her numb bottom. "Still, it would be nice to have something to eat."

"I hear you!" agreed Kate, flexing her stiff back. "If we are stopping here it would be great to get off and move around."

As if on cue their driver, who had been silent the entire three hours, called from the front bench.

"Varossa ahead. We'll stop here to feed and water the horses and you can stretch your legs. Just thirty minutes, mind. There's a lovely marketplace with music and food. Don't get too distracted. We all need a rest but don't want to delay too long, there are still a few hours to go and we are losing the day."

The next few minutes passed in eager anticipation as they leaned at various angles out of the cart, craning their heads to peer at the town as it loomed larger and larger ahead of them. After the simple pleasures and Crafting of the E-Langren village they had high hopes for this much larger town.

The expansive green fields soon gave way to large brick and stone buildings, many painted brightly and glowing warmly in the late afternoon sun. Heavily built-up streets ran in every direction off the main road through town, giving the impression of size and the expectation of a large population. Flower boxes bursting with beautiful blooms gaily decorated shuttered windows.

The lovely streets were filled with houses and shops and businesses, but there were hardly any people around.

After a few long minutes they clattered into the main square. A conspicuously quiet square. Festive bunting fluttered forlornly across closed doorways. Brightly lettered signs advertising cafes and hot food hung above empty restaurants. The handful of people buying fresh goods at the smattering of market stands shrank back as the cart approached and turned away.

"Something's wrong," murmured Kate to Asher. "Where is everybody?"

"That is a very good question," replied Asher, the back of her neck prickling with tension. "Joseph?" She called to the driver, "Is this normal?"

"No," he said slowly, the single word loaded with apprehension.

Levi caught Ash's eye, his eyebrows raised in query and concern. She shrugged nonchalantly but worry churned in her belly.

Joseph drove the horses and cart towards an empty bay just beyond the square where the horses headed gratefully for a large trough brimming with cool, clear water. As soon as the cart was steady the three of them climbed gingerly down, their muscles screaming.

"Seriously, this is the sorest I have ever been," moaned Levi, stretching his long frame one way and then the other. "I have never been so grateful to stand on solid ground."

Ash exhaled deeply as she stretched her own furious muscles. "Oh I hear you."

"Miss".

Joseph's deep voice full of concern interrupted her amateur yoga.

For the first time since they had snuck out of the manor Asher looked properly at the man who was helping them. A lifetime of driving carts in the sun and rain had weathered and marked his skin; his eyes, once a vibrant blue, were now watery and pale. It was an old face, a kind face, and right now it was a very worried face.

"This is highly unusual. Varossa is a vibrant, artistic town, usually full of wonderful Crafter items in the marketplace and plenty of music and people."

Kate and Levi joined them and the four of them exchanged worried looks.

"I think it best that we move on as quickly as possible," continued Joseph. "Stay close to the cart and we'll set off again soon."

"I'm sorry," interrupted Kate, "I don't mean to be a nuisance, but I really need to use the loo."

Joseph looked confused. "What's a loo?"

"The toilet," said Kate in a small voice, her face flushing pink. "Is there one nearby?"

"It's in the square, at the Hall of Gathering."

"Could you wait until we are out of town Kate?" asked Levi.

"I'm sorry," repeated Kate, jiggling from foot to foot, "I *really* need to go."

"We'll go together," decided Ash, "safety in numbers and all that." She grinned feebly, but no-one grinned back.

"Do you have coins for the toilet?" asked Joseph.

Asher rattled the small sack that Cook had tucked into her pocket. "Yes."

"Good," nodded Joseph, "use the small silver coins with the dragon's head, one each."

He disappeared back to the front of the cart and his horses.

"Alright," said Levi, "Let's move with purpose, like we know exactly what we are doing. The Hall had a huge plaque on it. Just head straight there."

The sun was still warm but Asher felt a shiver crawl down her spine as they walked into the quiet square. It felt like a hundred eyes were peering at them through closed curtains and from behind darkened doorways. Her heart was beating fast. She felt exposed, seen.

"What are you humming?" hissed Levi.

"What are you talking about?" she whispered back.

"You are humming under your breath."

And so she was. Humming the tune that had swirled in her mind her whole life, a tune that belonged to a girl who was unremarkable, so plain, so very uninteresting that nobody would really remember her, really see her. The tune that made her invisible, in plain sight. She fervently hoped it was working now.

The walk across the cobbled stone marketplace to the imposing red brick Hall of Gathering seemed to take eons, yet some-how they made it without encountering another person.

At the foot of the large steps Kate and Ash faltered.

"Confidence, remember? Stride in like you own the place," murmured Levi before bounding up the steps two at a time.

The heavy wooden double doors were open at the top. Normally a welcoming gesture it felt ominous under the weight of the strange atmosphere in the town.

The hall beyond the doors was huge and bright, with polished floors and a lacquered black staircase soaring into the light-filled void. It hinted at the grandeur of the floors above. Gleaming marble statues of important people long dead shared space with jolly portraits of Varossa's finest citizens.

Armchairs covered in heavily embroidered lush fabrics gathered in clusters, waiting for guests to sink into them. It felt like a building that should be bustling with people. Instead it was deserted.

On one side of the grand foyer glass cabinets displayed treasured Crafts whose energy tickled the tips of Asher's fingers. She steadfastly ignored the cabinets and the urge to touch the contents. Instinct warned her to stay far away from anything Crafter related. There was trouble in Varossa, and potentially danger. She layered the charm further.

Levi strode to a large information desk staffed by a young girl with dark hair and wary dark eyes. Following behind him Ash and Kate could clearly see the moment the full force of his charm impacted the attendant. Colour flooded her face and she sat up taller.

"Good afternoon! We would like to use the toilets please. My friend Samantha will pay you."

He waved grandly at Kate, who obediently stepped forward with the three silver coins Asher shoved into her hand.

"Thank you," whispered the girl to Levi as she slotted the coins into a metal box, her cheeks rosy under the force of his smile. She glanced quickly at Kate then away. She didn't acknowledge Asher at all.

The three of them stood waiting, Kate bouncing on the balls of her feet.

"Which way do we go?" asked Levi gently when it became apparent that no instructions were forthcoming.

"Just around to the left there," the attendant said softly, dropping her gaze as she pointed.

"Thank you," said Levi, his warm voice full of kindness. "Have a lovely day."

Kate took off quickly in the direction of the toilets, Ash close behind. They had moved beyond earshot when the woman called out.

"Excuse me," she called, softly.

Levi turned back around.

"You are new here." It was not a question.

"Just passing through."

"You are kind."

Levi smiled cheekily, his eyes lighting up with humour.

"You could have said that while my friends were here. For some strange reason they don't always agree!"

A ghost of a smile tickled the attendant's lips, then guiltily she glanced around the empty foyer, frightened some-one would see her.

"This used to be a wonderful town. We are known as a cross-road for Crafters and traders, travelling across Andera. Everyone has always been welcome. But now things are different. Armed Squads come regularly. They used to come seeking information. Now they take the Crafters themselves. In the beginning we fought back."

Huge tears shimmered at the edge of her lashes. "It is impossible. They say the great Weaver herself is ridding the land of Crafters who will not join with her to overthrow the Queen. She is gathering all power to herself."

Her soft voice had now dropped below the hush of a whisper. Levi took a step closer to hear.

"Don't linger long. People are frightened and strangers attract too much attention."

Levi nodded slowly, digesting the information.

"Thank you," he said genuinely, "that was very kind of you. We will heed your words. Take care."

Levi had already used the male toilets and was waiting on the steps outside when Asher and Kate returned from the bathroom.

"Why do girls always take so looooong?" he moaned.

Kate swatted his arm and huffed past him in dignified silence. Asher grinned.

The prospect of being back in the safety of the cart with Joseph and leaving the gloom of Varossa behind made them all walk quickly. They were almost at the far end, they could see the horse bay beyond the square, when a harsh voice stopped them.

"Hey! HEY! Stop where you are!"

Startled into compliance they stopped and turned around.

A small group was gathering. Five or six angry men and women circled around them, fear gleaming in their eyes.

"What are you doing here?" demanded a burly man with wild blonde curls and an impossibly long moustache. "Why did you go into the Hall of Gathering?"

"We are just passing through, we simply wanted-" Levi did not have the chance to finish his sentence.

Accusing voices clamoured over one another.

"Who sent you?"

"Where are you from?"

"The Squads are always looking for strangers, *Crafters* in disguise."

"They take our children, torture our families, thinking we are hiding Crafters. We won't protect you!"

The words were fast, furious, full of loathing. Questions from every angle. Levi turned from person to person, trying to explain, placate.

"No, no, we are simply... we only wanted to use the facilities... definitely not Crafters, never met one, just on our way to..."

"Grab them!" yelled a woman from the back. "Maybe we can trade them for our stolen sons and daughters."

Heavy hands grabbed at their clothes. Asher could feel Levi and Kate's panic. Fear and fury roiled within her, the music began to swell. *By all the stars no...* She wouldn't be able to control it.

"STOP!" boomed a deep voice from beyond the melee.

Everyone stopped, including Ash. The music froze.

Joseph forced his way through the crowd, now numbering close to fifteen.

"Leave these young people alone!"

Joseph wrapped his strong arms around Kate and Levi. Asher found herself forgotten, protected by her charm. Carefully she edged backwards through the people.

"How dare you!" Joseph admonished the men and women, his voice loud and stern. "How dare you frighten these young people like that. You should be ashamed. What is happening here?"

The heightened emotion of the pack was easing, replaced by shame and grief. Joseph was well known to them all, a regular merchant in their town. His solid, familiar presence was a reminder of all they had lost.

Apologies now flooded where accusations had been. People began to sob as they shared their stories. Families torn apart. Crafters tortured and stolen. Fear and division everywhere.

Asher stepped further away from the group. Quietly she turned, knowing she should slip off to the cart.

"Crafter, come quickly."

The grip on her arm was firm. Though not painful it was startling. She pulled away sharply, trying not to panic and set off the cacophony. Instantly the hold was released. Ash spun around to face her assailant.

"My apologies, I don't mean to accost or frighten you."

Asher raised both eyebrows in disbelief. "Really? Grabbing my arm is an odd way to not accost or frighten me. Particularly after that mob."

The heavily cloaked woman nodded once, acknowledging Asher's point.

She was not much taller than Kate, and though she had the voice and strength of a woman in her prime, her actual age and features remained a mystery to Asher, hooded as she was.

"Again, my apologies. Walk quickly with me, I can offer you safe passage from Varossa. Truly Crafter I mean you no harm. Rather I am ecstatic to see you."

Ash strode alongside the other woman, only willing to walk with her in the same direction as Joseph's cart. Soon the townsfolk would be placated and he, Kate and Levi would join her to leave.

"Why do you call me Crafter?"

Laughter bubbled from within the deep green cloak.

"A woman who no-one else seems to see? A furious energy so strong the water in the fountain bubbles in response? Please do not play me for a fool. I was not gifted but I grew up among the most powerful Crafters in the region, and I know a Crafter when I feel one."

Truth vibrated through her words and finally the hammering of Ash's heart started to ease. She hadn't betrayed her to the angry mob. Perhaps this woman was friend not foe.

"I don't need passage, I am travelling with Joseph."

"Then I will speak quickly for you must leave at once. You must get to the Queen, tell her of the Weaver's betrayal, tell her of the bloodshed and kidnappings. We must rise up against the Weaver and restore our lost Crafters. Please."

Ash stumbled in shock. "What are you saying? That you think the Weaver is behind these attacks?"

"Of course. The Squads are wearing her crest. They always announce they come in the name of the Weaver. At first we did not believe them and we sent emissaries to her for help. Their lifeless corpses were returned to us with the very clear message to comply. Only the Weaver has enough power to allow the Squads to defeat Crafters. I fear the

Queen cannot prevail against such power, but she is our only hope."

They had reached the cart. Not far behind them the crowd was dispersing. Her friends would be with them in a few minutes.

Emotion churned within Asher, but this time it was not fury. Notes of sadness, confusion, fear and frustration danced a melody in her head. *"Quiet!"* she commanded. When the music subsided what was left was calm.

"Will you show me your face?" she asked.

The woman hesitated for a moment, then pulled back the long hood.

Puckered burns and barely healed scars ravaged a face that once had been whole. It was impossible to tell what beauty had been hers. Asher recoiled in shock.

Quickly the woman pulled the hood back over her head.
"How did-"
"This is what happens when you oppose the Weaver's squads. They stole my Crafter sister then burned our house down, with me trapped inside. I survived. The skin on my face and body did not."

Asher was silent for a long moment, considering what to say.

"Please, show me your face. I want you to see my eyes when I tell you this truth."

This time Asher was prepared for the damaged face before her. As dreadful as the scarring was, Asher would not shame either of them again with her horror.

Gently she took the woman's gloved hands in hers. "You said you can feel Crafter energy?"

The woman nodded. "When the Crafter is a strong as you, then absolutely."

"So can you feel my truth now?"

The woman nodded again.

"Then hear me when I tell you. The Weaver is not behind this. The Weaver is your friend and ally. She was unaware of these raids and destruction until very recently. She is working to save you all. Believe me, please believe me."

Asher could feel her companion's uncertainty warring with the small kernels of hope.

"She is not the enemy?"

Ash shook her head vehemently. "Absolutely no. Trust in her. Tell the others. It is time to spread the truth."

Golden brown eyes filled with hope bored into hers, but still the woman with the ruined face was hesitant.

"Why should I believe you?"

Asher reached into memory for the energy of the blood-bonding completed nearly sixteen years earlier, of a woman and a baby bound by duty and destiny. When she smiled the echo of ten thousand generations smiled through her. Music swirled around her, so loud it seemed the air was vibrating.

"Do you feel this? Do you know who I am?" asked Asher as energy pulsed between their clasped hands.

The woman nodded, her eyes now glowing. "Yes I do."

"Tell the others the truth about the Weaver."

The woman shook her head, her fingers tightly entwined with Asher's.

"They will not believe me. They are too afraid and broken. Revealing the source of my knowledge will only put you in danger..." she trailed off, wonder in her voice.

Footsteps announced the arrival of Asher's friends.

Her companion dropped Asher's hands and pulled her hood over her head in one fast, fluid movement.

"What is your name?" asked Asher quietly.

"Raya."

"And your sister?"

"Simeona."

"I promise you this Raya. If your sister lives I will find her. And I will bring her home to you. On the Threads I promise you this."

Raya's gloved hands grabbed Asher's fingers once again. A hot tear splashed on their clasped hands. "Thank you Crafter."

"My name is Asher. And now I ask a promise of you. When the Weaver calls for help, answer her call."

Chapter Thirteen

The Mountain Man of Groush

"I love this cart," sighed Levi, happily scoffing lamb sandwiches and biscuits as he bounced with each pothole.

"Really?" asked Kate incredulously, "my how your tune has changed."

Levi rolled his eyes at her. "Well I do. I'll be sad to leave it when we arrive at Mat'drin. My experience of towns in Andera has not really been that welcoming."

Kate nodded glumly in agreement. After their hostile welcome at Varossa they had approached the next town of Harthe with no small amount of trepidation.

A significantly smaller town, there had been no grand square or large streets lined with houses. But still the empty streets and the wariness on people's faces added to their uneasiness.

Joseph had stopped to water and rest the horses while he delivered wine barrels, and the three of them had climbed down to stretch their legs, deliberately staying close to the cart. The minutes ticked by uncomfortably while they waited for Joseph's return.

A mother with a small child glared at them before whisking her wide-eyed child through a nearby doorway. Two men carrying boxes muttered curses in their direction. Asher, Levi and Kate stayed quiet and still, trying to be as unnoticeable as possible.

Joseph brought them hot tea from a nearby café which they gulped thankfully, and then they climbed back onto the cart and huddled among the blankets and crates until it was time to leave.

A few minutes after the cart and horses had lurched into movement they had come to an abrupt halt.

"Merchant! State your business."

Asher felt her heart stop, then resume beating with such a loud thump that she almost gasped. Buried under the blankets beside her, Kate reached out and grabbed her hand, then Levi's. Fingers squeezed tightly.

"What on earth is going on?" asked Joseph, surprise clear in every word. "I've just delivered an order of wine to the Inn and now I am on my way to Mat'drin. Like I do every week. Is that you Rohill? And wearing the livery of the Queen?"

A murmured assent indicated that the accoster was indeed the man known as Rohill.

"What's this all about then?" continued Joseph.

The response was less demanding, but still surly.

"I'm on night patrol. Got to check the comings and goings. There has been talk of Crafters turning against their own townsfolk. It is said the Weaver is behind it, planning an uprising against the Crown. I've been recruited by the Queen's Advisor to detain any suspicious people. Any

Crafters. If they are in league with the Weaver they will be dealt with. If they are innocent they need to be rounded up for their own protection."

"That's what is said, is it?" responded Joseph softly, "and what do you think Rohill, son of Nagarie? She who was one of the greatest Potter Crafters ever to grace Andera, and good friend to Hestawen. What would she think of this?"

A long silence followed this gentle question.

"The Weaver was always good to my mum, and to us. Never seemed to want more power than she had. Kept herself to herself mostly. Maybe she's not at fault, but then why isn't she helping? Both my sisters taken, my da shrinking into a shadow of himself -" Rohill hesitated.

Another rough voice called out in the twilight, a muffled question, a threat.

Rohill's resolve hardened. "I have to check your cart Joseph."

The older man answered sadly. "Do what you must Rohill."

So he had given the cart a once-over, poking at the blankets and checking a few boxes of bottles. But he had become distracted and disinterested after only a few seconds, unable to concentrate on the task at hand. It was almost as though he could not actually see the backpacks heaped under the benches, or Levi's left foot sticking out from the blankets, clad in a black trainer.

Kate and Levi barely dared to breathe during the agonising seconds. Asher could feel them squeezing her fingers, but her entire focus was on extending her aura of invisibility to encase them within it.

The whole experience had been unpleasant and frightening. They had felt like fugitives, with no way of knowing what they were fleeing from or to. The cart had indeed become their safe place, and dear Joseph a steadfast friend.

"Maybe we should continue on with Joseph to Ostrin tomorrow," suggested Levi. "Meet up with Hesta. Get this whole mess with Darven sorted. Restore order and eradicate the angry mobs."

"Or we can go to Groush, rescue Evie and go home," replied Asher bluntly.

"What about the small problem that the whole country thinks their Weaver has betrayed them and is torturing and destroying Crafter families who won't join her uprising? Hmmm? Don't you think we should do something about that?" Levi's tone was light but his dark eyes were serious.

"No I don't. That's nothing to do with us. Hesta can handle that."

But the words sounded hollow as she said them, and Asher felt something like shame coil around her gut. She looked away from Levi, unable to hold his gaze.

"Well if you won't help *your grandmother*," though whispered, the words still managed to sound accusing, "what about the woman in Varossa? You swore on the Threads that you would find her sister and return her. I'm not an Anderan, but that sounded pretty binding. Like a pinky promise between seven-year olds."

"Shut up Levi!"

Her friend just shrugged without remorse.

"It's kinda cool that you get so angry and grumpy these days. You spent so many years just being perfect and calm and so accommodating that it was like you were just a shadow of yourself. Maybe now you can actually deal with all the stuff you shoved down for so long. Feel all the feels. Much healthier in my professional opinion."

"Professional pain in the rear end," retorted Asher.

Levi rolled his eyes.

As always, among the nonsense he had a point. With each click of the horses' hooves and jarring pothole encounter they moved closer to Mat'drin and the journey to Groush. She did not know how they would facilitate the trek up the Mountains and had no idea what awaited them there.

Her burning desire to find Evie and get safely home to Earth now sat uneasily when she thought of Varossa and Harthe. How many times over was this same tale of loss being written across Andera? Towns and villages that were once like the village outside E-Langren, filled with joy and camaraderie, were now filled with suspicion and dread. How long would it be before the wave reached E-Langren and its village?

Darven was spreading fear and hatred among the people against the only person who could save them. Crafters would soon willingly align themselves with him to rid Andera of their Weaver. He would be unstoppable.

As for Levi's second point... Asher sighed heavily. By all the shape-shifters in the dragon universe Levi was right. She had sworn a rather epic pinky promise with Raya and she had to make good on that.

Her head was spinning trying to make sense of what to do and how to help everyone relying on her.

"One step at a time," said a reassuring voice. It seemed Kate was reading her mind. "And no, I'm not reading your mind, just watching the stress on your face. We just break it down into small steps and work our way through it. We can do this Ash. We're a team."

Levi and Kate reached out their hands and grabbed hers, reassuring her with their presence and unwavering support. She smiled at them gratefully, the lump in her throat making it difficult to speak.

"Thanks," she croaked.

"Righto, Mat'drin about half an hour away," called Joseph from the front. "Where are you kids planning to spend the night?"

***

Kate bustled around their compact campsite, straightening guy ropes and re-fixing pegs while Levi nurtured the small flames of their fire. Asher had been tasked with organising dinner, a job Levi had wanted but could not be trusted with.

Cook had stocked them as well as she could considering they had to carry everything on their backs. Fruit, sandwiches, cold sausages and cake were retrieved from Asher's pack and laid out on a makeshift log table. She frowned as she contemplated their supplies, then carefully re-packed some of the food. Who knew how many days they would have to last.

The lights of Mat'drin twinkled merrily in the distance. They had asked Joseph for a safe and unobtrusive place to set up camp, but within walking distance of the town. His choice was so far perfect. They had parted ways with the kind merchant with many heartfelt thanks, and no small amount of trepidation. For the first time they were truly on their own in Andera.

As the hours passed and the evening lengthened into night, the group felt relaxed and at ease. Now that night had fallen it seemed no-one was on the road, and their two little tents and small fire would not be noticed, tucked deep into a low-lying field.

As soon as the sky was dark enough Levi had pulled his small telescope from his pack and turned his attention to the unfamiliar stars above. He was most excited by a small constellation of bright orange stars that were actually moving around, almost as though they were dancing. He had been so entranced in the skies that he had not noticed how quickly the temperature was dropping.

His shivering body soon brought his attention back to more worldly matters.

"I wish we could have brought flasks of hot chocolate," said Levi wistfully, shivering lightly in the cool night air. "I'm cold."

"Put a jumper on," instructed Kate unsympathetically.

Kate was already well rugged up, and Asher had donned her mother's warm woollen coat. Obediently Levi reached into his pack and pulled out a worn and faded hoodie, yanking it over his head with a sigh of pleasure.

"Better," he declared, "but I'd still like a hot chocolate. Can you believe this is actually only the end of our second full day here?"

He propped himself up against his pack with his long legs sticking out towards the fire and contentedly munched on a muesli bar. The small telescope lay discarded at his side.

"It definitely feels like longer," agreed Kate. "You know, being here is almost like camping at home."

"Yup, the lack of wi-fi and phone reception adds an authentic touch."

"You brought your phone?" asked Kate, her voice incredulous.

Levi shrugged. "Of course. Never leave Earth without it. Fat lot of good it's done me. No service on the other side of the universe. Funny that."

Asher listened to the light-hearted chatter without really paying attention. She was twisting her harmonica between her fingers, warming the cold metal while an internal argument raged as to whether she should play or not.

Cook said no Crafting... There won't be Crafting, it's just music... I've played the harmonica hundreds of times without magic happening .... Some-one might hear .... There's no-one around! One song won't hurt... We're camping, this is part of camping ...

Giving up the fight, Asher raised the harmonica to her mouth. Gently she blew a scale, moving the small instrument lightly along her lips. Pleasure surged through her. She launched into a country reel. Levi and Kate fell silent, but they couldn't stay still for long.

Within a minute they were tapping their feet and clapping their hands, Levi joining in the music with the occasional "yee-ha!"

Music wafted through the clear night air. With nothing to stop them the notes seemed to dance across the fields, fading eventually into the distance.

As Asher played she was careful to control her Crafting, to dampen down the energy she could feel swirling inside her. She was being reckless enough playing out here in the open, she knew she couldn't draw additional attention from those seeking Crafters. But the music simply had to be played. She couldn't keep the notes inside her any longer.

As the reel drew to a close her friends burst out clapping. Asher took a bow.

"Bravo!" called a voice from beside her. "How sad you're done. Music is fun for everyone!"

Asher spun around in shock.

A rather dishevelled old man was perched on a large log a few feet away from their group, away from the illumination of the fire. Even in the dark it was clear his tangled white beard would benefit from a cut and wash, and what was left of the hair on his head needed similar attention. His clothes were a motley collection of shapes and sizes, giving the impression he had simply layered on each item as he had encountered them. On washing lines, in rubbish heaps, or a seamstress' discard pile. He was tatty and ratty and full of excitement, clapping happily.

"Where on earth did you come from?" asked Levi in bewilderment, peering through the shadows.

"Over there, over there, from the ground and in the air," was the cheery reply, accompanied by a vague gesture towards the town, the surrounding fields, the mountains beyond and perhaps even the sky.

"Well that clears that up," responded Levi drily.

"Who are you?" blurted Asher.

She had been completely shocked by the man's unexpected appearance, but strangely she was not scared. Her mind and body thrummed with the power of her music. The certainty that she could draw on that energy to overpower one strange old man gave her confidence.

"Play something else!" he demanded exuberantly, "Something else!"

His pleasure was flattering and Asher raised the harmonica to her lips before she had considered his request, and the wisdom of playing for this odd man.

A gentle blow produced a harsh note. No. Not the harmonica. Quickly she went to her pack and rustled around, before returning to her log seat with her flute, wrapped in a soft velvet cloth. She clicked the pieces together and blew again. Perfect.

Without conscious thought Asher found herself playing a slow melody she had never heard before. A gentle song of loss and longing. Of youth squandered and love sacrificed to ambition. Of vanity and arrogance long regretted. It was not a song she had ever learned, instead it seemed to be written on the wind, the notes playing themselves as she lightly blew into the gleaming instrument and pressed the keys.

It felt like the song had been waiting for her.

The final notes were gathered into the night and their little campsite descended into silence. On the other side of the crackling fire Kate was quietly swiping away tears and Levi had buried his face in his hands.

After letting the energy in her mind and body settle Asher turned her head to glance at their mysterious guest.

In the dancing firelight he seemed younger, taller. His scraggly hair was thick and lustrous, a rich rusty red. His now trimmed beard glimmered the same colour, and his face glowed with the energy and possibility of a man in his prime. But his eyes... his eyes were faded and knowing, the decades no longer on his body still reflected in his eyes. The young man pulsed with the energy of hope, the old eyes brimmed with pain.

The windows to the soul... thought Asher wonderingly. Then smoke tickled her vision and she blinked a few times hard.

When it cleared the young man had vanished and their ratty, tatty tramp was once more in place. A tear marked a trail down his grubby face. Ash resisted the urge to reach out and grab his hand.

"Perhaps once more?" he said softly.

Asher shook her head regretfully.

"I cannot play it again. It was given to me just for this moment."

He said nothing.

"You have waited a very long time for some-one to play it."

He nodded sadly.

"You are released," she whispered softly. Perhaps it had given him the peace he had been craving.

"A gift beyond price, for which I have yearned," he finally croaked. "Now Crafter I offer you something in return."

He reached into the masses of material, muttering as he pulled out trinkets and items which were then shoved straight back into pockets or dropped unheeded to the ground.

"Not that... maybe this... no! What is that doing there? I thought you were lost...as for you, you were told to stay - AHA!"

With gleeful triumph he pulled out a small blue whistle, about the size of her thumb.

"For you!" he presented the dusty whistle to Asher with a flourish.

"Thank you," she replied, twisting the whistle curiously in her hands. It felt oddly incredibly heavy and yet weightless. She shook it lightly.

"Should I blow the whistle now?" she asked.

"NO!"

Asher jumped, startled by his vehemence.

"No! No! No! It must only be used when the need is so dire that a truth or an answer is what you require, the problem so big and the answer unknown, that you cannot see clearly all on your own."

"Oh yes, that's super clear," muttered Levi.

"What does it do exactly?" asked Asher, trying to cut through the nonsense.

"It is a dream," whispered the old man, "it is a future. A moment when the Great Loom stills and the Threads can be spun any which way."

Despite the warmth of the fire Asher felt a cold shiver run down her spine. Her skin prickled with warning.

"Like a prophecy?" asked Levi carefully.

Their guest cackled. "Everybody is so obsessed with prophecy. It becomes rather tiresome. I prefer possibility. With every weave there are countless patterns that can emerge. But sometimes there is only one that should. The art of She who Weaves is to know which moments those are."

"Interesting that he doesn't have to speak in rhyme all the time," murmured Levi to Kate, "though it does seem fun to rhyme words off your tongue. It's hard to stop, once you've begun."

Kate rolled her eyes and attempted to ignore him, but her lips twitched and she coughed lightly to clear what might have been a giggle.

The old man's eyes bored into Asher's and suddenly they seemed sharp and clear.

"She needs the courage to weave as she must. No matter the pain, no matter the cost." His tone was ferocious.

The eyes, the tone, the intensity... it all seemed so familiar, but how? Her tired brain struggled to make the connections. Then he turned away and the moment was gone.

"Time to go!" he declared and leapt to his feet, unexpectedly sprightly. "Safe travels to Ostrin!"

"We're not going to Ostrin, we're heading to Groush," explained Kate, then she immediately reddened when she realised she had given away their plans to a complete stranger. In a hostile land. Her hand flew to her mouth. "Ohh!"

The old man cackled again. "No need to go to Groush. What you seek you will not find. The answers are at Ostrin, leave other paths behind."

Asher peered at the scraggly man now looming above them. Slowly she stood up and looked him up and down, trying to see beyond the dirt and rags.

Even with age he was still tall, taller than her. His lean face and proud shoulders were now so clearly familiar she was annoyed she had not seen it earlier. His appearance was unexpected, but not surprising.

"*You* are the Mountain Man of Groush. The Sorcerer who trained Darven."

He nodded sombrely. "Indeed, that sin is mine."

"And you are also Brawn, brother of the Weaver."

Behind her Kate and Levi sucked in surprised breaths. The old man shook his head.

"That man is gone."

Asher took two small steps and closed the gap between them. Gently she took his filthy, weathered hands in hers. His grey eyes, so like her own, filled with tears. She wondered when he had last felt the compassion of human touch.

"I played his song. Brawn lives within you. When you are ready, come home. All will be forgiven."

He shook his head, tears rolling down his face. "You cannot offer that. It is not yours to give."

Asher gave a small smile. She responded without conscious thought. "I am the Weaver."

The words whispered on the wind. They stood there together for a long moment, hands clasped, sharing energy and peace. Finally the old man smiled, his face calm and his eyes less pained.

"No you are not young Crafter. Not yet."

He pulled away, fussing around as he gathered bits and pieces that had fallen from his person. When satisfied he had all his treasures he turned to face her.

"I cannot right the wrongs that I have done. Great damage has been done and I played a part. But I can do this one thing for my sister. She who was raised beside me and raised my child as her own."

He held out a vial to Kate, who obediently jumped up and took it.

"What do I do with this?" she asked tentatively.

"I gave away her secret and now we'll have to pay, A Sorcerer-King without a crown, the Threads in disarray. Thistlewort will knot the thread, a single sip will lay her dead. The only hope to is yours to keep. Three careful drops from death to sleep."

Kate twisted the vial in her hand curiously as Brawn stared at her, as though seeing her for the first time. His face was unreadable. When he finally spoke his voice was almost kind.

"There's a long dark night coming for you little Phoenix. May you have the courage to survive it and rise again."

"What does- " Kate began, but the Mountain Man had finished with her and spun back to Asher for a final time.

"The answers are at Ostrin, tread with careful feet. All is not as it appears, haste will bring defeat."

The smoke billowed and the three friends bent over and coughed as they wiped stinging tears from their eyes. When they raised their heads he was gone, and so were the sausages.

Chapter Fourteen

Asanya

"I will accept any form of apology or acknowledgement of my general rightness, any time you are ready."

"Your what now?" asked Kate, trying to match her stride to that of the strutting Levi.

Which wasn't easy considering how heavy her pack was and how long Levi's legs were. He, meanwhile, was so caught up in his 'general rightness' that he had not noticed she was struggling with the pace.

On her other side Asher strode along quietly, lost in her thoughts.

The road was smooth and well tarred. Along its edges wildflowers danced in the breeze, proudly displaying a multitude of colours, shapes and scents. The fields of yellow and purple decreased in size as they walked further away from farmland and closer to the town. In the near distance the mountains rose relentlessly skyway, confident in their immortality.

"Oh you know, I say something and I am generally right." Levi puffed out his chest. "Like, yesterday, when I said let's continue on to Ostrin and sort out this mess with Hesta and *other people* thought we should go to Groush."

"Yes Levi, you were absolutely right." Asher apologised mildly, a smile dancing around her eyes. "You and the squalid old mad man from the Mountains think alike."

Levi frowned. "Hmmmm. That doesn't sound as good as I thought it would."

Asher didn't try to hide her smirk. They trudged along the empty road in silence for a few minutes more.

"Oh the sausages," moaned Levi.

The girls laughed. When they had discovered the theft last night he had been outraged, and though he had eaten well on cold ham and egg sandwiches this morning the lost sausages were clearly still bothering him.

"I think he needed them more than us Levi," responded Kate.

"Yes, I know," he conceded, "I don't begrudge him the food. I hope he's going to be okay."

"Me too," added Ash. The cool air on her face was invigorating as she walked. The exercise combined with the beauty of the colourful fields eased the anxiety which had been a constant companion for days.

The experience with Brawn's song was not something she had ever felt before. There had been other moments in her life when music seemed to form around her. The rise and fall of each note tripping effortlessly from her fingers. When that happened she was able to create her best compositions, but never before had she felt and understood the connection between the song and its owner.

In the early morning light the previous night's happenings seemed like a dream. Only the vial and the little blue whistle were concrete reminders that the Mountain Man had indeed been with them by the fire.

After he had vanished the three of them had sat up for a while longer, talking through everything that had been said and done. They had each taken turns twisting the vial and peering at the liquid within it, trying to make sense of the Mountain Man's rhyme. Finally they had dampened down the fire, tucked their new gifts carefully away, and rolled into their sleeping bags.

Levi had fallen asleep immediately, judging from the snoring wafting from his tent. Kate and Asher had talked a little longer, wondering what the next day would bring, but soon they too were asleep.

Asher was certain they would sleep deeply after the physically and emotionally demanding journey, but she had been awakened during the night by Kate thrashing in her sleeping bag, trapped in nightmarish dreams.

Gently she had laid a hand on her friend's shoulder and whispered that she was safe and just having a dream. That seemed to help Kate settle, but she had been quiet and withdrawn in the first few minutes of the morning.

Now, after a light breakfast and carefully packing down the camp, they were on the road to Mat'drin, hoping to find Joseph or another form of transportation to Ostrin.

Their solitary trudging was interrupted shortly before they reached the town.

Asher had been mindlessly staring over the fields as they walked, not really focusing on anything in particular as her thoughts raced over everything that had happened yesterday. So she wasn't sure how long the figure had been peering at them from behind a giant hay shed before she truly noticed it.

"Don't make it obvious," she muttered from the side of her mouth, "but I think we are being watched."

Immediately Kate and Levi stopped walking and spun around, peering in all directions.

"Seriously?" huffed Asher. "What part of 'don't make it obvious' did you not understand?"

"I can't see anyone," said Levi. "Where did you see them?"

"Behind the barn."

"Which barn?"

Asher resisted the urge to point.

"At 2 o'clock," she muttered.

"Where is 2 o'clock?" asked Kate, looking at the collection of buildings scattering the countryside.

"What do you mean, where is 2 o'clock? Two points after 12."

"But where are you marking from? Where is 12 o'clock? Is it where we are standing?"

"No that doesn't work," disagreed Levi, "because then we would be at the top of the clock and everything would be either behind us, or in front of us, and they would be diagonally opposite depending which way we were facing."

Asher sighed impatiently. This was becoming ridiculous.

"Mat'drin is 12 o'clock," she said curtly, "and we are the middle of the clockface. 3 o'clock is directly to our right. 6 o'clock is behind us."

"Got it," said Levi. "Which means you are talking about that big shed over there."

He pointed directly at the barn.

"Levi!" huffed Ash.

"Sorry," replied Levi. "So you saw some-one there. It's probably some farmer's kid who has been told to stay away from Crafters and strangers."

"Whoever it is, I don't think they are a danger to us," said Kate, "the hostile people have been rather forthcoming. This person is deliberately hiding from us."

"Maybe it's Brawn?" suggested Levi. "Stalking us for more sausages?"

"I think we should check it out," said Asher, surprising all of them, herself included.

Levi's brows shot up.

"Really? Why? Have you already forgotten the experience at Varossa?"

Asher shook her head. "No, of course not. But this is different. Kate is right. This is not some-one threatening us. I can't explain it, it just feels like we should investigate."

Levi shrugged in concession.

"Okay then. Get your harmonica ready though. Let's not be totally unprepared."

Harmonica in hand, Asher led her friends through the fields. The ground underfoot was softer than she was expecting, and they had to tread carefully in the mud, crushing grass and flowers beneath their feet.

The barn was built from a sturdy combination of wood and steel, anchored in the landscape. As they approached the large scale of the building became more apparent; it was easily the height of a three-storey building. Inside it was filled with enormous bales of hay and large barrels and crates.

"Hello?" called Asher as they walked through the open barn doors. "Anyone here?"

There was no response. Though well kept and clearly in regular use, it seemed to be currently unoccupied. Levi poked around the largest bales and came back to Asher and Kate, shrugging his shoulders.

"It seems empty."

"Maybe the figure you saw was just a trick of the morning light," said Kate.

Asher shook her head. There was energy here. Strong energy. The globe against her skin was pulsing and murmuring, and though Asher could not discern its message it was clear that it was agitated.

She closed her eyes and tried to feel where the energy was coming from. A moment later she had her answer. She opened her eyes and put a finger over her lips, warning Kate and Levi to be quiet. Then she signalled that she was going to walk towards the barrels, but that they should head towards the doors, talking as though they were leaving. They nodded in response.

"I guess we'll leave then," said Levi loudly, "seeing as there is nobody here."

He started stomping noisily towards the entrance. Kate rolled her eyes at his theatrics, but fell into step beside him.

As the other two talked and stomped their way slowly around the barn, Asher slipped deeper into the large space, weaving her way soundlessly towards the barrels and the storeroom that lay beyond them. The energy vibration became more pronounced the closer she came to the small storeroom door. She paused for a moment, breathing quietly as her body tingled with adrenaline. Her focus sharpened as her mind raced through all the potential possibilities.

Despite what she had said earlier, she could not be sure that the hidden person was not dangerous. It might be incredibly foolhardy to persist, particularly when the person clearly did not want to be found. Asher considered turning and leaving, until the muffled sound of crying drew her attention.

Quietly she opened the door to the storeroom and stepped into the poorly lit space. No light or lamps illuminated the room, but a small window devoid of blinds or curtains allowed enough natural light in so that Asher could see the boxes and cupboards filling the room.

At first glance there was no-one to be seen, and now that the crying had ceased it would be easy to believe the place was empty, but strong pulsing energy drew Asher towards a tower of crates stacked neatly on the right side of the room. A sharp intake of breath confirmed that she was heading in the right direction. Her presence had clearly been noted.

With every step the tingling running up Asher's spine increased, until her whole body was buzzing. She paused before the crates, breathing shallowly, trying to convince her suddenly leaden body to keep moving.

After a few seconds of frozen forever, Asher lurched forward and pulled off the highest most crate and peered straight into the face of the shocked thing hiding there. Asher's startled scream mingled with the weak roar of the small creature. She stumbled backwards, dropping the crate which landed on the stone floor with a loud crash.

Fast, heavy footsteps announced the arrival of Levi and Kate.

"Ash! Are you alright?" demanded Levi, screeching to a halt beside her. "What's happened?"

Asher pointed in the direction of the crates as she sucked in a few deep breaths. Her friends automatically turned their heads that way.

"What on earth is that?" murmured Levi as Kate yelped in surprise.

Now that the initial shock had eased, Asher's equilibrium, and curiosity, were starting to return. Carefully she edged closer, trying to identify the creature before them.

It seemed small, though it was hard to really understand its true size as it cowered behind the remaining crates. Its head was turned away from them, hidden beneath large red and gold feathered wings that grew from its tawny coloured lion's body. A long lion's tail was curled around its body. Its fur was filthy and matted from the mud outside, and there were dark stains around the hind legs that looked like dried blood.

Beneath the quivering wings Ash could hear muffled sobs of fear and pain.

"It's okay," she said softly, "We're not going to hurt you. We will help you if we can."

There was no response.

"It's okay," repeated Ash, deliberately staying very still. "We will not hurt you. We have food and water if you need some."

Nobody moved for a few long minutes, and Ash was wondering if she should say something further, when there was a slight rustle, and one of the wings pulled back ever so slightly. A large golden eye peered through the feathers.

Without taking her own eyes off the creature, Ash indicated to Kate, who rummaged around in her pack, before carefully stepping forward with a bottle of water and three cupcakes and two sandwiches. She placed them on the crates and then hastily returned to her place next to Levi.

The small lion raised its head from beneath its wings and eyed the food hesitantly. Its wary gaze flicked between the cakes and Ash. Sensing the creature's wariness Ash took a few steps backwards.

As soon as she was further away, the hungry lion inched forward and grabbed a cake in its jaws, barely chewing and swallowing before gobbling the next one and the next.

"A winged lion," breathed Kate in awe.

"It's a pegalion!" said Levi excitedly. "Fly my pretties, fly!"

Kate stared at him. "Seriously? More Wizard of Oz?"

"It's a fitting reference. Except it's a winged lion instead of a monkey, and we are travelling with the witch."

"Does that make you the scarecrow? The one without a brain?" teased Kate.

"Do we have anything to pour the water into?" Asher quietly asked her friends, ignoring their nonsense. "It won't be able to open the bottle with its paws."

"How about that?" said Levi, pointing at a shovel hanging with other tools on the wall. "The metal head will hold some water."

Ash nodded. "Yes, I think that will do."

Levi strode over and grabbed the shovel off its peg. The winged lion stumbled backwards in fear but did not cower beneath its wings. Instead it mewed its little roar and bared its teeth.

"Levi, stop," commanded Asher softly. "I think the lion thinks you are going to attack it."

He stopped.

"Lay the shovel down here. I'll pour the water onto the head and then we should all back away. Okay?"

The other two nodded. Moving slowly, Asher retrieved the water bottle and filled the metal head of the shovel with as much water as it could hold. Then the three humans moved a few metres away and waited.

After a few minutes the small lion crept out from behind the crates, eyeing them nervously. Wary step by wary step the creature moved closer to the water, clearly favouring one hind leg over the other. It seemed very reluctant to put any weight on its right leg, using its wings to hop along instead of walking.

"I think there is a gash along that thigh," whispered Kate. "I have a small first aid kit. If it lets me, I could clean and bandage the cut. I've tended to worse on the farm."

The lion crouched beside the shovel and lapped eagerly at the water. The humans stood as still as they could, trying to radiate non-threatening energy. Once it had drunk its fill the lion limped back from the shovel and raised its head.

Large, intelligent brown eyes moved slowly from Kate to Levi, coming to rest on Asher. The globe on Asher's chest burbled and buzzed. She crouched down to the floor, maintaining eye contact the whole time.

"My name is Asher," she said quietly. "Can you understand me?"

The pegalion nodded its head.

"Do you need our help?"

The small creature hesitated, then nodded again. It bent a wing to indicate the bash along its hind leg, covered in dried blood.

'Hurt,' it whispered in her mind.

"Did you just hear that?" asked Levi, "I thought I heard it speak, but in my mind."

"I heard it too," murmured Kate. "Now shush."

Asher's focus was entirely on the hurt creature before her.

"My friend Kate can help you, if you let her."

The pegalion flicked its gaze between Asher and Kate, working out how much it could trust them. Then it nodded slowly.

Kate pulled the first aid kit from her pack and walked slowly toward the lion. Once she had crouched beside it, she opened the kit and showed the contents to the creature, quietly explaining what she was going to do. The little pegalion nodded as she spoke.

Carefully Kate washed away the blood from the wound with the water from the water bottle, then rinsed it with sterile saline from the first aid kit. Once she had cleaned the gash and slathered it with antiseptic cream, she pulled it back together and fastened it with steri-strips, which she covered with wide sticking plasters, before wrapping the whole area in a bandage.

During the entire procedure the lion jerked a few times but did not cry out or pull away.

"That will stop any further bleeding and help with the healing, but you really need to rest the leg," said Kate gently.

'I need to get home,' it whimpered sadly.

"Perhaps we can take you," said Asher, "where do you need to go?"

'Far away from Andera, across the darkness to Elliptica.'

The humans shared surprised looks.

"You have travelled across the Void?" asked Asher. "By yourself? Why?"

'To see Andera. Perhaps to meet the Weaver. When she comes I am not allowed to meet with her, they say I am too young. I'm not allowed to do anything or go anywhere because they say I am too young. So I thought I would prove them all wrong. But I have injured myself now, which means I am not strong enough to cross the darkness. My mother will be very angry with me.' Its voice was sorrowful.

"How did you open a portal?" asked Ash.

The pegalion tucked its head on its front paws and covered its head beneath its wing, muffling its response.

"I'm sorry, I couldn't hear that," said Ash.

The wing lifted slightly.

'I took something of my mother's, something she had told me not to touch. And I wished to be in Andera. I simply focused on the Weaver's shining globe. The portal opened and I flew-ran through. But I must have done something wrong, for I have not found the Weaver, and now I'm stuck here. I'm not powerful enough to make it work again. I've tried and I've tried but the portal won't open. And even if I can open it, now my leg is injured my wings are not strong enough on their own. My whole body must work as one, or I'll get too tired and get trapped in the darkness.'

A large tear plopped onto the ground near the creature's front paws.

Asher screwed up her nose as she considered what to do. As eager as she was to get to Ostrin and retrieve her sister, she could not simply leave this pegalion child here by itself, injured and unable to return home. Especially as the little lion had come to Andera looking for the Weaver and had affixed her destination to the globe. A bubble of guilt burbled in Asher's chest.

Then she remembered the mind conversation with Hesta when she herself had still been on Earth.

"Could you call for your mother? Perhaps we can open the portal this end and she can travel through to collect you."

The little lion did not respond for a minute, then a soft sigh escaped from under the wings.

'She's going to be rather cross,' it said.

"Yes, she may be. But then she will take you home. Surely that is better than being alone here."

The child lifted a wing to look at Asher as it considered that. *'Yes, I suppose so,'* it conceded.

"Then let us see if we can open the portal and you can call for help. Where is your item of power?"

The lion instinctively shrunk back beneath its paws and wings, hiding whatever it had stolen from its mother. Large eyes peered out.

'I'm not allowed to show anybody. That's even worse than crossing the darkness by myself.'

"That's okay, no problem." said Asher, thinking fast. "I'm going to close my eyes and lean in close to you, so I won't see your charm. Then you can touch your charm to this bangle, and the portal will open, we hope. You do not have to focus your energy on opening the portal, just on sending a call to your mother. Does that make sense?"

The pegalion nodded.

"Okay then, let's give this a go, think of home," said Asher encouragingly to the little lion, pulling off the bangle.

"Here goes nothing," she muttered to herself.

With her eyes closed, Asher held out the bangle. A few seconds later she felt a jolt of powerful energy rush through her hand and up her arm, as the lion's item of power made contact with hers. Then the little creature let out a mewing roar as it sent its thoughts tumbling across the galaxies.

Silence engulfed them for two anxious minutes, and then that little mew was answered by an enormous roar, the force of which shook the barn and sent Asher, Levi and Kate stumbling backwards to the ground.

Asher looked up in time to see a giant tawny lioness leap through a shimmering portal, massive red wings beating powerfully.

She roared again, tearing apart the air around them. The small pegalion mewed in response, its little head hung low in contrition. Then the lioness bent low to her child and licked its head, before spreading a wing to capture the little one and pull it close. The small lion mewed happily within that warm embrace.

Tentatively the humans stood up from where they had landed on the hard floor. Without conscious thought they huddled together, acutely aware of the huge lion, at least three times the size of a regular Earth lion, staring at them with fierce, unfriendly eyes.

Asher's heart was beating so fast she felt like she couldn't quite breathe. Carefully she took a few deep breaths and willed her body to calm down. The lioness's gaze burned into her, but she didn't dare look away. She was half afraid that if she dropped her gaze for even a millisecond, the furious mother would pounce on her and rip her to shreds.

'Which of you injured my baby?' growled the lion softly, menace in every word she sent thundering around their minds.

Asher and her friends rapidly shook their heads.

"None of us," said Levi quickly. "It was already injured when we arrived."

The lioness narrowed her eyes at him, but he did not step back. Asher marvelled at his courage.

The small pegalion mewed to its mother earnestly, and then carefully shifted to show her the now bandaged leg. The lioness turned her unrelenting stare to Kate, who gulped nervously.

'Asanya tells me you cleaned and bandaged the wound.'

There was less menace, but the thoughts were still intense. Asher wondered if her friends' heads were throbbing as much as hers. Kate nodded jerkily at the lioness, her face pale.

'My thanks to you.'

Kate wilted with relief as the lioness turned her attention to Asher.

'And who are you?'

"Asher," she whispered huskily.

'Who?' roared the lion.

Asher cleared her throat. "Asher," she said more clearly, though still a little hoarsely.

'You are the Crafter who opened the portal for Asanya.'

"Yes."

The large lion stared at her for a long moment, and Asher had the distinct feeling she was trying to read Asher's mind. On instinct she clouded her thoughts.

'How did you open the portal? That is a difficult thing to do for one so young and inexperienced.'

Asher held out the bracelet, thankful that her arm only trembled slightly. The lion leant forward and sniffed at the piece of jewellery.

'A mighty piece indeed," she said. *"Where did you find it?'*

The implication that she had either found or perhaps stolen the bangle stung at Asher, and she straightened her back and raised her chin.

"I did not *find* it, it is a family heirloom. It was a gift from my mother."

'And your mother's name?'

Asher hesitated too long. The lion bared her large sharp teeth.

"Ginarwen," she blurted quickly. "Ginarwen el Hestawen."

'The Anderan Weaver's daughter,' said the pegalion without surprise.

Asher nodded jerkily, worried she had given too much away.

'I thank you Asher el Ginarwen for opening the portal. The debt is now mine to repay. As for you,' her intense golden gaze returned to Kate, *'a gift of thanks. A healing for a healing.'*

Kate frowned in confusion as the pegalion shook her wings, shaking free one large, gleaming red feather that floated softly to the ground at Kate's feet.

Then in a blur of powerful wings and legs, and with a final roar of perhaps farewell, the mighty lioness and her cub disappeared through the portal and across the Void, leaving the three awe-struck humans staring after them in silence.

Chapter Fifteen

The stones of Mat'drin

Asher, Kate and Levi trudged along the road to Mat'drin, each lost in their own thoughts. Their encounter with the pegalions was already starting to feel like a confused dream, and every now and then one of them would say 'were there really two winged lions back there?' and the others would nod and respond 'aha'.

Kate held the feather in her hands for a long while, running her fingers along its length, before carefully tucking it into her pack.

Forty-five minutes later the town rose up before them. The buildings did not organically transition from the fields as both Varossa and Harthe did. Mat'drin was a walled town, designed to be fortified and protected. Massive stone walls shielded the buildings within, and the only way to enter was via equally large iron gates that were currently open to travellers.

Mat'drin was the entrance to both the Mountain pass and the road to Ostrin. It was the last line of defence before the royal city. The seriousness of the town was not designed to fill a heart with joy or excitement. Its dark grey buildings and sombre street frontages were a stark contrast to the beauty of Varossa. Yet for all its beauty Varossa had not been a pleasant experience. Nervously they approached the enormous gates, wondering what welcome they would encounter within.

At the entrance two guards lounged against the stone pillars, one sipping from a steaming mug of tea, the other leafing through a pile of papers. Neither seemed to be armed, or particularly interesting in guarding.

Nonchalantly they eyed the approaching trio, looking Kate and Levi up and down and barely glancing at Asher.

"Good morning," offered Levi, surprisingly subdued. Even his spirits were dampened under the weight of the cold, grey stone. Or perhaps it was the residual effect of the encounter with the pegalions. Whatever the reason, he seemed to realise that now was not the time or place for frivolous chatter.

"Morning," replied the tea drinking guard. "State your business."

Good question, thought Ash, *rescue a missing Terran and countless stolen Crafters, overthrow a Sorcerer, restore the reputation of the Weaver and travel across the Void to Earth. Hmmm...*

"Visiting our aunt," Kate blurted. "It is her 70th birthday this coming week, and we are celebrating with her. These are my cousins."

Asher tensed, waiting for the barrage of questions she was sure would follow. *Their names, the address of the old aunt, how long were they staying, where had they come from...* Nothing.

The guard nodded and jerked his head, indicating they should continue on through the gates.

With small smiles of gratitude they hurried past the men, who had already lost interest in them.

"Sheesh!" exhaled Levi when they were out of earshot, "that was tense. Well done Kate. Now what? Where do we go from here?"

They peered around them. Four storey high stone buildings towered above them on each side, all seemingly identical in design. Their height blocked a large amount of the morning sun, so the wide stone cobbled street was shadowed and cold.

Some of the windows had been thrown open for the fresh morning air, and from inside one building they could hear singing. Otherwise everything was still and the streets were empty.

"I imagine Joseph will have spent the night at an inn or hotel. Annoyingly Mat'drin doesn't seem to embrace street signs," murmured Levi.

"Follow me," declared Kate, striding confidently along the street. Further ahead a junction offered them three options. With barely a glance Kate chose the one that veered right.

Deep into the town they walked, Kate confidently choosing their direction.

Around them the town was waking up, more windows were flung open, voices and chatter wafted onto the streets. Occasionally a door swung wide and a person would emerge, acknowledging them with a sharp nod. People began to join them as they walked, keeping a careful distance, but clearly walking in the same direction. Soon enough they walked into a large square bustling with traders, stalls, sounds and smells. Mostly fresh baked goods.

"Whoa!" breathed Asher and Levi.

Kate beamed with pride, as though she had built the square herself. "Da-da!" she flung her arms wide.

"How on earth did you know?" asked Levi.

"I followed the widest road each time, I figured they were designed for carts to bring items into the town. If we followed the way of the carts we would find the place where the horses were fed and rested, and hence, the inns!"

"Well that is clever indeed," said Levi with an admiring smile.

"This is nothing like I was expecting. In my head Mat'drin was a small town," said Asher wonderingly. "This is like an old city in Europe."

"Exactly!" replied Kate. "That's what I thought when we first walked in. It's a walled medieval city. The first few layers are designed to intimidate intruders, but deep inside is the beating heart."

They looked around, relishing the sights and sounds of the heart of the old city.

"What next?" asked Asher, turning to Kate. She hadn't been around this many people since her Crafting had been unlocked and the intensity of the energy around her was making her feel a little light-headed. Thank goodness Kate was thinking clearly.

"I think we should find Joseph as quickly as we can. So he doesn't leave the city without us."

"Then pastries and hot chocolate?" Levi wriggled his eyebrows hopefully.

The girls laughed.

"Yes Levi, then pastries and hot chocolate. Now, this way I think."

Kate led them around the edge of the square, now teeming with people. Nobody paid them any attention apart from two small children who were captivated by the rolled up tents swinging from their packs and swatted at them as they strode past.

Kate led them to a courtyard clearly set up for horses. A large trough ran the length of the middle, filled with fresh water. Iron rings designated spaces for horses to be tied up, and beyond the courtyard stables and sheds housed the animals and carts.

"Always follow your nose," declared Kate, tapping her own with her pointer finger.

They wandered along the stables and sheds. Levi called out with excitement when they spotted Joseph's wine cart tucked inside a stall.

"He's still here!" he shouted, grinning madly.

They all smiled with relief, both at finding Joseph's cart and the freedom they felt after hoisting their packs under the oh so familiar wooden seats and stretching their backs.

"But how do we know where he is?" asked Levi. "If we head into the square he might leave with our packs. If we stay here and wait we could be here for hours. And miss out on pastries." His face was glum.

Asher climbed onto the cart. "I'll stay. You go explore."

Her friends frowned up at her.

"Are you sure?" asked Kate, uncertainty clear on her face.

"Absolutely. I think I need to clear my head. Here, you'll need this." She threw the bag of coins to Levi who deftly caught it with his left hand. "Be careful, okay?"

Kate and Levi nodded, then turned and headed quickly back in the direction they had just come. With a long exhale Asher lay down on the bench and focused on settling her swirling thoughts.

The feeling of Brawn's song still echoed within her. She had created music her whole life, sometimes simply feeling the music that wanted to be written. But this had been completely different. She had not been the creator, merely the instrument it had been waiting for. Other musicians may have come and gone, and the song would have remained silent. It had wanted only her.

Asher lay on the hard wood with her eyes closed and tuned in to the energy around her.

At first she could only feel the horses stabled nearby, snorting and munching. There were five of them in total and their energy was vibrant and very alive. Carefully she pushed her awareness further afield, becoming aware of human energy vibrating behind the heavy stone walls. And then unexpectedly she felt the energy of the stones themselves.

Centuries of human experiences and emotions were captured within the heavy fabric of the buildings. For millennia before that the stone had lain in the ground, part of the great energy of the planet. All of this was still within into the very fabric of the rock, the energy deep and complex.

Intrigued, Asher pushed deeper into the layers of the stones, wondering if she could separate any particular layer from another. Carefully she wove her way through the energy, pushing deeper and deeper. Then without warning she was trapped.

Her tiny self was suddenly overwhelmed by the dark, the depth, the heaviness.

Asher struggled to open her eyes, to take a deep breath. It felt like her chest was being crushed, her arms and legs pinned in place. Weakly she twisted her body while trying to pull her energy free from the stone. The more she struggled, the heavier the stones became, the more constricted she became.

She was going to be caught here forever, her life-force trapped in stone. Panic threatened to overwhelm her.

A sudden freezing splash of cold water over her face brought her mind and consciousness immediately back into her body. With a huge gasp Ash threw herself upright and opened her eyes. Standing before her was the quiet man who had driven them from E-Langren.

"Joseph!" she spluttered. "Thank you."

The wine merchant looked at her briefly then looked away, tucking the now empty bucket back under the seat and busying himself with tightening barrels on the cart.

"No idea what you mean. I meant to wash the benches, didn't see you there at all."

His meaning was clear. They would not discuss it further.

Asher nodded her understanding as she took deep restorative breaths and shook out her arms and legs. He might not want her thanks, but she was incredibly grateful. Joseph had saved more than her life just now.

"So our plans have changed," she said in a small voice, "may we continue on with you to Ostrin? With everything that's happening in the towns I understand if it's too much trouble-" she added in a rush.

"No problem," said Joseph, putting up his hand to halt her waterfall of words. And so it was agreed.

Asher murmured a small "thank you" then lay back on the seat. Her head pounded with an ache she was sure would accompany her for the rest of the day. The whole experience had reinforced that there was still so much she did not know about being a Crafter, about being the Weaver.

She realised how very small she really was.

Chapter Sixteen

The Queen and the Sorcerer

Levi and Kate returned from the marketplace chattering excitedly. Levi was carrying a paper bag full of something delicious smelling and Kate was wearing a new sweater.

Asher gritted her teeth against the head pain and sat up with what she hoped was a carefree grin.

"Jeepers Ash! What's wrong with your face? Your mouth is all twisted like you ate something sour, and your skin is a confusing combination of dull and flushed. And is your hair wet? Or super sweaty?"

"Thanks Levi," she answered, giving up the pretence of the smile, "don't waste your charm on me."

"Seriously Ash, you do look rather dreadful," added Kate.

"I just have a splitting headache."

"Oh well that's easy to fix," said Kate, jumping onto the cart and rummaging around in her pack. "Paracetamol or ibuprofen?"

She brandished the packets towards Ash with a flask. With relief Asher downed two tablets with a gulp of water. Thank the stars for the ever organised Kate.

Now that her head pain was taken care of, her sense of smell was coaxing her stomach back into action.

"What do you have in there Levi?"

"Donuts!" He passed the bag to her. "We've already had a heap. They are *delicious*. We couldn't bring you a hot chocolate, they don't seem to do take-away cups here. And I wasn't sure if we'd have time to return a proper mug to the woman."

"Shat's ohk'y," mumbled Asher, her mouth full of cinnamon and sugar yumminess. "Shoooow good!"

"Have you seen Joseph?" asked Kate.

Asher swallowed her last mouthful of donut wonderfulness.

"Yes, he's okay with us hitching a ride to Ostrin. He should be back shortly, he went to finalise some errands. I like your new sweater Kate. It's really pretty."

Kate beamed and gave an excited twirl. The sweater was a soft blue colour which perfectly complimented Kate's fair hair and blue eyes. The wool was incredibly fine, giving the v-neck sweater a beautiful shape and texture. Asher could feel the Crafter energy imbued in every stitch and loop.

"I couldn't resist. We were walking past all the stalls admiring the craftsmanship of the various objects and this sweater just called to me. The woman insisted I try it on and once it was on, well, that was it. It just felt like mine."

"It really suits you. Like it was crafted just for you."

Kate nodded brightly. "Yes, that's what the woman said. Every sweater knows its person and this one was crafted for me! I just love it!" She twirled again.

Her pleasure was contagious, and Asher could feel the ache in her head begin to ease. Whether it was the result of the pain killers or the joy Kate was exuding, either way it felt good.

Footsteps clattering across the stone announced Joseph's return. After helping him heave out the cart and hitch up the horses the three friends once again climbed back onto the wooden benches and settled in for the final ride.

They exited the courtyard via a different route, winding through Mat'drin and finally leaving the walled city from a completely different gate than the one they had entered through. Behind them the Mountains indifferently witnessed their departure.

The scenery varied greatly from the open fields they had travelled through yesterday. Houses and buildings lined the road now. Clearly defined orchards and well laid vegetable gardens were being tended by men and women wearing large hats to protect them from the midday sun.

"The equivalent of urban sprawl," said Levi, "I guess there is only so much room in a centuries old walled city. You have to expand somewhere."

"Joseph, how long until we reach Ostrin?" called Kate over the rumble of the wheels.

"Not long, about an hour. These villages are all part of the Castle lands. The majority of these people work for the Queen, either on the land or in the castle itself."

An hour! Bubbles of anticipation and trepidation gurgled in the pit of Asher's stomach. She had no idea what awaited them at Ostrin but hoped with all her heart that they would find Evie.

Each passing mile brought them closer to the castle. After a time they could see the towers rising out of the horizon, and then the shape of the large stone walls.

"Might be time for you lot to lie low," suggested Jospeh, "and do that thing you do. I assume you don't want to be announced."

So when the cart rattled across the bridge and through the enormous portcullis they were tucked quietly under the blankets and missed all the glory and grandeur of the imposing entrance to Ostrin.

The castle guards were more thorough in checking the cart than Rohill's rather inept attempt. But Asher's charm held firm and they were not discovered. Holding their breaths until the cart rolled away from the entrance the three of them exhaled a huge sigh of relief in unison.

Unable to see where they were going Asher imagined the path they were taking through the courtyard, down the road around the side, left, then right, until her nose informed her that they had neared the stables.

With a lurch the cart pulled to a stop. Joseph called a cheery hello to some-one in the yard, making it clear to Asher and her friends that there were others about.

As he fussed with the wine barrels and bottles stacked around them Joseph muttered quietly, "in ten minutes all will be clear, then I will show you the way into the castle."

True to his word, ten minutes later Joseph helped them climb down from the cart and haul their packs onto their backs. Kate grimaced as she adjusted the large pack on her small frame, but she didn't complain.

Now that they were free of the blankets they took the chance to look around. They were in a cobbled courtyard with stables lining two sides and cart storage along the other two sides. The number of other carts and horses already stabled and resting gave the impression of a busy yard full of merchants and traders. Roads led off into the castle precinct. Looming over them was one of four towers, the East Tower as Joseph explained. This housed supplies and where he would be depositing the last of his many wine barrels and bottles. He would share a meal with the other merchants in the common dining hall then spend the night in Ostrin's village.

The Queen and her Court were in the main building that ran between the South and West Towers. The North Tower was used for armoury and was off-limits to visitors. The Towers were all connected by huge walls that housed apartments and rooms, which was how they would move through the castle.

"If you're looking for her Majesty head to the main building. If it is some-one else you seek, then I cannot advise you further, though there are rumours of dungeons deep below the castle itself."

Asher shivered, an image of Evie shackled in a cold and frightening cell tormenting her mind.

"It might be best to hide those packs away and don the garb of servants. They move with ease throughout the castle. There are plenty of uniforms in the stores."

"Thank you Joseph," she said, every word bursting with gratitude. They might never have made it this far without him.

He looked her calmly in the eye, his expression kind but his thoughts a mystery to her.

"Be careful young Crafter. I don't know why you need to be here or what you need to do, but these are dangerous times for one such as you."

"Thank you," she whispered, "I will not forget your kindness. If I can ever repay it..."

He brushed off her thanks. "Follow me into the store-room and I'll tell you where to go from there. The rest is up to you."

Quietly they followed behind as he led them through a heavy oak door at the base of the tower. They stepped into a huge storage room filled with crates and barrels of all shapes and sizes. A door at the back led to a cool room full of cheeses and milk. The thick stones walls kept the room cool, and Crafter energy murmured from the glass chests that contained solid blocks of ice. Asher kept her consciousness far from the stones.

Wooden stairs to the right of the room led upstairs, where the linens were kept. That was where Joseph suggested they store their packs and change their clothes. From there they could exit along a corridor that housed the servants' quarters and move through to the main castle.

Voices outside in the courtyard cut short his explanation and Levi, Kate and Asher dashed up the stairs. At the top Asher hesitated, turning around to say a final goodbye, but the merchant was gone.

The room she walked into was like a department store. Huge shelving ran the length of the large space laden with sumptuous quilts and sheets and towels and pillows neatly piled in categories. At the other end more shelving displayed table clothes and napkins in an assortment of colours. Bunches of dried herbs hung around the shelves, keeping everything fresh and sweet smelling.

Hanging racks held every manner of uniform the royal house could need, from guards to scullery maids and every job in between.

"More costumes!" declared Kate happily, "these are like a Victorian era film."

"Which ones do we choose?" asked Ash, bewildered by the range.

Kate muttered to herself as she browsed through the clothes, finally settling on an outfit for Levi and two for her and Ash.

"These should do the trick. A footman and two lady's maids."

"How on earth do you know this stuff?" asked Levi.

Kate's cheeks reddened and her neck flushed. "I love a period drama," she declared defiantly, "I'm not ashamed."

Asher grinned and pulled the white and grey dress over her jeans and t-shirt.

Kate hissed in horror. "Aren't you going to change properly?"

"Nope." Asher twisted experimentally, tugging at her layers. "A bit bulky, but comfortable enough."

Asher wriggled her brows at Kate's beautiful blue sweater. "If you change completely you'll have to leave that in your pack. What if it gets lost?"

After a long minute of sighing and muttering Kate threw up her hands. "Fine!" She yanked her own white and grey maid's dress over her sweater and jeans.

Levi emerged sheepishly from a small ante-chamber wearing black trousers with his ankles sticking out, and a long sleeved white shirt that didn't reach his wrists. Asher burst out laughing.

"For goodness sake!" Kate returned to the rack and rummaged around until she found a taller size. "Here, try this."

When they were finally dressed to Kate's satisfaction they found a place to pile the packs. Asher pulled out her harmonica and tucked it into the deep pocket of the skirt and then they headed to the door that would take them into the castle corridors.

With her hand on the knob of the closed door Ash hesitated.

"I'm not particularly good at big speeches." Kate and Levi grinned. Ash rolled her eyes. "Anyway, I just want to say thank you. For coming with me. You know, to Andera and to Ostrin to rescue Evie. It means a lot."

Her friends crushed her in a bear hug until she squealed and pushed them away, all of them laughing.

"Seriously," her tone immediately sobered them, "I have no idea what happens next. I don't even know if we'll get back to this room to collect our packs. As soon as we find Evie I'm going to open a portal and take us home."

Unconsciously she toyed with the heavy bracelet hidden under her sleeve. The other two nodded.

"Alright," said Asher resolutely, mustering her courage, "let's do this."

They followed the corridor along the length of the huge castle wall, marvelling at the many rooms that opened off it. Bedrooms for the servants lined each side, with bathrooms interspersed. They encountered quite a few people dressed as they were, who nodded greetings as they wandered past. Nobody challenged them or even spoke to them, though a couple of young girls gawked at Kate's cart messed hair and giggled. As usual they paid no attention to Asher. Occasionally a trolley was pushed past them, laden with supplies from the stores.

At the South Tower they walked into a huge kitchen that was teeming with staff. Multiple cooks and serving staff dashed from bench to bench, all working together in an unspoken rhythm. Platters of food were being laid out for the waiting staff to whisk away.

Levi's stomach grumbled mightily and Kate threw him a look.

"Sorry," he muttered, "It just smells so good! And we haven't had lunch."

"You there!" An imperious voice cut through the din. "Young man!"

They turned reluctantly towards the voice. A large man with red cheeks and a white chef's hat perched precariously on his head was pointing at Levi. A huge apron wrapped over his body was stained and splattered with the sauces of the many dishes the kitchen was creating.

"Take this meat to the Dining Hall. And make haste! The Queen is entertaining. The Weaver is in attendance!"

An excited flurry of activity accompanied this announcement.

Hesta is here! Ash's fingers tingled and her face flushed.

"You girl!" Now it was Kate's turn as the bossy finger turned her way. "Take this wine and wait upon the Weaver. Do not speak to her, do not leave her side. Respond to any requests. Do you understand?"

"Yes sir," responded Kate in a small, compliant voice, taking the jug that was thrust into her hands.

"You!" Asher thought she had been spotted, but another maid stepped forward. "Take this plate upstairs to the Gold Room. Now!"

"What now?" hissed Levi as he walked past Ash, laden with a platter of hot meat.

"You two follow orders and find Hesta. I'm going to slip off and find Evie. I'll bring her to the Dining Hall and Hesta can help send us all home."

Her friends nodded quickly, then disappeared with the tide of servants heading from the kitchen.

Ash followed at a slower pace, deliberately falling further and further behind. At the end of the corridor the group moved through an unobtrusive servant's entrance into an extravagant Dining Hall.

Huge chandeliers hung from massive wooden beams, gleaming in the bright sun that poured through coloured windowpanes. The largest table Ash had ever seen was centred in the room and could easily seat one hundred guests. Today it was laid only for four.

Along the walls massive mahogany sideboards groaned under the weight of candelabras and ornaments. The walls were layered with tapestries and landscape paintings of the fields and villages around Ostrin.

The servants bustled around, laying food neatly onto a serving table and giving the spotless glassware a last minute polish.

Asher backed quietly out of the room, leaving Kate and Levi in the gaggle, and back-tracked to the small door just off the corridor before the dining room. To the left of the door a plain, narrow, windowless staircase gave her the option of up or down.

Asher hesitated then decided to see what was beyond the door first. Carefully she pushed it open, its well-maintained hinges not making a sound. She swallowed the urge to gasp. *Wow.*

She was peering into a huge sitting room, filled with lush settees and lounges, sofas and armchairs, arranged artfully in social groups. In one corner a Grand Piano shone, its polish as brilliant as the day it was assembled. Large golden lamps with cream linen shades graced gleaming ebony tables. A plush woollen cream carpet covered the entire length of the wood floor. Panelling painted deep navy lined the room, and glass cabinets showed off priceless Crafter objects for guests to wander among and admire.

To the right a grand oak staircase led down to the lower floor. Clearly the royal inhabitants and their guests did not have to skulk unseen behind the walls like the servants.

A familiar head of auburn hair caught Asher's eye. Hesta was seated by the large fire on the other side of the room, quietly contemplating the flames. Her back was to Asher hiding at the servant's entrance. Penn stood silently by her side, his eyes roaming the room. Any moment now he would see her. With a large thump of her heart Ash jumped back out of sight and pulled the door closed.

It was a relief to see Hesta. Somehow she felt braver, more certain of success. Knowing the Weaver was close at hand gave her strength.

'Hesta,' impulsively she sent the thought, *'I am here.'*

'I am aware,' was the dry response. *'Did you enjoy your cart ride?'*

Asher felt her cheeks redden. Of course it was impossible to hide anything from the Weaver.

'Be very, very careful Asher. And stay cloaked.'

At the stairwell she chose to head down, hoping that she would find a way to the dungeons and to Evie. At the bottom of the stairs there was another heavy wood door. Slowly she pushed it open and stepped into a meeting room of sorts. Bookcases lined the walls and an oval board-room style table was surrounded by black chairs. To her left two oversized French doors were ajar, leading into a private study. She could just hear the wisps of a conversation, the speakers unseen.

"Now Magda, you must do what I say. We have discussed this enough. There is no time for more childish questions or disagreements."

The man's voice was smooth and pleasant, though firm. His tone was unyielding.

"If you say so Darven. If you really think this is the right thing…" the child-like voice trailed off, clearly hesitant and wanting to be reassured.

The man offered that assurance immediately. "Of course my Queen. This is best for all of us." He paused. "Particularly the Princess."

"Oh the Princess!" the joy in the Queen's voice was clear. "Well then of course Darven."

"Good". A rustle indicated he was standing up. "Time you greet our Weaver." He said something else under his breath and laughed, a chilling sound that made the hairs on Ash's neck prickle.

Asher stepped closer to hear better.

"Oh Darven, I'm not suuuure," wavered the Queen, her whiny voice cutting through his laugh. "Maybe you should-"

"I cannot. I have explained this at length to you. You must be the one. Listen here Magda," all pretence of subservience was gone. "We have discussed this enough. You know what to do."

What? What was she to do? Asher took another step closer to the doors, then another.

"Should I bring Evelyn to meet the Weaver?"

Asher's heart stopped.

Darven laughed again. "Oh yes. Send for Evelyn indeed. How will the Weaver react when she comes face to face with her stolen *grandchild*? She might want to take her home." His voice was sly.

"No!" shouted the Queen petulantly. "I'm keeping her. Hesta cannot have her! No!"

"And she will not Your Majesty," soothed Darven, "just do as I say and all will be well."

But the Queen was fretting now. "Where is she? Where have you put Evelyn?"

Darven sighed impatiently. "She is safe. She is in the Gold Room, resting."

The Gold Room! Where had she just heard that? Asher held her breath while she sifted through memories. Some-one else had mentioned... Cook!! He had sent the maid *upstairs* to the Gold Room.

Asher spun around, ready to leap back up the stairs, but in her haste she tripped over the carpet, or her own feet, or maybe even the long dress. Whatever the cause, within seconds she landed with a thump against the wall.

"Who's there!" called Darven immediately, his voice stern. "Show yourself at once."

Asher righted herself, breathing deeply to steady the crazy beating of her heart. Slowly she moved around the wall and stepped through the doors into the study, slouching her shoulders and directing her gaze towards the ground.

The room was richly decorated with heavy mahogany furniture and objects gleaming marble and gold, but Asher barely noticed the surroundings. Her attention was drawn immediately to the small blonde woman sitting regally by the fire, masses of hair piled high on her head, her cream skin glowing in the firelight. She was clothed in a shimmering deep blue dress that tucked in at her waist and was designed to billow around her when she stood. Her face was uncertain and confused, as though she was unsure of her own thoughts. Standing at her side a man dressed in gold and black towered over her.

So this was Darven. The man who had caused such chaos in her own life and was now ripping Andera apart.

From under her lashes Asher studied him.

He was no taller than her but gave the impression of a man of great height. His cold presence filled the space around him, dominating the child-like Queen. His face was very handsome beneath his golden hair, but there was a cruelness in his eyes that no amount of beauty could hide. Around his neck layers of gold and silver hung with pendants and charms burning with trapped Crafter energy. Asher could feel the energy twisting and churning, desperate to be free. This was not Crafting, this was something ugly and unnatural. Her face felt cold and numb. Her fingers tingled desperate to free the stolen life-force. Every instinct was on a high alert. Danger, danger. Carefully, lightly, she layered the invisibility charm.

"What do you want girl?" he demanded.

Ash bobbed an awkward curtsey to the Queen, a wobbly movement she had never made before in her life. She hoped it was sufficient.

"Your Majesty, lunch is ready." She bobbed again. "I apologise for the noise, I fell down the stairs."

"Go then." Darven dismissed her with a wave, already losing interest in the clumsy maid.

Asher went, rushing through the rooms and up the stairs, the hidden servant's door closing soundlessly behind her.

Once she was gone the Sorcerer offered an arm to his Queen.

"Come then Magda. Time for you to collect Freya and share one last meal with your Aunt."

Chapter Seventeen

The rescue of Evie

Up the stairs Asher bounded, past the dining room floor and onwards to the rooms that lay above. She burst out of the door at the top of the staircase and ran straight into a stylishly attired woman who was exiting a hallway to Asher's left.

"Oh my goodness, I'm so sorry!" cried Asher, reaching out her hands to steady the older woman.

"That was a very exuberant entrance," responded the woman calmly when she was on firm footing once more. "You seem in a hurry."

A thousand responses flitted through Asher's frazzled thoughts. This woman was clearly not a servant, so what was she supposed to say?

"The Weaver is here," she blurted.

The woman smiled, her warm face filling with pleasure.

"Ah, is it your first time meeting the Weaver? She makes everyone nervous."

Clearly the woman expected her to nod, so she did.

"You will be fine child. She will most likely pay little to no attention to you."

Asher nodded again. "Thank you," she croaked.

"I am Lady Freya," smiled the woman, "you must be new. Are you here for the Princess?"

"I'm looking for the Gold Room," Asher replied, hoping she did not sound as impatient as she felt. She cared nothing for princesses, she only wanted to find her sister.

Lady Freya nodded. "Indeed. Follow this hallway around. It is the second room on the left."

"Thank you," Asher bobbed another curtsey. Her balance was better this time, but it really was a ridiculous thing to do.

Lady Freya smiled warmly and headed for the wide, splendid oak stairs. Asher spun around and hurried along the hallway, paying no attention to its decorations or ornaments.

At the second door on the left she hesitated. Her hands were sweating, her heart was pounding and her stomach was churning.

She hoped that beyond that door was Evie. Finding her had been the driving focus of the last three strange, unsettling days, and her sole purpose for coming to Andera at all.

She had feared for Evie's life, been terrified that her sister was being tortured for her sake, prayed to the universe that she would find her safe and whole, and promised on the Threads that she would bring her home.

And now she was so close she could almost hear her breathing. If all went well they would be on their way home in a few minutes. This was the happy ending. But something felt terribly wrong. Disharmony in the Threads, a discordant note.

You are being ridiculous she scolded herself. Shaking off her apprehension Asher took a deep breath and turned the handle. Heart pounding, she stepped into the room.

Evie was sitting alone staring out the window, her back to the door. She was beautifully dressed in a fitted cream woollen dress that fell just below her knees. Her hair gleamed from a hundred brush strokes. On the table beside her plates of meat and salads and fruits were untouched.

Relief rushed through Asher, followed quickly by anger. How dare Evie just be fine, sitting here like a pampered lady, while she and mum were worried sick about her! Then just as suddenly as it had come, the anger was gone. None of this was Evie's fault.

"Evie," she called as she walked into the room and closed the door.

Her sister whipped around, her eyes wide with shock. In one quick movement she jumped to her feet, then she ran to Asher and threw her arms around her. They squeezed each other tight, laughing crazily.

"Oh my goodness, Asher!! How did you get here?"

"It's a long story. We have to be quick. Levi and Kate are downstairs. It's time to go."

"Levi and Kate?" Evie shook her head and stepped back. "What are you talking about? Go where?"

"Home. Home to Earth, to mum."

Something hard flickered across Evie's face and she resolutely pursed her lips.

"No Ash, I'm not leaving."

"Not leaving?" Asher was incredulous. "What are *you* talking about? I'm here to rescue you."

Evie laughed. She waved her arms around. "Look at this room Ash. Look! What do I need rescuing from? I'm not lost, I'm *found*!"

As instructed Ash looked around the room. It was indeed impressive, with a beautiful sitting area by the window, a lovely gilded table with two fancy golden chairs, and a huge marble fireplace which was currently unlit. Through another doorway was a marvellous bedroom with a giant four poster bed. And everywhere everything gleamed gold. It was everything Evie had ever wanted, bemoaning her life in the Beast. It was a room for a princess. A Golden Princess.

Realisation hit Asher hard in the chest.

In shock she stared at her sister. "Oh Evie..." she breathed, "*You* are the princess."

Evie nodded. Mutely they stared at each other, then Evie grinned.

"And you are a maid!" She giggled.

With a flash of temper Asher yanked the dress over her head, throwing it on the floor. A dull clunk reminded her that the harmonica was tucked in its pocket, so she grabbed the offending garment, fished out her harmonica and threw the dress back on the carpet.

"Better?" asked Evie cheekily, still grinning.

"Much," huffed Ash. Wonderingly she looked around the room again. "How?"

"Darven rescued me."

"No, Darven kidnapped you," corrected Asher. "He thought you were me and he took the wrong sister. I've come to rescue you."

Evie screwed up her face in anger.

"Why is everything about you Ash? You think you are so special. Well guess what? You're not. Darven didn't want you. He wanted *me!* He rescued me from the woman who kidnapped me as a baby, who pretended I was her child all these years. He brought me home."

Evie was no longer grinning. Her face was flushed with anger, her words building in volume and passion.

"I was born a princess, born to be a queen! And Jennifer stole me! Magda, I mean Mother, has been grieving for nineteen years. I belong here with my real mother and my real home. I will never return, never! I matter here. I'm not some after-thought in a family full of self-absorbed artists. I'm a real-life princess! Darven says I'm the most important person in Andera and I'm going to change the world!"

She was raging, making no sense. None of this behaviour was anything like normal Evie. Asher stepped forward to grab her.

"What are you talking about? This is ridiculous! You are being ridiculous."

Wrong choice of words. Fury erupted from Evie. She screamed in anguish and shoved Ash hard, forcing her to stumble backwards to the ground.

"Don't you dare call me ridiculous! Leave me alone!" sobbed Evie, "Get out!" She grabbed the bowl of fruit and heaved it hard at Asher's head.

With no time to think, Ash brought the harmonica to her lips and blew. The heavy silver bowl froze in mid-air for a few seconds then landed with a dull thud on the thick carpet. Fruit spilled everywhere.

Asher pursed her lips and frowned a little. She had been trying to return the bowl to the table.

Evie's blue eyes were wide with shock. "How did you do that?" she hissed.

"Neither of us are who we were," said Asher sadly as she stood up. "On Andera you are a Princess and I am a Crafter."

"A Crafter..." Evie breathed the words in fear. "You are one of *them*."

Asher frowned at her tone. "What does that mean?"

"*Crafters,*" Evie spat the word, "working with the Weaver, tormenting ordinary people, planning to overthrow the queen, plotting to steal the kingdom."

"That's not true!"

"Really? That's why they stole me. That was the beginning of the Weaver's treachery. Then she came to recruit you for her army. You heard mum, *Jennifer*, say the Weaver wanted a war! How well do you know the Weaver Ash? You met her what, three days ago?"

Asher couldn't speak, her thoughts racing and colliding, tying her tongue. Evie was misinterpreting everything. *Wasn't she?* She thought of Gin's own anger and doubts about her mother, her fear they were being played as pawns.

Her head was beginning to pound.

"I could say the same thing about Darven and the Queen," she blurted.

Evie shook her head, refusing to hear it.

"Can you really trust these people Ash? Our *mother*, a woman who lied to us our entire lives, who stole me, perhaps even you, from a distant planet and pretended she was some-one else on Earth? The so called Weaver who turns up at our house in the middle of the night trying to convince you to leave with her, a complete stranger? Has she been completely truthful with you? Hmmmm?"

Asher's head was spinning. The words Evie was saying were not untrue, but they just weren't truth. Not as Ash understood it. Darven was weaving a tangled plot, turning the queen against the Weaver, the Crafters against the Weaver and the people against the Crafters. Turning sister against sister. He would end up with ultimate power and be considered blameless by the people who were left.

"Evie please come home," she pleaded, "Let's just go back and leave all this madness behind. It's nothing to do with us."

Evie's eyes were uncertain, but stubbornly she shook her head. "I belong here, where I am loved. Magda loves me. Everyone loves me. They treat me like I am some-one special. And one day I will be Queen."

Asher could feel tears welling. She held out her hands to her sister. "*We* love you. Me, and mum and dad. *We* are your family."

"No!" Evie flung herself onto the large golden settee, turning her face away from her sister. "Darven has explained it all. They were never my family. Jennifer stole me,

STOLE ME, when I was only a baby. She hid me on Earth and it has taken him nineteen years to find a way to rescue me. He *saved* me." Her voice caught and she swallowed hard. "And now I have to stay. I *want* to stay. You go back to *those people*, and your boring life and the dreadful Beast, but I won't come with you."

A long silence hung uneasily between them. Evie was no longer sobbing, but her body shook with great quivering breaths.

Asher felt like she could burst into tears herself. None of this made any sense. She knew nothing of kidnappings or princesses, but she was sure mum could explain it all. Mum loved Evie fiercely, of that there was no doubt. She would never have done anything to harm her. She had been willing to risk her life and cross the Void to save her. There must be an explanation. It would all be sorted out. At home.

"Evie..." she implored.

"When I was seventeen and had my heart broken, all I wanted was my mum to hold me tight and tell me that he was a douche-bag and everything would be okay. But she was deep in her breakdown over *you* and her damn painting. When I was accepted to university we were meant to go out for a family dinner, but she was too unwell to attend. Another damn migraine. There was never space in her heart or in her life for me. It was only ever you."

She sounded like she was holding back tears.

"I hadn't realised how unloved and unwanted I was until we left Earth, and I saw it all clearly for the first time.

Darven tells me I slept for the last few days. And I dreamed of every rejection, every heartache."

Suddenly this whole situation made much more sense. Evie had been badly impacted by the Void, her deepest fears amplified and distorted.

"Evie, none of this is true. It's an effect of the Void. Mum loves you to the moon, and beyond."

"No Asher. Just leave me alone." She did not turn around. "I said, leave me alone."

After a long moment Asher nodded slowly. A great wave of weariness washed over her, sadness filling every nook and cranny of her heart.

"Okay." She walked to the door, then hesitated. "What do I tell mum and dad?"

"Tell them I'm finally home. Tell them goodbye."

Asher was exhausted, she was confused, she had come a very long way to learn only that her sister wanted nothing to do with any of them. The tears could not be held at bay and Asher started to cry.

"Please Evie…"

On the settee Evie dashed away silent tears of her own, but she refused to turn around. She had chosen her future, and it was golden.

After a few long minutes Asher took three or four deep shuddering breaths, forcing herself to stop crying. Roughly she wiped away the moisture on her face with her t-shirt. *Enough.*

"Evie, I love you," she said softly as she opened the door and stepped through.

"Asher?" from within the Gold Room the princess called.

Asher stopped moving but didn't turn around. She did not want Evie to see the heartbreak on her face.

"Leave quickly. Darven is punishing Crafters who collude with the Weaver to steal my mother's throne. I don't want you hurt..." her voice trailed off. "Anyway, it will all be over soon. Today marks the end of the Weaver's reign. Right now Darven and Magda, I mean Mother, are taking care of that. Soon there will be no more Weaver and everything will be alright again."

No more Weaver! The words were like a punch in her stomach. Her vision became blurry and dark. Instinctively she knew the Threads needed to show her something. Asher closed her eyes and let them spin.

Without the Weaver to protect them, creatures of magic would be persecuted and eradicated. A thousand stars would die. Magic across the universes would shrivel and mutate, desolating planets and species untold. A million possibilities would cease to exist. Children that would cure illnesses would never be born, stories that would inspire generations would never be written, life-forms of beauty and wonder would simply vanish. On and on the threads tangled, weaving faster and faster until Asher was dizzy. All was chaos.

With a horrified gasp Asher opened her eyes. It could not be allowed to happen.

Magic must always exist. The balance must always be maintained. There must always be a Weaver.

She spun around to face the Princess Evelyn, heir to the Throne of Andera, glowing in the reflection of her golden cage. Her sister. Evie's beautiful blue eyes were sad and serious.

"Stay away from the Weaver Asher. Don't let Darven see you. Go home and be safe."

If the Weaver fell, nowhere would be safe for people like her, and mum.

"Goodbye Princess," said Asher sadly. "I hope you are happy here."

'ASHER...' Hesta's voice was weak in her mind. By the Threads it was happening.

Evie had made her choice, now Asher must make hers.

She ran for the stairs.

Chapter Eighteen

The Tangled Threads

While Asher and Evie argued upstairs, downstairs in the dining room the four residents of E-Langren resolutely ignored each other, pretending no acquaintance at all. Hesta merely nodded when Levi offered her the platter of meat and shook her head when Kate offered the decanter of wine. Penn stood quietly along the wall and didn't look at them at all.

It was all very awkward, but that seemed to be the theme of the lunch.

The Queen was seated at the head of the huge table, the Weaver to her right and Freya to her left. The final setting remained empty.

Of the three women the only one who seemed genuinely happy was Freya. She chatted merrily across the table to the Weaver who had answered curtly, though not rudely, her mind clearly elsewhere.

Every time Hesta raised a glass to her lips, or food to her mouth Penn would stride forward and insist on tasting it first.

"One would think you were insulting our hospitality Aunt," tittered the Queen. "Is the food at my table not good enough to eat without a servant tasting first?"

The Weaver had turned her fathomless eyes on her niece and said nothing. Under that all-knowing gaze Magda coloured furiously and looked away.

"We are thrilled to see you Hesta," smiled Freya, "but why the unexpected visit?"

"There is trouble outside these walls Freya. Beyond Mat'drin the country is in disarray. Crafters are going missing. There is violence and bloodshed. The people are afraid."

Both Freya and Magda frowned.

"That cannot be so," said the Queen, "Darven assures me all is well in the land. He goes on many trips in my stead. It has been many years since I have left this castle, but he takes good care of everything. Oh how I wish I was stronger." She sighed deeply, then brightened when a spoonful of curly carrots was carefully scooped onto her plate.

"Oh look! How pretty." Happily she munched on the carrots, the unrest beyond the Castle already forgotten.

Freya leaned forward. "What is the problem Hesta? Who is behind this?"

The Weaver raised her brows and tilted her head slightly towards the oblivious Queen.

"Darven?" mouthed Freya.

The Weaver nodded once.

"Have you come to take my princess?" demanded Magda unexpectedly, her child-like voice cross and squeaky.

"Absolutely not Magda, don't be absurd. I have no desire to take your daughter."

"You did once" the Queen accused petulantly.

Freya sucked in her breath. "Magda! How can you accuse the Weaver of such a thing!"

Hesta sighed. "I had no idea Gin had taken her. I didn't even know who she was until yesterday. I have no interest in Evelyn."

"She's mine now."

"Yes dear, nobody is taking your princess," soothed Freya, shooting Hesta a look of concern.

"I need to speak with Darven," said Hesta. Her voice was hard and firm.

The little Queen fidgeted. "Well, ah, he's busy. Yes busy. You have to eat with me." Her bright blue gaze refused to meet the Weaver's.

Standing deferentially at a distance Levi and Kate made bug eyes at each other. Evie, a princess? In a rather crazy way it made sense. They wondered whether Ash had found her yet.

"Magda." The Weaver was not to be put off. "Send for Darven. This nonsense ends today."

"Yes," murmured the Queen wonderingly, "that's what Darven said as well. This ends today."

She turned to a silent footman standing by the door. "Ask His Excellency to join us."

The young man sped off to do her bidding.

"Well then!" said the Queen brightly, motioning a young maid to refill their water glasses. "What news of your travels through Andera Hesta?"

Freya threw another concerned look at the Weaver. Clearly the Queen had already forgotten their conversation of only moments before.

"Is this common?" asked Hesta.

"More and more so," murmured Freya worriedly.

The Weaver contemplated the Queen for a moment, then raised the water glass to her lips. Immediately Penn was at her side. Wordlessly he took the glass from her and sipped. After a minute he returned the glass to Hesta who drank.

Within seconds the Weaver pushed back her chair, clutching at her chest, gasping for air.

"Hesta!" screamed Freya, "what is wrong?"

Levi and Kate lurched forward, but Penn was already there, cradling the Weaver as she collapsed to the ground.

ASHER... called Hesta, sending the last of her strength through the castle.

"Weaver, Weaver, what has happened?" Penn's voice was low and urgent. "What do I do?"

The Queen looked confused. "What is happening?" she asked no-one in particular, standing up from her seat to peer at Hesta on the ground.

Darven strode into the dining hall just as Asher leapt through the entrance to the servant's corridor.

Levi and Kate rushed to Asher's side in a panic, fear clear on their faces.

Time slowed. Blood rushed to her head, filling her ears with a whooshing sound and making her legs weak. Asher felt like she was moving in quicksand, trying to get to Hesta quickly but barely moving at all.

'Wait, do not reveal yourself,' whispered the Weaver in her mind. Her voice was weak.

Vicious laughter filled the air, echoing off the stone walls.

"Well, well, well. The mighty Weaver lies at my feet. What's that? Sorry cousin dear, I cannot understand a word you're mumbling."

Fury shone on Penn's face and Ash could see he was struggling between holding the Weaver steady and safe or jumping to his feet and throttling the older man. A thought passed between Hesta and Penn, and the Protector begrudgingly pulled in his rage.

"Well done Magda," congratulated Darven, his handsome face twisted with glee.

The Queen looked like a child caught misbehaving.

"What have you done?" hissed Freya.

"Nothing!" whined the Queen. "I only flavoured the water with thistlewort, like Darven suggested. It's so rare on Andera. He said it would be a nice surprise for Hesta."

"Oh my goodness," whispered Kate. "Thistlewort to knot the thread... They've poisoned her!"

Darven circled the fallen Weaver menacingly, gloating gleefully.

"Oh dear, look at you down there. Not so demanding now are you Weaver, hmmm? Oh how easy this was in the end. All the Crafter blood I've shed to try and make a charm strong enough to thwart you. You should have heard their groans of pain, their pleas for mercy! And nothing would work. Nothing!"

He grabbed a glass from the table and smashed it against the wall. As suddenly as it erupted his temper was gone, and the sorcerer was grinning once more.

"But how simple it all was in the end. A very small secret so carelessly shared, and here we are! You know what my favourite part is? Hmmm?"

Nobody answered.

"Evelyn! You missed that completely. Hahahaha. You've been so focused on your precious missing Crafters that you neglected to research the old prophecies. It was all so clear!

When the lost one returns to the place of her birth
The might of the Weaver will fall to the earth
Power will rise from the Mountains and Sky
The future re-woven, torn Threads re-tied."

He laughed merrily, taking a large swig of the thistlewort infused water.

"Ah refreshing! And it only grows in Terran soil. I found it by chance in your own daughter's garden which only happened because I was rescuing Evelyn. That's the fun thing about prophecies – the twists and turns!"

They had been so wrong. Darven hadn't taken Evie in mistake. He had wanted the missing princess, not the missing Heir.

"It's me! I'm the power from the Mountains and Sky," he chortled with glee, "and you have fallen to the earth! It's just too wonderful! This is the end of the Weaver. The mighty Hestawen brought low by a simple plant. Her useless daughter cowering on Earth, unable to return and take up the Threads. No other Heir trained to take her place."

Asher could feel music rising within her. Strong, angry, fierce. It was wild, like in Hesta's study, but she needed to control it. She couldn't let it rip her apart.

The Weaver's breathing was shallow, her face a ghastly grey.

'Hesta, what do I do?'

'Leave quietly...' her energy was weak. *'Take Levi and Kate. Go home.'*

Her breaths were shorter, she was losing consciousness. She knew she was going to die.

'What about you?' implored Ash.

'Will... not... die... here... at... his... feet.' Every thought was wracked with pain.

Fear roiled and churned in Asher's gut. She did not know what she would do, but she could not just leave Hesta here alone.

Step by small step she and Levi and Kate moved quietly closer to Penn and Hesta.

"How long does this take?" burst Darven impatiently, "five minutes? Twenty? By all the Threads this is dreary."

In one quick motion he grabbed a carving knife from the table and lunged at Hesta's heart.

Everybody screamed and Penn reflectively threw his body over Hesta's. A thunderous crack ripped through the air and Darven was thrown backwards onto the ground. Even at her most vulnerable, Hesta's aura was too powerful for Darven to penetrate.

"Argghhhhh," he moaned as he sat up gingerly. "Still dying on my floor she is protected from me. Damn you," he groaned. The Queen hurried over to him.

"Now," whispered Levi, pushing Kate forward.

Still garbed as a maid Kate ran forward, drawing the attention of no-one. She slipped in beside Penn.

"Quickly, give her this. 3 drops. It is the antidote."

He assessed her in one look then nodded, deciding she was trustworthy. As Darven pulled himself up off the floor Penn uncorked the tiny vial and dropped the precious liquid into the Weaver's mouth.

One...

Darven looked over, realising immediately what was happening. "Noooo!" he screamed.

Two....

The sorcerer raised his hand, lightning crackled from his fingers. He couldn't attack Hesta, but he could destroy Penn before he gave that last drop.

"Three!" shouted Levi throwing a handful of firecrackers at Darven's feet.

The sorcerer lurched back in surprise, yelping as the little crackers exploded around him. As soon as he realised they were harmless he pointed a furious finger at Levi. Eyes wide, Levi stepped backwards and bumped against the table. There was nowhere to go. He would not be able to move fast enough to escape the Sorcerer's magic.

Music leapt in Asher's mind.

She grabbed hold of the rampaging notes, tussling them into submission. She was the Musician and the music would obey. Her whole body shook with the rising energy.

She raised the harmonica to her mouth and blew with all her might, running her hands over the small instrument, summoning the notes, commanding them.

Rough music burst forth, mingling with all the anger and fear she was feeling for Hesta, all the grief and loss she was feeling over Evie. Energy raged around her.

Darven was flung back against the wall, his eyes wide with shock. Then he crumpled to the floor.

The stolen Crafter life-force burst free from the collection of charms and pendants around his neck, weaving in with her own energy. The very air began to crackle. Still Asher blew into the harmonica, a song of darkness and pain. The combined powers of the many Crafts roared like a storm. They swirled around her, within her. Asher could feel herself being caught in the swell, could feel herself being pulled under. She was going to go mad. Feebly she tried to keep her head above the wild current, to keep focused on the room, but it was too hard. She closed her eyes as the music pulled her into the maelstrom.

And then somebody grabbed her and yelled her name, pulling her back from the edge. She turned her full attention to the feel of the hands on her shoulders, their warmth, their urgent pressure, and she opened her eyes.

"Ash! Ash!" Levi was shaking her, "Stop now, we have to go."

Asher felt the wildness retreat as pulled her focus back towards her friend. Around her the energy eased and the power dissipated.

"Where's Hesta?" she demanded as her head cleared, "and Penn?"

"Gone," said Levi quietly. "It was like a ghost appeared and they were pulled through the air."

"Is she alive?"

He shook his head. "I don't know. I don't know. The three drops went in, we counted. Ash, we have to go. Can you get us home?"

For the first time since this whole adventure had begun Levi sounded afraid. Asher looked around at the damage she had wrought. The dining table and all its contents were scattered and smashed. The Queen and Freya were unconscious on the floor, breathing heavily. Darven had taken the hardest hit, but even now he was starting to stir, his own powers protecting and rejuvenating him at an unnatural rate. The servants had fled.

Asher felt horrified at what she had unleashed. She had been so worried that she didn't have the power required of the Weaver's Heir, so concerned that she was not strong enough. But now, looking at the chaos, Asher was finally convinced that she was worthy of Hesta's belief in her Crafting ability. But what good was Crafter power if she couldn't control it? This wasn't creating, this was destruction.

A moan from Darven brought her back to the present.

"Come quickly!" she spun around and ran back through the servant's corridors, through the kitchen and to the storeroom. Her mind and body were exhausted, but pure adrenaline fuelled her haphazard flight. Behind her Levi and Kate banged and clattered. Around them startled servants leapt out of their way with shouts and curses.

They crashed into the storeroom, slamming the door shut behind them and heaving a solid chest of drawers in front of it.

"Grab the packs."

Wordlessly they pulled them on, Levi helping Ash shrug into hers.

"Please let this work…" murmured Ash, yanking off the bracelet and the globe. As soon as they touched each other Asher felt the air around her rip apart. She focused on her living room at home, trying to recall every minute detail.

There! That's where I want to go. She held the image in her head, pouring it into the energy of the bracelet.

"Hold on!" she yelled, "no matter what, don't let go!"

The maelstrom began to spin around them, filling their senses with everything, and then strangely nothing.

The Void.

She had ripped open a portal and they were standing on the edge of the Void.

'MUM!' she screamed, *'Mum, I need you!'*

Far on the other side of the Void a pinprick of light appeared. Ash blinked rapidly, fearing she was hallucinating. But it was still there, and it was growing. Gin was holding open the door to Earth.

'Asher! Thank the stars. The Threads are in disarray, you need to cross now. Run towards me. Now!'

"Asher, let's go." Levi held out his hands to her and Kate.

In the corridor they could hear raised voices and doors opening and banging. The search was getting close.

Asher stepped forward and grabbed her friends' hands firmly. "Ready?" she asked.

Levi nodded and they took a step towards the portal. But Kate refused to move. All colour had drained from her face and she was staring in horror into the Void.

"I can't," she mumbled, her breath tight. "I can't do that again." She tried to pull her hand from Levi's tight grasp.

"No, let me go!" She yanked her arm loose and twisted away from Levi and Kate.

"Kate, we have to cross now. It's okay. We are all together, let's go," said Ash urgently. The panic in Kate's eyes was scaring her.

Heavy bodies banged into the barricaded door. The chest of drawers shuddered under the attack. There was only a minute before they were through.

"Levi, can you carry her?"

He nodded.

"Carry me? What do you mean?" Kate's voice was rising with hysteria. "Just leave me here, just leave me."

Asher laid a gentle hand on Kate's head. *Please let this work.*

She brought to mind the Beethoven sonata she had played back in Hesta's library to inadvertently waken her friend, and softly she hummed the same tune. This time she imagined the notes soothing and lulling Kate into a dreamless sleep. Within seconds Kate slumped in Levi's arms.

Thank the stars.

Ash grabbed Kate's pack and hooked her hand through Levi's elbow.

"This is going to be awkward," she warned.

"Piece of cake," he mustered a grin.

And they stepped through the portal into darkness and despair.

An eternity later they finally stumbled into the Blake's living room. Gin was there to pull them through. With a shout of thanks she threw her arms around them all, kissing their faces and squeezing their arms. Then carefully she helped a half-awake Kate stumble to the sofa.

Levi collapsed to the floor. He would never admit it, but crossing the Void while carrying his pack on his back and Kate in his arms had been the hardest thing he had ever done, mentally and physically.

Terrible images had filled his mind as he had forced his way across the Void, of Kate falling from his arms into the darkness, screaming as her sanity was ripped from her. Now, safe in the warmth and light of the familiar, small convulsions shook his body as pent up adrenaline coursed through him. Lying where he had fallen, Levi took deep, shuddering breaths to release the mental tension and physical pain of the crossing.

Gin grabbed Asher and held her tight. Asher burrowed her head in her mother's shoulder, relishing the safety and security of her embrace.

Home, they were home. They had only been gone for three days but it felt like everything had changed. And none of them would ever be the same again.

"Evie?" Gin asked, a thousand questions wrapped up in that one word.

Asher pulled away from the embrace to see her mother's face. Was she imagining it, or did Gin seem nervous?

"She is fine and she has chosen to stay. She is at Ostrin with the Queen." Ash watched her mother closely. "She had quite a tale to tell, of a stolen royal baby and a diabolical Weaver plot."

Gin's face shuttered, sharing nothing. Ash could see the pain deep in her mother's eyes, but she was not prepared to let it go.

"Mum, do you want to explain what she's talking about?"

Gin shook her head. "At least she is unharmed and safe, that is what matters."

"Mum, I think I deserve to know."

There was no response. Gin stepped away from Ash, wiping away silent tears before hurrying over to kneel beside Kate and check on her.

Ash knew that one day Ginarwen would have to tell the tale of the stolen princess, but it seemed it would not be today. She shoved down her frustration and the hard knot of resentment that was burning within her.

I've endangered my friends and myself and you won't even tell me what is really going on...

"Can you really trust these people Ash? Our mother lied to us our entire lives..."

Evie's words mocked her, inflaming her own doubts. She did not want to feel that way about her mother, her kind and loving mother. And besides, there was the rather pressing matter of the injured, perhaps dead, Weaver to sort out.

She took a deep breath and swallowed her uncomfortable thoughts and emotions down deep inside.

"Mum. We need to go back. You and I need to go to Andera and find Hesta and restore balance to the Threads somehow."

Gin didn't turn from her inspection of Kate as she shook her head. "No we don't. We need to stay here, away from Hesta and Darven and all the chaos the two of them have unleashed. We can be safe here."

"But the magic..."

"Is not our concern," said Gin firmly, finally twisting around to look her in the eye. Her face was set, her eyes unreadable. "Hesta will work it out."

"But what if Hesta is dead? We saw her collapse after Darven poisoned her!" burst out Ash, struggling to understand why her mother was being so obtuse. If the Threads fell apart, nowhere would be safe.

For a moment Gin seemed truly shocked, then she pulled herself together. "No," she replied firmly, "that is not possible, I would have felt that."

"We need to do something mum. We can help. All those stolen Crafters – they are relying on us, on me."

Gin turned her face away, busying herself with wrapping a warm blanket around the now sleeping Kate.

"Mum..." pleaded Ash.

"Enough Asher." Gin's voice was firm. "Your friends are exhausted, *you* are exhausted. It is time for you to get into your bed and sleep. Kate can sleep here on the couch. Levi –"

Gin turned to Levi who had pulled himself to his feet. He was determined to stay upright, but there was a definite grey pallor to his normally warm olive face that suggested he would not be vertical for long.

"Levi, you go upstairs to Evie's room. No arguments."

Levi nodded, visibly relieved, and made his way slowly up the stairs.

Asher's head was spinning. It had been an incredibly difficult day and now she was left trying to work out what she needed to do next. She had thought Gin would sort it out, but she was realising that Gin wanted nothing to do with Andera, Hesta, or the tangled, twisted Threads.

How could she be so heartless? So uncaring? With a rush of insight, Asher understood.

Gin wanted her small, normal, unobtrusive life, and Asher could not blame her. It was what Ash herself had always wanted. To be here in the safety and warmth of her ramshackle home, surrounded by the people she loved. Safe, small. An unremarkable girl living an ordinary life.

But now everything was different. She had seen what would happen if she let the Weaver die, and she could not simply walk away from that.

"I cannot go back Ash," said Gin in a small voice. She did not raise her face to meet Asher's eyes. "This is not my fight."

Asher had never seen her mother so unsure of herself, almost apologetic. For reasons that were still unknown to Ash, her mother had chosen to run away from her destiny, from her responsibility.

"And it is not yours." Gin's voice was very, very weary. She stood up came, over to Ash and gave her a squeeze.

"Go to bed Asher. We can talk more in the morning. I'm beyond grateful you are all home safe. Sleep well sweetheart."

And she too headed up the stairs.

Asher stood still, staring blindly at the flickering, dancing flames of the fire, immobilised by confusion and doubt and frustration. Finally, with a sigh, she stepped away from her sleeping friend and crossed the room to the stairs.

A few minutes later she was in her own bedroom. She had no conscious memory of getting there, but her feet had taken her there on auto-pilot.

Ash looked around at the familiar desk and lamp, at her music score strewn across the desk, the dressing gown hanging across her chair, and the heavy quilted comforter laying across her bed. The same one she had wrapped around herself on that strange night when she had first met Hesta.

Everything was so familiar, and yet she felt so out of place.

Asher walked to the bed, pulled back the cover and climbed inside, fully clothed. Immediately her battered body sank into the soft mattress in relief. Her eyes drifted shut. Soon enough Asher was asleep.

And she dreamed.

She dreamed of a thousand Weavers, standing side by side in a line that stretched back through time and space. Around them danced innumerable worlds filled with wonder and magic. She dreamed of a princess crying in a golden room, and a painter asleep at her easel, her hands and face smeared with paint. And she dreamed of Hesta, dying at Darven's feet.

With a deep gasp Asher woke up.

She loved her mother deeply, but she knew that Ginar was wrong. She had been wrong to turn her back on her destiny, wrong to deny her daughters the knowledge of their birthrights, their true identities. She had been wrong to hide away on Earth leaving Hesta to hold the Threads alone. And she was wrong to tell Asher that they had no responsibility to save the Weaver and stop the sorcerer.

Ginarwen was determined to forsake her destiny, as surely as Asher was being pulled towards hers. Ginarwen's illumination in the Threads was diminishing, as Asher's was increasing.

As her mind struggled to make sense of this new dynamic, a strange feeling was blossoming inside Ash. Strength and obstinacy that she had never realised existed were pulsing and growing.

A part of her really she wanted to stay, to fade back into her simple routines and her uncomplicated life. But that was not possible. It may not be Gin's fight, but at some point it had become hers, and she could not walk away.

Asher had no idea what she was going to do, or how she was going to do it, she simply knew that she had to take a chance. She had to try.

"She needs the courage to weave as she must. No matter the pain, no matter the cost."

Before she could change her mind, Asher climbed out of bed and heaved the pack onto her back. Her muscles clenched in protest. She pulled the globe and bracelet from the pockets of her jeans and rubbed them together. Beside her desk the air began to shimmer.

Certainty settled within Asher. There was still fear, and confusion and a sense of dread, but she was sure of what she had to do.

"There must always be a Weaver. I understand what that means now." Her voice was soft in the quiet room. "I was born to weave the Threads, that's what she keeps saying. So maybe it's my turn."

Asher entwined the globe and bracelet together, the air crackled, the portal opened.

Hesta, the library... She pictured the bookshelves, the star maps on the floor. Before her the Void beckoned. She shuddered at its bleakness and took a deep breath to steady her nerves.

She remembered sharing the wonder of the universes with Levi and her excitement over the Dragon Planet. The image of the map took hold. *The Library... the Dragon Planet...*

In the distance the portal opened on the other side. *The Library... the Dragon Planet...*

She felt a rush of air over her shoulder as her bedroom door flew open. Asher did not turn her head. She knew if she looked at her mother her resolve would falter.

"Asher no!" Gin leapt forward desperately, determined to grab her.

It was now or never. For a split second Asher allowed herself to imagine closing the portal and staying safe and small in her room. But beyond the Void the universe seemed to be calling her name, and she felt her heart leap in response.

Asher jumped.

***

Asher sat up slowly, rubbing her sore head. The crossing of the Void had been fast and furious, and she had crash-landed awkwardly into the ground. The feel of grass beneath her hands and the hot sun on her face was disorienting. Clearly she had not arrived in Hesta's library but somewhere outside.

Carefully she collected the pendant and bracelet that were lying next to her and placed them back on her neck and wrist. She breathed deeply to steady her racing heart and then took a good look around.

She was lying in a field and the Manor was nowhere in sight.

An ear-splitting roar tore the air around her. Something large whooshed above her head, sending vibrations all around her body. In terror Ash flung herself to the ground, covering her face.

The thing landed with a light thump not far from where she lay. Asher shook with fear, trying to disappear into the long grass, fervently hoping it had not noticed her. Heavy footsteps moved closer. The earth trembled beneath each step.

Warm breath caressed her head.
It had definitely noticed her.
Gathering all her courage, Asher raised her head.

** End of Crafter, Book One of The Weaver's Heir **

Printed in Great Britain
by Amazon